Erotic Fantasy

Hans-Jürgen Döpp

Author: Hans-Jürgen Döpp

Translators: Philip Jenkins, Jane Rogoyska, Dr. Jane Susanna Ennis, Susana M. Steiner

Layout: Baseline Co. Ltd.

127-129A Nguyen Hue, Fiditourist, 3rd floor

District 1, Ho Chi Minh City, Vietnam

ISBN 10: 1-85995-061-2

ISBN 13: 978-1-85995-061-6

Printed in Singapore

Erotic Fantasy

Hans-Jürgen Döpp

Contents

Danse galante

Introduction

Love's Body
Reflections on Fragmentation of the Body

The subject of the essays in this book is not the body as a whole, but rather its separate parts. As we fragment the body, we make its parts the subject of a fetish. Each individual part can become a focus of erotic passion, an object of fetishist adoration. On the other hand, the body as a whole is still the sum of its parts.

The partitioning that we carry out here brings to mind the worship of relics. Relic worship began in the Middle Ages with the adoration of the bones of martyrs and was based on the belief that the body parts of saints possessed a special power. In this respect, each fetishist, however enlightened he pretends to be, pays homage to relic worship.

At first, this dismemberment only happened to saints, in accordance with the belief that in paradise the body will become whole again. Only later were other powerful people such as bishops and kings also carved up after their deaths. In our cultural survey of body parts, we are particularly concerned with the history of those with "erotic significance." Regardless of whether their significance is religious or erotic, they all attain the greatest importance for both the believer and the lover because of the attraction and power inherent in them. This way, fetishist heritage of older cultures survives in both the believer and the lover.

> O Body, how graciously you let my soul
>
> Feel the happiness, that I myself keep secret,
>
> And while the brave tongue shies away,
>
> From all that there is to praise, that brings me joy,
>
> Could you, O Body, be any more powerful,
>
> Yes, without you nothing is complete,
>
> Even the Spirit is not tangible, it melts away
>
> Like hazy shadows or fleeting wind.[1]

Anatomical Blazons of the Female Body appeared in 1536, a newly printed, multi-volume collection of odes to each body part individually. These poems, praising parts of the female body, constituted an early form of sexual fetishism. "Never," wrote Hartmut Böhme, "does it sing the 'whole body,' let alone the persona of the adored, but rather it is a rhetorical exposition of parts or elements of the body."[2] In these poems, head and womb represented the "central organs." It was to be expected that representatives of the church scented a new form of idolatry in this poetic approach and identified a sinful indecency in this depiction of female nakedness:

1. Margit Gaal, 1920.

"To sing of female organs,

To bring them to God's ears,

Is madness and idolatry,

For which the earth will cry on Judgement day."

This is how such condemnation is expressed in a document entitled *Against the Blazoners of Body Parts*, written in 1539[3]. The poets of the *Blazons* were "the first fetishists in the history of literature."[4] "The *Anatomical Blazons* represented a sort of a sexual *menu à la carte*: from head to toe, a series of fetishist delicacies (and in the *Counterblazons* from head to toe a series of sensual atrocities and defacements). Such a gastrosophy of feminine flesh is only conceivable when the woman is not regarded as a person. The fetish of the female body involves the abolition of woman as such."[5] From this perspective, the *Blazons* would be womanless.

The poetic dismemberment of the female body satisfies fetishist phallocentrism, which, as Böhme points out, also lies at the root of male aggression. Today it would be called "sexist."

"A woman is a conglomerate of sexual-rhetorical body parts, desired by men: one beholds the female body in such explicit detail that the woman herself is negated. A courtly, cultivated dismemberment of a woman is celebrated in the service of male fantasy."[6] Is the female body thus reduced to a plaything of lust?

Böhme's analysis echoes much of contemporary feminist critique: The corporeal should be given homage only when it is united with personality, as if the body itself was something inferior.

What Böhme refers to as "phallocentrism," can be observed even in the context of advanced cultures: the progress of civilisation has been accompanied by an ever-increasing alienation of the body – this process is repeated in each stage of history.

The lustful preoccupation with the body is the primary interest of a child. Children are able to experience desire in the activity of their whole body to a much greater degree than adults. In adults, this original, all-consuming childhood desire is focused in one small area – the genitals. This is how Norman O. Brown describes erotic desire in *The Resurrection of the Body*: "Our displaced desires point not to desire in general, but specifically to the desire for the satisfaction of life in our own body."[8] All morals are bodily morals. Our indestructible Unconscious wishes to return to childhood. This childhood fixation is rooted in the yearning for the pleasure principle, for the rediscovery of the body, which has been estranged from us by the culture. "The eternal child in us is actually disappointed in the sexual act, and specifically in the tyranny of the genital phase."[9] It is a deeply narcissistic yearning that is expressed in the theory of Norman O. Brown. For him, psychoanalysis promises nothing less than the healing of the breech between body and spirit: the transformation of the man's "I" into the bodily "I" and the resurrection of the body.[10]

This dichotomy between body and spirit defines our culture. Dietmar Kamper and Christoph Wulf discuss this in their study of the destiny of the body throughout history and conclude that "...the historical progress of European imprinting since the Middle Ages was made possible by the distinctively Western separation of body and spirit, and then fulfilled itself as 'spiritualisation' of - life, as rationalising, as the devaluation of human body, that is, as dematerialisation."[11]

In the course of progress, the alienation of the body evolved into a hostile estrangement. The body with its variety of senses, passions, and desires was clamped into a rigid framework of commandments

2. Anonymous, 1940.

3. *Intense Pleasure*, 19th century
   Photograph.

and taboos and was made into a simple "mute servant" through a series of repressive measures. Therefore, it needed to regain its value in an alternative way.

This estrangement consisted of an unstoppable process of abstraction, of the ever growing estrangement of people not only from their own bodies, but also from other people's bodies. The progress in the name of conquering nature in the past two centuries has increasingly led to the destruction of nature, and not only in the external world, but also in the inner nature of man. The dominion of people over nature led at the same time to dominion over human nature. The "love-hate relationship with the body" is the basis of what we call "culture": "Only culture views the body as a thing that one can possess, only in the context of culture did the body first differentiate itself from the spirit – the epitome of power and authority – as an object, a dead thing, a 'corpus.' In man's devaluation of his own body, nature takes vengeance on man for reducing it to the level of an object of mastery, of raw material."[12]

Due to the demands of the intensification of work, discipline, and increased mental control, the body becomes increasingly transformed "...from an organ of desire into an organ of production."[13] In accordance with the principle of division of labour, industrialised societies separated work from life, learning from work, intellectual from manual work. The result has been turning the body into a machine.

On it own, the "freedom of sexuality" changes little in this disfigurement of the inner nature of man. "Sexuality is, at least in its modern reduction to 'sex,' a term too narrow to correctly describe the fullness and versatility of emotions, energies, and connections," concludes Rudolf zur Lippe.[14] In the digital age, the body completely loses its substantial meaning. Volkssport and swinger clubs represent an attempt to reanimate the estranged body.

In the thought of Friedrich Nietzsche, the first modern philosopher of the body, that which had been despised previously was brought to the foreground. As he first observed, the destruction of humanity in the age of capitalism began with the destruction of the body. He praised the living body as the sole carrier of happiness, joy, and self-elevation[15], and heavily criticised the view of the body characteristic of Christian morality. "All flesh is sinful," taught Christianity, and while it praised work, it diminished the flesh to being the source of all evil. The sinful flesh had to be subjected to the ascetic spirit. Christianity was for him "the hatred of the senses, of joy in the senses, of joy itself."[16]

He replied to the "despisers of the body": "There is more reason in your body than in your best wisdom."[17] Here the spirit would be inclined to interpret itself falsely, advises Nietzsche, to escape from the body and "use it as guide... Faith in the body is better manifested than faith in the spirit,"[18] a thesis that today is being confirmed through psychosomatic research.

Nietzsche anticipates the psychoanalytical insight that everything having to do with soul and spirit is rooted in physical experience: "'I' says you, and are proud of this word. But the greater thing – in which you are not willing to believe – is your body with its great wisdom; it does not say 'I,' but does it."[19]

One needs to be wary of misunderstanding when interpreting Nietzsche, especially in the face of fascist ideology which justified its barbaric conception of man through references to his writings. "Today we are tired of civilisation": fascism used this complaint voiced by Nietzsche to support naked violence. Such violence is exactly what the progress of civilisation that Nietzsche criticises

4. *Erotic Wooden Sculpture,* work of the Makombe in Tanzania.

was based on from the very beginning. The liberation of people is based not on an excess of reason and enlightenment, but, rather, on its shortage, bodily reason notwithstanding. The fascist cult of the body was only the ultimate manifestation of the process that silenced the body. Those who exalted the body in the Third Reich, "…had the same affinity with killing as the lover of nature has with hunting. They viewed the body as a movable mechanism, with the joints as hinges and the flesh as the padding of the skeleton. They related with the body and worked with their limbs as if they were already separated."[20]

The new Man is a body-machine: his physique is mechanised, his psyche eliminated.[21] "I am not following your path, you, the despisers of the body!" was Nietzsche's answer to such philistines. Did the "sexual revolution" liberate the body? Only to a certain degree. Indeed, what appeared to be liberation, was often nothing more than propagation of the socially mandated self-objectification and mechanisation of the genitalia. "The so-called 'Sex Wave' movement addresses the needs that were banned for so long from morality and from the public sphere using the technology of mechanical production and propagation, thereby degrading those needs even more."[22] Sexuality and erotica are no longer the expression of resistance to the ongoing process of socialisation, but rather its victims.

Meanwhile, in the private world of a fetishist, the body, with its sensuality, experiences a libidinous revaluation that potentially reimburses it for what the socialisation process has taken away. This is how Eberhard Schorsch attempted to rehabilitate perversion, which he saw as a complement to an all around curtailed sensuality: "Perversions reveal the narrowness, the one-dimensionality, the amputated desire of exclusively genital, partnership-based heterosexuality."[23] He explains:

"Exhibitionism and voyeurism expose the restriction of sexuality produced by the introduction of intimacy and a sense of shame… Fetishism points out the narrowness of the ideology of personality and partnership as necessary for sexual fulfilment. As a result, an emotional attachment, or 'love,' is projected onto objects. A sadomasochistic relationship represents the possibility of unlimited, unconditional mutual love to the point of the obliteration of one's own person, thereby showing the limits imposed by individuality in the context of accepted sexuality."[24]

Schorsch's rehabilitation of perversion is valid, however, only on sociologic-analytical level: "Perversions as phenomena manifest the utopia of sexual freedom, the utopia of unrestricted desire, because they expose the great limitations and narrowness of what is socially accepted as sexuality." This sounds nice, but, on the other hand, from the subjective, psychoanalytical standpoint, perversions can be also seen as great obstacles. In any case, they illustrate the dynamism and explosive force of sexuality.

Freud considered perversions to be symptoms of neurosis, whereby that which is suppressed in neurosis is expressed "directly in resolutions and acts of fantasy."[25] As Volkmar Sigusch summarises this thesis: "Perversion is the affirmation of normality. It is not its reversal and distortion, but its emphasis and pinnacle."[26]

Thus, the fetish of a pervert focuses on the sensual experiences of childhood, while for a "normosexual" a vague, more or less mild fetish of certain body parts and features of the so-called sexual object would not at all be conceivable without otherwise normal sexual desire. The apparent directness with which the sexuality of a fetishist relates to things or, rather, objects, "allows a

5. Anonymous, *Tit Fuck*, 1850.

Ein Maskenball in Domino,
Schon der Gedanke macht mich froh,
Doch ein noch höherer Genuß,
Ist ein Ball in Naturalibus!

6. *Images of Spring*, coloured shunga,
18th century. Silk on card.

perverse act to appear as seemingly primal and vital, akin instinctive carnal desire and animalistic lust. Yet, Sigusch observes the closeness of a fetishist act to poetry: "The surprise: a perverse act is comparable to poetry writing."[28]

Which brings us back to the *Anatomical Blazons.*

All the body parts focused on in the following essays can become the subject of poetry as much as of fetish: an ecstatic face, a beautiful backside, breasts, a leg or a foot. Through the psychoanalytically oriented cultural-historical approach it becomes obvious that the body, as we experience it, is not something naturally given, but rather, first of all, something historical. Other essays in this volume deal with the oral and the sense of taste. The oral desire, as well as sense of taste, are modes of sensual appropriation of the world; as this book is illustrated with pictures of erotic art, the sense of sight should be appealed to equally. The chapter "Delights of a Whip" and "Lesbos" refer not only to real gender-relationships – the phantasm that they are based

7. David Greiner, *Love Games I*, 1917.

on is even more significant. The central phantasm, essential to both the history of culture and of life, is the "phallus." As a *Basso Continuo*, it is present in every sexual maturing, even when its power is renounced.

"There is more reason in your body than in your best wisdom": An awareness of the bodily that can bridge the separation between body and spirit and allow the body to be understood as a cultural-historical product has yet to develop. Everything that is exclusively erotic, however, joins together in praising the whole body:

> So we would like to praise the Body duly,
>
> Pay homage to it as to Lord and Master,
>
> So that the sprit, that only nourishes thoughts,
>
> Without body, neither happiness nor sorrow does excite us:
>
> The Body makes its energy praiseworthy,
>
> The force that completes us, consumes us.

8. David Greiner, *Love Games II*, 1917.

The Erotic Orient

Bound Happiness
Chinese Eroticism

The aim of Taoist art and culture was to reach that state of harmony which would lead Man, perennially confronted by a chaotic universe, towards a new serenity. In this spiritual context, love represented for the Chinese a force which they believed to unite sky and earth in balance and to maintain the reproductive cycle of nature. Eroticism thus became an art of living and formed an integral part of religion (to the extent that such western notions can be applied to philosophical thought of this kind).

Taoist religion assumes that pleasure and love are pure. "In order to gain some understanding of Chinese eroticism," writes Etiemble, a great connaisseur of Chinese art, "we need to distance ourselves from the notion of sin and the duality between the corrupt body and the holy spirit," an ideology which lies at the very base of Christianity. Erotic Chinese art reflects the extent to which we are "morally corrupt" and "full of prejudices."

The Yin-Yang pairing introduces us directly into the world of Chinese eroticism: "The path of Yin and Yang" signifies nothing less than the sexual act itself. One of the best-known sayings of ancient Chinese philosophy, "Yi yin yi yang cheh we tao" ("On the one side yin, on the other yang, this is the essence of Tao") indicates the fact that sex between a man and a woman expresses the same harmony as the changes between day and night, or summer and winter. Sex symbolises the order of the world, the moral order, while our culture stigmatises it as evil.

In this sense, master Tung-huan wrote in his Art of Love: "Man is the most sublime creature under the skies. Nothing which he enjoys can be compared to the act of sexual union. Formulated according to the harmony between the sky and the earth, it rules Yin and dominates Yang. Those who understand the sense of these words can preserve their essence and prolong their life. Those who do not grasp their true significance are heading towards their doom."

The split in the Universe between Yin and Yang is all the more important because these two inseparable principles mutually influence each other. We know of a great many Chinese manuals whose purpose was to provide an education in the art of love-making for young couples; this education would cover desire, morality, and religion. In these texts, the sexual act is always referred to metaphorically with terms such as "the war of flowers," "lighting the great candle" or "games of cloud and rain." The texts are also full of images referring to various sexual positions:

    unfurling silk
    the curled-up dragon
    the union of kingfishers
    fluttering butterflies
    bamboo stalks at the altar

9. Wedding book illustrating love positions, 19th century. Japan.

10. Wedding book illustrating love
    positions, 19th century. Japan.

11. Wedding book illustrating love
    positions, 19th century. Japan.

the pair of dancing phoenixes
the galloping tournament horse
the leap of the white tiger
cat and mouse in the same hole

In Chinese aesthetics, nothing is ever named directly and obviously. Instead, things are referred to obliquely; any transgression of this tradition is considered vulgar. Even the European notion of "eroticism" is much too direct. They would prefer to substitute the term "the idea of spring." In the verses of a popular Chinese song, physical love is praised without pretence but also without vulgarity:

"The window open in the light of an autumn moon,
The candle snuffed out, the silk tunic undone,
Her body swims in the scent of the tuberoses."

In the erotic images of paintings on silk or porcelain, wood engravings or illustrations, sexuality is never shown in its crude state or in a pornographic manner, but always in a context of beauty and harmony. Symbolic meaningful details enrich these illustrations, evoking the tenderness which occupies a favoured place in Chinese iconography. Nevertheless, these details are difficult for Europeans to decipher: the cold and impassive faces of the lovers are a long way from our idea of a blaze of passion.

Thus it is that one of the most fertile and ancient cultures in the world invites us, through its religious practices, to make love. Taoist manuals advocate the technique of holding back from ejaculation, a truly prodigious invention which allows the man to satisfy the woman. By doing this, a subtle alchemy is achieved: the man receives Yin from the woman, who obtains from him the pure essence of Yang. For this reason, coitus reservatus is considered in Taoism and in Tantrism to be the most subtle form of sexual union, because it allows the crossing of the divide between masculine and feminine energy. The creation of a new life is not the principal aim of the sexual act. Rather the act has more to do with identification with cosmic forces than with the forces of life.

The "theory of juices" holds that sperm passes through the spinal column directly to the brain. During the seventeenth and eighteenth centuries, European medicine laboured under the same misapprehension. How frightening it must have been to be a young boy masturbating and believing that doing so would lead to a degeneration of the spinal chord and a drying-out of the brain!

Whilst ejaculation provides a mere instant of pleasure which is very swiftly lost and finishes in the relaxation of the entire body, a buzzing in the ears, tiredness of the eyes and a dry throat, coitus reservatus or coitus interruptus provokes a growth in vitality and an improvement in all the senses. Among the best-known manuals are those of Sou Nu King and Sou Nu Fang, which among other things recount how the legendary Yellow Emperor, Huang-ti (2697-2599 B.C., according to traditional historical reckoning) used experienced women to teach him about the art of love-making. In *The Treaties of the Bedroom* there is a conversation between the Emperor and one of his mistresses, a simple young girl:

'The Yellow Emperor asks the simple young girl: My spirit is listless and lacking in substance; I live constantly in fear and my heart is full of sadness. What can I do to cure myself? The young girl

12. Wedding book illustrating love positions, 19th century. Japan.

13. Wedding book illustrating love positions, 19th century. Japan.

14. Wedding book illustrating love positions, 19th century. Japan.

replies quite simply: "All human weaknesses come from an unhappy union of bodies during the sexual act. As water wins in the fight against fire, so woman gains in the fight against man. Those who are skilled in pleasure are like good cooks who know which five spices to add to a soup." Those who understand the art of Yin and Yang can unite the five modes of pleasure; those who do not know this die before reaching the age of maturity and without having had the slightest pleasure from sex. Should one not forestall this danger?'

And in another lesson in the same work: Huang-ti asked: "What does one gain from practising sex according to the path of Yin and Yang?"

"For man, sex makes his energies surge – for woman, it serves as protection against sickness. Those who do not know the right path think that the sexual act can be harmful to health. In truth, the sexual act has only one purpose: physical pleasure and joy, but also peace in the heart and strength of the will. The person feels neither sated nor hungry, he is neither hot nor cold; the body is satisfied and the spirit likewise. Energy ebbs and flows majestically, and no desire troubles this harmony. This is the result of a well-accomplished union. If one follows this rule, women will achieve full pleasure and men will always remain healthy." Thus answered Sunu.

All of these manuals advocate making love as often as possible and even at an advanced age: "Whatever his age, man would not be happy living without a woman. If he is without a woman, his concentration suffers because of it. If his concentration suffers, the forces of his mind grow weaker; if the forces of his mind weaken, the span of his life grows shorter…"

The bibliography of works of the Han era, which directly pre-dated the birth of Christ, includes eight books that are entirely devoted to the art of love-making. During that era the following maxim was adopted: "The art of having sexual relations with a woman consists of remaining master of oneself and preventing ejaculation in order to allow the sperm to return to the brain." From that

15. Wedding book illustrating love positions, 19th century. Japan.

moment on, every educated Chinese man felt obliged to be familiar with the technique of reinforcing masculine power named "drinking at the jade fountain": the man had to remain inside the woman while she had her orgasm and only leave her when it was over, without releasing any sperm in the process. The treatises teach that it was even possible to make love several times in one night with different women if one followed this technique. Taoist wisdom emphasises the positive aspects of this for the man's health:

'Those who are capable of making love several times a day without spilling their sperm will be cured of all illnesses and will reach a ripe old age. If sexual relations are not limited to one woman, the success of this method will only be enhanced. The best option is to make love with ten women or more during the course of one night.'

Sex, medicine and religion are thus closely linked in Taoism because of the large number of energy channels that flow through the body. There is a link between the exterior world in which man lives and the individual interior of every human being. Sexuality is thus called upon to play a central role in everyone's life.

This explains why men thought of satisfying several women sexually as a duty. And the aim was to do it without exhausting all their energy. So, men were supposed to learn different erotic techniques for giving several women multiple orgasms without, however, experiencing their own. Taoist education, from the simplest effort right up to the most elevated spiritual heights, was founded on the control of sexual energies. Tantrism, influenced by Buddhism, was in its teachings and intentions largely similar to Taoism.

The greatest development in erotic art was principally concentrated in the rich commercial cities in the south of China, during the early part of the period that is considered the beginning of the modern era in Asia. From the tenth century onwards, cities as famous as Suzhou, Hanzhou or Quanzhou were among the most flourishing in the entire world. Businessmen frequented luxurious

16. Wedding book illustrating love positions, 19th century. Japan.

brothels, wine houses and other places of pleasure such as tea houses or the baths. They formed a sub-culture which today is largely documented by writings and novels from that period. The culture of courtesans was a part of this.

The golden age of Chinese erotic art dates from the end of the Ming period (1368-1644), which was characterised by relatively great liberty and the flourishing of all kinds of arts and science. The prudery of Confucianism was the cause of the destruction of a great number of erotic paintings which illustrated the ancient Taoist manuals. Confucianism denied eroticism, and advocated the separation of the sexes as well as the subordination of personal passions to the laws of family and the state.

Later on, Christianity played a negative role in favouring these iconoclastic practices. What had survived all of these eras was finally destroyed during the Maoist cultural revolution. These philosophical detours can no doubt go some way to explain the delicacy of Chinese eroticism. Like a mantra, these pieces of information are repeated again and again in books about China. And yet Asian eroticism still remains very enigmatic to western understanding.

As Europeans, we cannot help but wonder how sexual ecstasy can be combined with a technique that is so precisely worked out and that is controlled by such a myriad of instructions and recommendations. Does it not lead to a loss of spontaneity in one's feelings and passions? Is this whole culture of delicacy, of the small and the pure, perhaps obeying a process of distancing things from reality and idealisation? Is what is really happening actually a change in the opposite direction? Does this oh-so-subtle control of natural impulses perhaps indicate repressed anguish hidden by the official and ideological explanation of love?

For a man to avoid having an orgasm is clearly in this day and age a very reasonable method of birth control, but when this practice is advocated because of the loss of vital energies, one suspects quite another motivation. Is there not here a fear of orgasm, in the form of a fear of the oneiric dilution of one's self?

Orgasm, indeed, means "little death", because during an orgasm the barriers of the individual are broken down for a moment. To flee death ... would that not mean, in this male-centred sexuality, fleeing union with woman? Does the fear of death really mean a fear of women's power? Chastity can only be dangerous, but seeing the loss of sperm as the loss of the very substance of life is no less so.

If a young man neglects his sexual life, he will be haunted by phantoms which will rear up in his dreams in the form of seductive young women. If he gives in to them, they will suck out his vital energy. It is exactly on this point that Chinese and European traditions meet. In this dream, it is the unconscious which is reclaiming its rights. Thus, regular sexual relations are recommended.

In this sense, Chinese sexuality seems to be held hostage between two distinct fears: on the one side, there is the fear of losing one's vital energy because of sexual abstention, and on the other is the fear of losing one's vital energy by ejaculating.

Sharing, as we all, do the human condition, that is, having all been born of a mother and a father who, in one way or another, have been able to come to terms with the Oedipus complex, sexuality can only consist, even in China, of a mixture of pleasure and pain. It is exactly these elements that one must seek behind these endless affirmations of eternal harmony.

What, for example, is the significance of that fact that, in hundreds and hundreds of depictions of the sexual act claiming to offer a complete guide to all conceivable sexual positions, I have only found two or three images of cunnilingus? Was this position forbidden? In 1,000 erotic images, only three represent this theme. Isn't that strange?

17. *Images of Spring*, coloured shunga, 18th century. Silk on card.

18. Wedding book illustrating love positions, 19ᵗʰ century. Japan.

Likewise, another theme can give us an insight into repressed fears: In all the images that we have seen, women wear their shoes, even if they are naked. Unshod feet are never shown. For the Chinese, these feet, enclosed in their embroidered shoes, represented the most sublime erotic quality, and small feet exerted a very specific charm over men which we find difficult to understand today. During the Ming period, the custom of foot-binding developed rapidly. Concubines, courtesans, and also simple, mainly peasant women, had their feet broken in childhood and then had them bound for the rest of their lives. Any refusal of this custom was considered shameful. When in 1644 an attempt was made to abolish the custom, the women of Manchuria practically revolted. Indeed, this sign of nobility was held particularly dear among the poorest elements of the population. The bound foot represented at the same time the most powerful taboo: if a woman allowed her foot to be touched without resisting too strongly, one could hope for anything from her.

This custom was finally abolished by Mao Tse-Tung in 1949. Some authors have posited the theory that this 'walk of the golden lotuses' tightened the vaginal muscles, but there is no medical proof to sustain the idea.

Etiemble suggests that the bound feet of Chinese women "has nothing to do with what was, and still is, the essence of Chinese eroticism: the theory of Yin and Yang, the coitus reservatus, the

respect for the partner's orgasm and the naturalness of feelings." But perhaps we are seeking to separate things that are in fact connected. If one thinks about it – a clubfoot acquired through appalling pain, flattened ankles which sink into stockings filled with painful ulcers: this has nothing to do with Chinese eroticism. Is it not a symbolic castration of woman? A castration which found redress only in the woman's toe, the phallic significance of which was swiftly identified?

And what about the treatment of the female body during the nineteenth century? Does trussing women up in wired corsets not have some connection with European eroticism? The female body, sadistically laced up and suffocated by handcuffs and belts: is that not a fundamental indication of man's primal fear of woman?

It is clear that there persists a kind of ideology which glamourises Chinese sexuality but which is, however, nothing more than a misplaced sense of conscience. As Bougainville wrote in 1771, in his *Voyage Around the World*, as well as in other exotic accounts of the eighteenth century, people often remark that Chinese sexuality criticises our "fallen and decadent state" while hiding their own sexual conservatism and their outmoded morality.

Perhaps I, too, am nothing more than a desperately decadent European who will never be able to find the path to the noble art that is love.

19. Wedding book illustrating love positions, 19th century. Japan.

20. *Images of Spring*, coloured shunga,
    18th century. Silk on card.

21. *Images of Spring*, coloured shunga,
    18th century. Silk on card.

Between the Sublime and the Grotesque
Japanese Erotic Engravings

In contrast with classical Japanese art, books of Ukiyo-e woodcarvings show "images of a changing, ephemeral and perishable world." We know them under the name shunga, which means "spring picture."

The term "shunga" originally came from Buddhism and is associated with the idea of the painful vanity of all earthly things. Soon, however, its meaning changed as it gradually came to signify the joyful, carefree delights of everyday life, and a playful and unconcerned manner of abandoning oneself to the pleasures of the moment, of letting oneself go with the flow "like a pumpkin in the currents of a river." Thus, for the most part the Ukiyo-e illustrate scenes between courtesans and actors and are set in a world full of pleasure. The shungas allow us a glimpse into a universe where the greedy enjoyment of life is paramount and the pleasures of carnal love play an important role.

Japanese woodcarving developed over a period of the two centuries from around 1670 to 1870. Utamaro, the undisputed master of colour wood-carving, was active for only three decades of this period, between 1770 and 1800. This also happened to be the golden age of the Ukiyo-e. In his book on Utamaro, Edmond de Goncourt explains the fascination of erotic woodcarving: 'It is really worth studying the erotic paintings of the Japanese, if only because of the amazing pleasure to be had from their drawing, the impetuosity, the natural power of these sexual unions, or because of that uncontrollable desire to make love and push through the paper walls of the next room to do so. What a confusion of bodies, some entangled, some united, what greedy vigour in the arms which both attract and repulse the partner. Feet with curled toes fly through the air, long, deep embraces are exchanged. Eyes closed, eyelids downcast, their faces turned towards the ground, the women look almost as if they have fainted. And finally, look at the force and power with which the man's penis is drawn!'

Often, these books and scrolls would form part of a marriage dowry and were supposed to serve as an introduction to the art of lovemaking. In the form of printed or painted scrolls, the shungas thus became family heirlooms. In noble families, they formed part of the sexual education of the young daughter who was destined to become an insatiable lover. They were, therefore, intended not only to awaken her sexual imagination but also to bring a particular visual pleasure to the person who contemplated them.

Many of these books were destined for Yoshiwara, the pleasure district in the flourishing city of Edo in the seventeenth century. During the Tokugawa period (1600-1853), the rich bourgeois of the big cities who had during a long period of peace managed to enrich themselves still further, were enjoying a period of extraordinarily hedonistic pleasure. Districts full of dubious hotels grew at an astonishing rate until they became the centre of community life. Guides to these "houses of ill repute" were written which described in minute detail the charms and defects of the most famous courtesans, not omitting to mention the girls' prices, of course.

These "love guides" also contained information concerning the women's characters: which of the concubines was particularly clever and innovative, who was loyal and who was sincere. Other books gave lists of intimate details, with advice about how to behave with the women and explained the sexual practices that were specific to each one. For connoisseurs, there was even information about where one could find rare and unusual pleasures.

22. *Images of Spring*, coloured shunga,
18th century. Silk on card.

The collector and businessman, Hayashi Tadamasa (1851-1906), who was one of the first to bring these precious Japanese woodcarvings to Paris, owned no less than two hundred "guides to the houses of pleasure," describing the life of the courtesans of Yoshiwara.

Utamaro (1753-1806), the absolute master of coloured woodcuts, divided his life between his art and the Yoshiwara district. Goncourt, who wrote his biography, wrote of him that "He spent his days with his editor or in his studio and his nights in Yoshiwara." Since his publisher's office was situated right at the entrance to the infamous district, the path between his studio and the houses of pleasure was doubtless a short one. Perhaps we could consider him a Japanese Toulouse-Lautrec? There were fifty houses of ill-repute listed at that time, with nearly 6,000 girls, of whom at least 2,500 were courtesans offering various pleasures. Edo, which is now the city of Tokyo, numbered at the time over a million inhabitants. The greatest courtesans of the period owed the brilliance of their existence not only to the wealthy city bourgeoisie but even more particularly to the large number of provincial aristocrats who had ended up in the capital. These were men with no occupation and nothing to do; the hours they spent enjoying the pleasures of the Yoshiwara district made it easy for the police to keep them constantly under surveillance.

Just as European absolutism had declined in influence, so Japanese warrior ideology had lost an important part of its influence in Japan. Gradually love and sexuality came to replace the more bellicose activities of the nobility. So when the noblemen moved around the capital with their numerous suites, they travelled regularly by horse to the Yoshiwara district or were carried there by litter. The state police had, therefore, not hesitated to grant a licence to the pleasure district; it made their task of surveillance much easier to have this group of individuals all in one place. Yoshiwara was founded about 1600 on marshy land – then known as "rush land" – and was situated behind the imperial palace. In 1657, after the great city fire, it had to move to the area near the Merciful Temple of Asakusa, but its name remained unchanged. The district was then surrounded by walls and ditches and divided into nine separate areas. Entering this "town of perpetual daylight which glitters resplendent like a peacock's tail", the first thing one would have encountered was the main street with its fifty tea houses which really did serve tea and nothing more.

In a way, they acted as the antechambers to the brothels and as places where clients and prostitutes could meet and agree on terms. Parties took place there and everything was so incredible and splendid

23. *Images of Spring*, coloured shunga, 18th century. Silk on card.

37.

24. *Images of Spring*, coloured shunga,
18th century. Silk on card.

"one began to doubt whether one was still on earth." The "library" of these "houses of ill-repute" usually consisted of erotic books. As clients waited their turn, they would pass the time drinking tea and flicking through these albums with their risqué pictures and amusing stories. As with the Greeks, physical love signified an elevated state of being for the Japanese also. Like the Greek hetaera, the courtesans of Yoshiwara were proficient in different arts. They wore beautiful and costly garments just like real princesses. Jippensha Ikku, a friend of Utamaro, once said of the women of Yoshiwara: "They are educated like princesses. From a very early age they are given a full education. They know how to read and write, they learn all the arts, music as well as the tea ceremony, ikebana or the best way to arrange a bunch of incense." At the beginning, the courtesans used to use an old-fashioned poetic language, as had been the custom in the imperial palaces over a thousand years earlier, but which no longer bore any resemblance to everyday Japanese.

So, is the geisha a robot-like creature created solely for man's satisfaction? She is, as Théo Lesoualc'h has remarked, the product of a long transformation wrought by the Japanese to the image of woman: the flawless form in which all elements of "femininity" can be found condensed. Nothing

in a geisha's behaviour is left to chance. In the eyes of the man, she is the symbol of perfection, from her refined and artistic hairstyle or her way of wearing make-up and wooden-soled sandals, right down to the perfectly-judged manner of her behaviour, which clearly dictated how she should position her body, what her conversation should be and how she should express her feelings. "The geisha is the archetype of woman. She is the erotic fetish of feminine grace, although codified and reduced," wrote Lesoualc'h.

A Westerner looking at shungas will notice first of all the cold and detached expressions on the faces of the couples making love. Both sexes consummate the sexual act with a stoic impassivity as if they were only partially involved in the act. Only their stretched-out and curled toes and the cloth which the woman bites with all her might to contain her excitement betray the extent of their ecstasy. Following the traditional rules of this art nothing which could possibly move the observer is expressed here. One might also notice the extremely exaggerated, almost caricature-like dimensions of the male organ. Could it be a fear of impotence that lies behind these over-inflated penises? Or is it the product of a fantasy which itself hides man's fear of woman's untamed nature? However, what

25. *Images of Spring*, coloured shunga, 18th century. Silk on card.

26. *Images of Spring*, coloured shunga,
18th century. Silk on card.

we also find in these over-sized penises are reflections of the ancient phallic cult of the Shinto religion. Shintoism, which is the indigenous religion of Japan and a cult entirely devoid of all metaphysical dogmas, is an astonishing mixture of the most varied rituals in honour of over 800 polymorphic gods.

Thus the phallus quite naturally became a god to whom temples, or private altars at home, were dedicated. It was even invoked in prayer on some evenings in the pleasure districts during the seventeenth and eighteenth centuries. Even today one can still come across ancient phallic steles on the edges of fields which have been placed there as symbols of fertility. Festivals in honour of the phallus were a regular event and were the occasion for exuberant processions. An account dating from the end of the nineteenth century describes one of these processions in Tokyo: "A phallus several metres high, all covered in gleaming varnish, was placed on a sort of portable casket and carried by a group of young men, who were shouting or laughing at the tops of their voices. They zig-zagged along the streets and made sudden, unexpected charges in all directions. Real Baccanalian rites!" Thus the cult of the phallus was the backbone of the Shinto religion. In the temples, wooden, porcelain, stone or metal phallic figures were sold as good-luck charms. Japan never suppressed

sensuality as such; if there were laws and limitations, they were always socially based but never religious. To seek physical pleasure was considered a natural desire, even if it consisted of unusual practices. Thus, sodomy figured among the normal pleasures of the body. The word "sin", it seems, was never uttered. Even when we are shown "natural love" in its many varied forms in the woodcarvings, they always involve massive priapic fantasies.

Almost all masters of woodcarving produced erotic images, sometimes even in such precious materials as gold, silver or mother-of-pearl. And yet the shunga studios were for the most part clandestine. Artists did not sign their work, or else used a pseudonym. The number of copies made was always limited and most often sold on the black market.

Purity of line became a rule that could not be broken for woodcarving; the artist had to carve out the lines in the wood with extreme care. Parallel perspective was mainly dominant: lines that were parallel in nature were also parallel in the wood. Central perspective, which was a European invention, was only introduced in the nineteenth century. Likewise, the Japanese were not familiar with the effects of shadow and light which are so much a part of European art. The initial technique was to print onto paper with one sole block and then to colour the picture by hand which considerably restricted the

27. *Images of Spring*, coloured shunga,
18th century. Silk on card.

41.

28. *Images of Spring*, coloured shunga,
    18th century. Silk on card.

numbers which could be produced because of the time involved. For this reason, they started using several blocks in the eighteenth century. Katsushika Hokusai (1760-1848) is the last great figure of the Ukiyo-e. After him, woodcarving began to decline, giving way to vulgar copies produced in large numbers and designed to cater to the tastes of the masses. By the second quarter of the nineteenth century, it had, to all intents and purposes, become a popular art. For a long time, Europe ignored Ukiyo-e on the grounds that its content went beyond the boundaries of good taste. It was not until the universal exhibitions in Paris of 1867, 1878 and 1889 that a western audience had the opportunity to rediscover an art form that had hitherto been despised. After that, none would dare deny the major influence of Japanese woodcarving on the entire Impressionist movement.

The English artist Aubrey Beardsley probably possessed the finest collection of Ukiyo-e and shunga. His work, which is so characteristic of the late nineteenth century, is a perfect illustration of the influence of Japanese woodcarving on western art.

Toulouse-Lautrec also possessed a remarkable collection, a few photographs of which remain. These prints, with their images of cruel and violent ghosts, seem to have particularly affected him, especially the scenes where women are embraced by animals, monkeys, foxes, badgers or vampires.

By contrast, in Japan throughout the nineteenth century these prints were hidden and forbidden. As the land of the rising sun became more industrialised, it also became more open to western influences and the Ukiyo-e disappeared into people's desk drawers. In effect, from the moment when the Meiji emperors seized power in 1868, Japan started flirting with the idea of assimilating into Europe. For this reason, any over-obvious signs of fertility cults or their symbols, especially images of the phallus, were suppressed as they were considered unworthy of a modern nation. The American occupation after the Second World War dealt the final blow to Shintoism. Today, most of the classical shungas which are offered for sale in the West are bought by Japanese collectors who are returning them to their home country in this way.

However, it was not until a massive exhibition of Japanese woodcarvings took place in 1973 at the Victoria and Albert Museum in London, that the majority of art lovers were given the opportunity of re-learning how to appreciate the true value of these erotic works.

Perhaps today we need to look at these works with new eyes, forgetting that over almost 150 years they served as the languorous representations of our desire for a simple sexuality that rises above all notion of "sin".

29. *Images of Spring*, coloured shunga, 18th century. Silk on card.

44.

In Praise of the Backside

Our Arses Shall Be Symbols of Peace

Behind-thoughts[30] on the realm of the moons of flesh

For Jürgen Lentes

The arse is the proletariat of body parts. It is condemned to namelessness; we search the dictionaries in vain for suitable expressions. At most, the common or vulgar expression serves as a term of abuse. The gesture of showing the bare behind is interpreted as obscene and shocking. Sometimes it is the despised location where punishment is administered. Its presence is characterised by passivity. The work ethic internalised in bourgeois society places passivity, indolence and inactivity under a taboo from the aesthetic point of view as well. Thus the posterior has become an obscene part of the body, especially when its indolence is emphasised by the growth of adipose tissue.[31] The rear-end represents worthlessness within the framework of the body; it is held to be the most soulless part of the body and thus has every reason to groan sometimes, deeply and wordlessly.

Idealistic aesthetic theory, with its reservations about anything that "resembles bestial ugliness" (Rosenkranz), banished the bottom from the repertoire of beautiful objects worthy of representation. It is a physical representation of the opposition between spirit and matter. Where the spirit strives upward, its gravity drags us down. In his work, *The Nude,* (1958), Kenneth Clark analyses the classical conception of physical beauty. "Nothing which bears any relationship to the human being as a whole was removed or ignored." So the proportions of the body are discussed, the moulding of the stomach, the rounding of the hips, the play of muscles in the arms and legs, but not the posterior – as if it were not part of the whole.

In every respect the arse is the symbol of everything offensive. This verdict on the anal region is yet more effective and far-reaching since, from infancy onwards, it is linked with the experience of sexual pleasure. Lou Andreas-Salomé[32] argued that the first prohibition a child encounters is against taking pleasure in the products of the anal region. This prohibition is decisive for his or her entire future development. Freud explains; "It is in this context that the infant must first become aware of an environment hostile to its instinctive drives, must learn to separate its own being from this other, and then perform the first 'displacement' of its outlets for pleasure." From infancy onwards, the anal region remains the symbol of everything worthless, everything that must be separated from life.

Bourgeois aesthetics and the libidinous destiny of anality converge in one concept; "disgust". It is precisely the tabooing of the bottom, however, that gives its exposure a sense of potential anti-bourgeois protest. There have been many reports throughout the twentieth century of young women

30. Félicien Rops, circa 1890.

45.

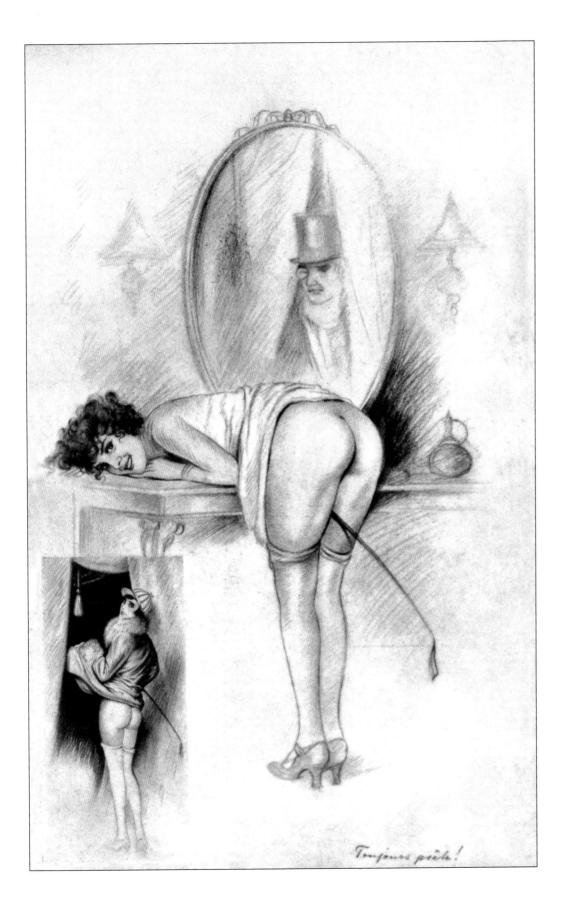

Toujours prête!

31. Berthomme de Saint-André, 1927.

32. Reunier (pseudonym of
Breuer-Courth), 1925.

and girls baring their bottoms in public – provocatively, boastfully, ostentatiously. Towards the end of the 1950s, there was talk of a new phenomenon – "mooning" by entire groups of young men. By the 1970s, this was increasingly the case among young women as well. Hans-Peter Dürr[33] has indicated that this was a provocative act of rule-breaking. The taboo, which continued to exist under the concept of modesty, was deliberately broken by anal exhibitionism.

Jean-Jacques Rousseau had already written about the pleasures of anal exhibitionism. In his *Confessions,* he informs us that when he was about eighteen years old – round about 1730, therefore – he used to look for "dark alleys and remote spots where I would show myself at a distance to young women in the posture I really wished to adopt close to them. What they saw was not the obscene member – I never ever thought of that – but its reverse, the ridiculous. The silly pleasure I took in mooning in front of them is indescribable. I really only needed to take another step further in order to experience the treatment I longed for, since I had no doubt that one or other more resolute girl would have done it to me in passing if I had had the courage to wait." Did he want to be spanked on his bottom? In any case, according to his own estimation, he gave the girls "more of a ridiculous sight than a seductive one. The cleverest pretended not to notice; others shrieked with laughter, while others took offence and made a fuss."

In spite of disgust and shame, people retain their fascination with this part of the body, with its functions and products – even, and especially, when they campaign against "obscenity". A secret, displaced pleasure can always be detected under cover of disgust.

We know of the twenty-one-year-old Mozart's letters to "Bäsele", presumably his first lover. In these, he celebrates scatological verbal orgies in a boisterous, almost infantile manner; this is probably the reason these letters were unpublished for so long. Untamed pleasure in anality ignites a verbal faecal-firework display. On 13 November, 1777, he wrote from Mannheim; "I'm sorry about the bad handwriting, my pen is already old. Soon it will be twenty-two years that I have been shitting out of the same hole, and it's still not torn! – and I've shat so often..." On 28 February he writes; "I just did a big fart! Our arses should be the signs of peace. Shit! – Shit! O sweet word![34]"

Anal eroticism seems to be an indisputable fertile soil of our culture, and psychoanalysis has shown that the drives which are interpreted as anal-erotic have an extraordinary significance for our inner life as well as our cultural life. The bottom is a place where instinctive drives and their sublimation can be localised, so that it could be said that it represents the cradle of our culture. The posterior as the other side of "high" culture? What is our concept of beauty? It is there even when not discussed. Does not the idea "And the Word was made flesh and dwelt among us, and we behold its glory" refer precisely to the buttocks?[35] Fashion has always been aware of this. Women have always tried to draw men's attention to their rears, whether by swaying them ostentatiously while walking, or by artificial padding for fashionable emphasis, as though their entire attractiveness depended on the attractiveness of their bottoms.

In the history of fashion, periods of slimness alternate with periods of voluptuousness. The cult of the callipygian is always found in those periods where rounded, curvaceous, voluptuous women embody the ideal of beauty. The posterior loses its aesthetic value in periods where slimness is the norm.

The Rococo was a period of sophisticated eroticism. It is evident from illustrations of the period that a lovely backside was admired just as much as a lovely bosom. A publication entitled *Servants of Beauty,* which appeared in Leipzig in 1774, gives the following opinion of what constitutes a lovely

33. Berthomme de Saint-André, 1927.

34. Achille Devéria, circa 1830. Lithograph.

35. Achille Devéria, circa 1830. Lithograph.

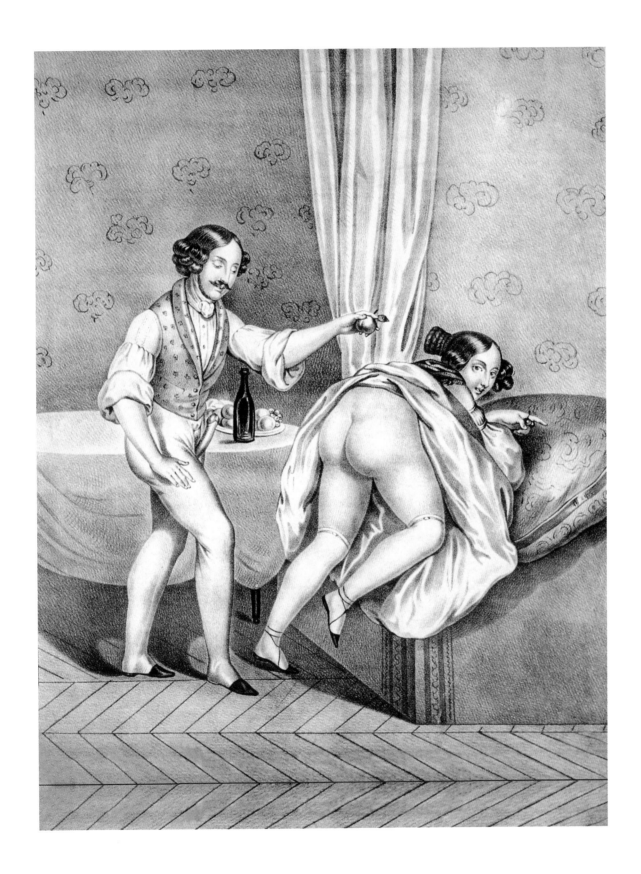

backside: "Those buttocks are considered beautiful that are evenly placed, not too high, and not uneven as in lame people whose hip-bones are displaced, that do not stick out like a bay window; not so large and fat that you could dance on them, but not so skinny and sharp that you could drill holes with them, but rounded, hard, taut, so that they have a pleasing resonance when slapped, smooth and white..." We see that the image of a firm bottom is not new, just the concepts change.

> Goethe was also aware of the charms of a lovely backside;
> "I know a girl who has a lovely mouth,
> And lovely round cheeks...
> And something else round as well,
> That I never grow weary of gazing on."

It was the fashion to emphasise these curves with extra padding, for instance with an item known as the "Cul de Paris". This was described in a women's dictionary of 1725: "A French backside is a rounded, soft and lightly padded cushion or loincloth that a woman wears beneath her skirts so as to pad out her rear end and draw attention to her figure". The "Cul de Paris" experienced its greatest triumph during the Biedermeier period, when it developed into a fixed steel frame which gave the impression of curves which often did not exist.

Men also took pride in having taut buttocks. During the Renaissance especially, opulent male figures were appreciated. Many contemporaries described the closely-cut breeches which particularly emphasise the buttocks as shameless. A chronicle from 1492 records: "Young men wore tunics that came no longer than a hand span below the belt, so that their breeches could be seen quite clearly, in front and behind, and they were so tight that the cleavage of their buttocks was obvious; a fine thing!" In the first half of the sixteenth century wide breeches which gave the impression of huge buttocks became fashionable, quite in keeping with the course sexuality of the period. In our own day the cult of the callipygian has gained a considerable improvement in status thanks to the modern fashion for trousers, especially the worldwide triumphal progress of jeans, for both sexes.

Nevertheless fashion has never managed to achieve a genuine "décolletage" of the buttocks. An erotic story from 1905 describes a "ball" of the buttocks: "Lovely lady, I think that bottoms have been condemned to suffer since the creation of the world; now it is time that they were honoured, it's only fair... Choose a form of exposure that corresponds to the form of its beauty. You are permitted to adorn it elaborately with pearls or diamonds, veil it with gauze, frame it with ruches and frills, drape it with blue or red, according to the colour of your hair. If you adorn this part of your body with the same artistry as you adorn your bosom, I can guarantee, ladies, that you will look divine, and the success of the festivities will be recorded for posterity." Only recently have "décolletages" for bottoms been seen at "Love-Parades"[36]

But there may be an archaic need to expose this part of the body which so fascinates one's sexual partner. This may well be a survival of the time when copulation took place exclusively from behind. J. Eibl-Eibesfeldt[66] claims that bushmen still prefer to copulate in this position even today. Even in our own culture, the archaic methods of copulation play an important role. Freud established that in all fantasies or memories of origins, *coitus a tergo*, in the manner of animals, is imagined.

36. Achille Devéria, circa 1830.
Romantic Lithography.

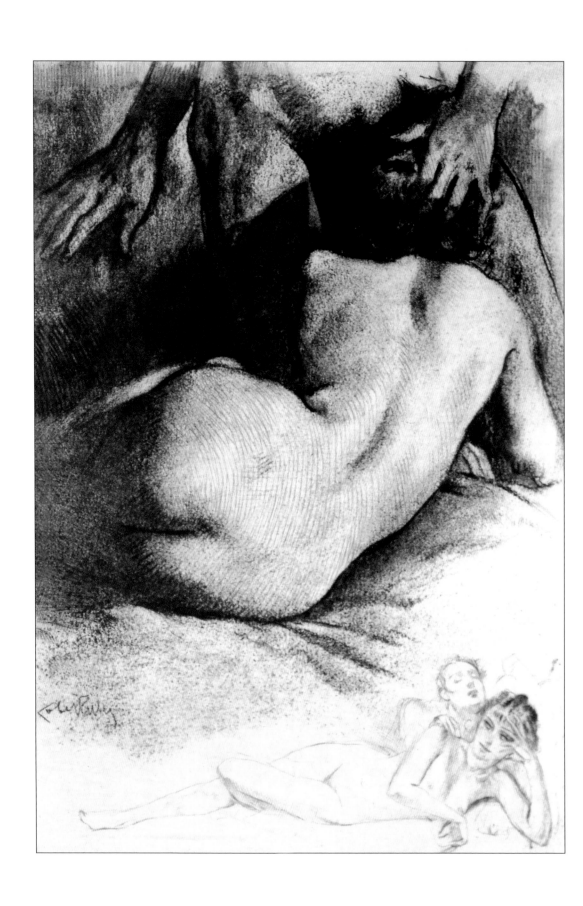

37. Lobel-Riche, 1936.

38. Lobel-Riche, 1936.

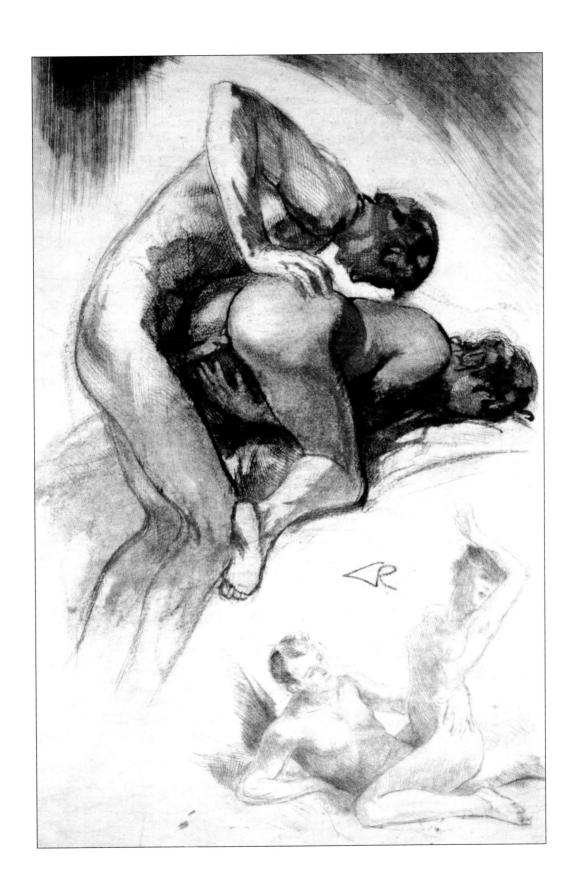

In antiquity, the admiring observation of the posterior was one of the common ways of evaluating a female. Competitions to discover the loveliest bottom were common. One of Alkiphron's "hetaerae[67] letters" describes a wild symposium held by courtesans in which the spectacular climax is a dispute between two of them as to who has the prettier and more graceful bottom. The dispute is arbitrated by an exhibition: "First of all, Myrrhina loosened her girdle – she kept on her thin silken garment[68] – and swayed back and forth, so that her bottom trembled like thick, creamy milk, and she looked over her shoulder to watch its movements; she uttered soft sighs, as though she were in the throes of love's ecstasy. But Thryallis didn't let herself be intimidated, but went even further in shamelessness.

"'I'm not going to compete in thin robes', she said, 'and I'm not going to be coy, but I'll be naked as in a wrestling match. Coyness has no place in this competition'. She cast off her garment and swayed her hips slightly. 'Look', she said, 'see how even the colour is, how spotless, how pure, see my rosy hips and how they shade into my thighs, there are no bulges of fat visible, nor any bones, nor any dimples. And indeed, by Zeus, it doesn't tremble like Myrrhina's – and she smiled slightly. And then she demonstrated the play of muscles and swayed her buttocks so that the muscles danced across her hips, and everyone applauded and victory was awarded to Thryallis." The decision was influenced not only by the appearance and characteristics of the posterior but also by the charm of the environment in which it was exposed.

The well-known *Judgment of Paris* is the model for such beauty contests. A similar competition in Syracuse is at the base of the legend of the founding of a cult of Aphrodite. The two daughters of a simple peasant were competing to see which had the prettiest bottom; to judge between them they chose a young man of good family who promptly fell in love with the older sister while his younger brother fell for the younger sister. There was a double wedding and the two girls dedicated a temple to Aphrodite, to whom they gave the name "Kallipygos", "She of the lovely Buttocks."

Exposure and demonstration of the buttocks is part of the repertoire of erotic gestures which prostitutes use to arouse their clients. Already in the fifth century B.C. admiration was being expressed for dancers who danced "with kilted-up skirts" and then undressed and allowed their posteriors to be admired.

The posterior gained aesthetic recognition thanks to this exhibitionism; it is unjustly despised, because the charms of a beautiful bottom appeal to the aesthetic sense of both sexes. F. Th. von Vischer[69] states that it is the "peach-like shape" of the bottom which creates aesthetic appreciation. The effect of these sculptural charms explains why many content themselves with seeing the buttocks and derive sexual pleasure from the sight.

We know from reports of the Papal Court of Pope Alexander VI that the erotic attraction of the posterior sometimes led to public orgies. One chronicle reports; "Once there was a dinner in the Apostolic Palace at which many distinguished courtesans were present. After the meal they were required to dance with the servants and guests, first dressed, then naked. After the dancing, flaming torches were placed on the ground and chestnuts were thrown between them, which the naked women picked up, crawling between the torches, bending and swaying a hundred times, while Cesare and Lucretia Borgia watched. This charming scene took place on the eve of All Saints' Day 1501." In England the predilection for the sight of callipygian charms gave rise to a particular type of prostitute known as "posture girls"[70]. This branch of prostitution seems to have arisen about 1750,

39. Paul-Emile Becat, 1848.

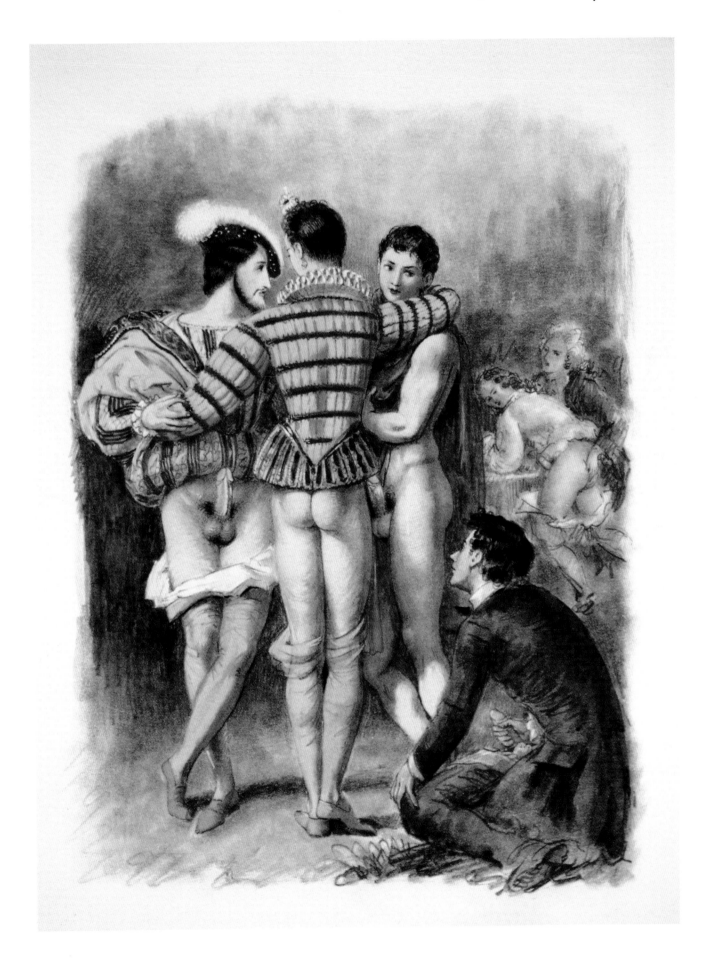

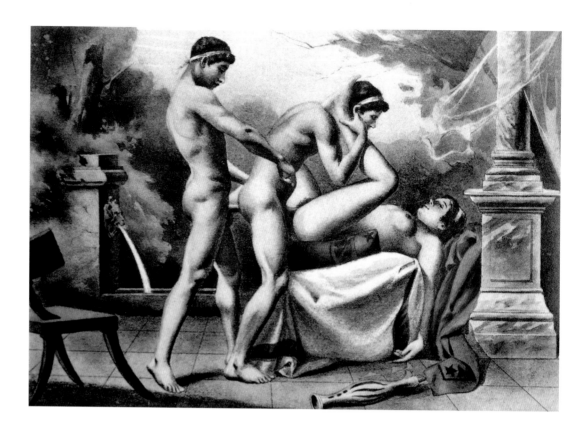

as it is mentioned for the first time in many erotic writings of that time. For instance, *The History of the Human Heart* or *The Adventure of a Young Gentleman* (London, 1769) refers to "posture girls", who "stripped stark naked and mounted themselves on the middle of the table"[42] in order to show off their attributes. The behaviour of these "girls" in a brothel in Great Russell Street is graphically described in *Midnight Spy*. Urbanus says, "There we see an object that arouses at once indignation and pity. A beautiful woman lies on the ground, showing that part of her body which, were she not dead to all sense of shame, she would eagerly seek to conceal. As she is given to drunkenness, she usually arrives at the house slightly tipsy, and displays herself in front of men in this indecent manner after two or three glasses of Madeira. Look, now she is being carried out like an animal. People mock her, but she is delighted to prostitute such incomparable beauty." This type of anal-erotic voyeurism was particularly common in England at this time.

This admiration of the posterior was definitely ambivalent, as expressed in accompanying fantasies of corporal punishment. That which is desired is also a "damnable" object, and not only in puritanical cultures. One's own fascination has to be suppressed by punishing the desired object. Thus in the idea of flagellation (for which England was particularly notorious) there is a defensive reaction against one's own desires. In *Our Mutual Friend*, Dickens has this to say of the cherubic Mr. Wilfer: "So boyish was he in his curves and proportions, that his old schoolmaster meeting him in Cheapside, might have been unable to withstand the temptation of caning him on the spot"[43]. A pedagogue in antiquity would undoubtedly have solved the problem in an entirely different way. A poem by Heine also satirises the motif of corporal punishment. In *Citronia*, from the "Last Poems", he describes a schoolmistress sitting in her armchair: "And a birch-rod in her hand, with which she beats the little brat. The little one, who

40. Paul Avril, circa 1910.

committed a trivial fault, is weeping. She lifts up the skirts and the little globes with their charming, lovely curves, sometimes like roses sometimes like lilies - ah, the old lady beats them black and blue. To be ill treated and insulted - this is the fate of beauty on earth." In normal editions of Heine, the middle section of the verse is omitted. Another stroke of the rod, this time from the pen of the censor against the delightful lines. It is not far from pleasure in exposure of the posterior to anal intercourse; a beautiful object that is desired must also be possessed.

In a study of *The Posterior in Antiquity*, Adrian Stähli indicates that, in vase paintings of the sixth and fifth centuries B.C. depicting the act of intercourse, the posture of anal intercourse is predominant or, if vaginal penetration is depicted, then it is in a position where the woman shows her bottom to the man, suggesting anal penetration to him or to anyone seeing the illustration. It is time to take a rear view of our idealised, posterior-less image of the Greeks. As Kenneth Clark emphasised: "This deeply rooted awareness, the recognition of the significance of physical beauty, protected the Greeks from the two evils of sensuality and aestheticism." No - sensuality was increased by beauty! The classical object of libidinousness was - the posterior!

As Stähli has indicated, this was in no way gender-neutral; in antiquity, anal penetration was perceived at least potentially as a homosexual act. "The female posterior and that of a boy whom a homosexual lover finds attractive are, in principle, interchangeable." In comparison with the much more highly valued charms of a boy's bottom, a woman's was always second best. "Homosexual epigrams from the Hellenistic period and the Roman Empire praise boys' bottoms every bit as enthusiastically as the eulogies to women's backsides". As in the case of praise of women's rears, the shape, form and colour of boys' backsides are praised and described in detail. Far more often than the

41. Paul Avril, circa 1910.

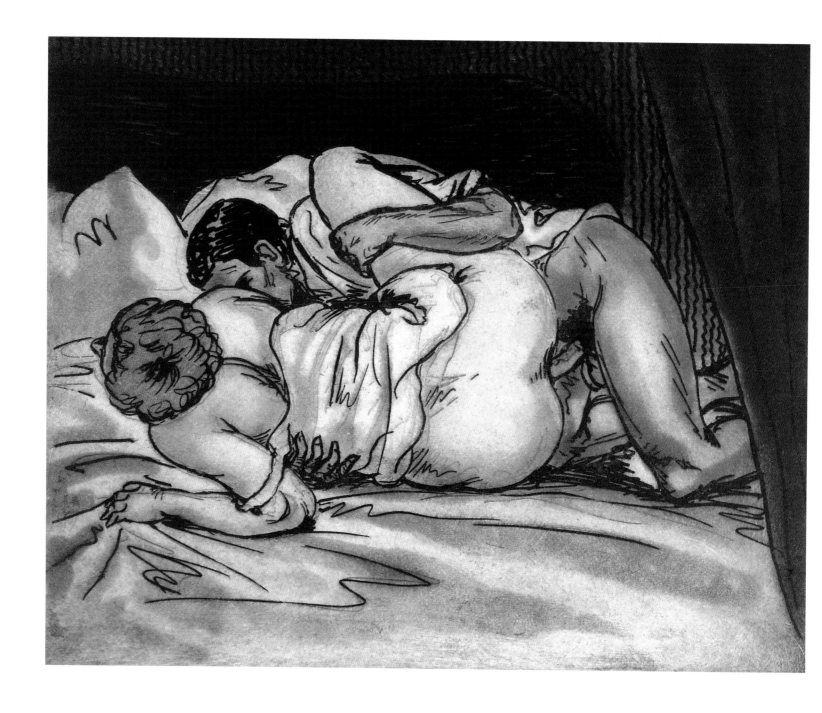

penis, the backside is seen as the decisive element of the desired boy's sexual attractiveness. The desire to penetrate male rears is diverted to females. This is also the part of the body where sexuality is an expression of male dominance.

Contempt for the posterior no doubt owes its origin mainly to Christianity, which must have seen in it a heathen place of worship. At least since the thirteenth century, "unnatural indecency", which included anal intercourse, was declared to be one of the worst of sexual sins, and the Church never ceased to condemn it most severely. Any danger that threatened the continuation of the species had to be abolished – thus, three sins against Nature were denounced more fiercely than ever; sodomy, masturbation and abstinence.

The Renaissance, however, did not only bring about a revival of the writings of the authors of antiquity. The new Humanism also led to an unusual valuation of sexuality. The confrontation with profane examples of classical literature led inevitably to recognition of the value of the erotic for Greek and Roman culture, a recognition that also encompassed the visual arts. For the "intellectuals" of the fifteenth and sixteenth centuries, the greatest happiness consisted of a symbiosis of intellectual, sexual and culinary pleasures. Aretino[44] wrote glowing praises of callipygian charms. In his "Dialogues" he writes: "then he held the cheeks of her bottom apart with gentle hands – it looked as if he were turning the white pages of a missal – and looked at her backside, absolutely enchanted. It was neither a spiky bag of bones, nor a wobbly lump of fat, but exactly the right size and shape, a bit tremulous and curvy, shining like living ivory. The dimples that one is so glad to see on the chin and cheeks of lovely women adorn her posterior as well. The cheeks were tender as a mouse born and bred in a mill, completely covered with flour. And all her limbs were so smooth that the hand he put on her flank slid down to her calf, like a foot turning on the ice." At least in Rome in the sixteenth century, anal intercourse was re-instated in its rights. This is the interpretation of several extracts from Aretino's *Sonetti Lussuriosi*, for instance the depiction of a woman grasping the erect penis of a man who is pretending to protest, in order to put it into her anus:

(She)
 Where do you want to put it? Tell me please,
In front or behind? Because it might annoy you
If during our play
It slipped into my arse.

(He)
 O no, Madonna, a ride in the cunt
Doesn't have that much sex appeal.
What I do, I do with the aim
Of not offending against custom.
But if you really want it anally,
Then it is decided –
Stick the arrow in the hole that we've always avoided.
You'll see, it will do you good
Like medicine to an invalid.

42. Courbouleix, circa 1935.

And when I feel your hand on my prick

I'm so happy – when we fuck,

I'll probably die of joy.

(Translated by Thomas Hettche)[45]

This is another very free rendering of another sonnet:

(She)

If you don't like my cunt, take me from behind

Only a liar would claim that he would ignore my arse.

(He)

This fuck in the cunt, the next in the arse.

I enjoy both, and so will you.

Aretino and many of his contemporaries were aware that many women disliked anal intercourse. The *Sonetti Lussuriosi* and the *Dialogues of Courtesans* repeatedly mention the fact that intercourse "from behind" was only a pleasure for the man:

(She)

From behind is a pleasure only for you.

 In front for both of us.

And so your maid says:

Do it by the rules or not at all.

At the beginning of the sixteenth century, pederasty was widespread among the educated aristocracy, just as it was in Greek antiquity – and also the desire to "treat women like men". Especially the senior clergy showed a particular predilection for this phenomenon, which thus acquired the label "prelate's dish" or "pleasures of the great and the good."

Most lovers of boys, whether clergy, poets or aristocrats, were not homosexuals in the strict sense of the word but bisexual. They experienced the same pleasure that they got from sexual intercourse with boys when they "treated a woman like a man". This pleasure was increased when the woman wore men's clothes and so appeared to give the optical illusion of being a boy. This was something unheard of as it disregarded the Church's strict prohibition. Nevertheless, Roman and Venetian courtesans were often happy to dress as men. Alfred Semmerau quotes a decree of 1578: "The licentiousness and brazenness of the courtesans and whores of Venice has grown to such an extent that, in order to attract and seduce young men, they have adopted, among other fashions, this new and uncommon fashion of dressing as men. Whores and courtesans are hereby forbidden to appear in the streets dressed as men, on pain of three years' imprisonment and perpetual banishment. Gondoliers who assist them will be sent to the galleys for eighteen months..."

In another work of the period, the origin of the term "bugger" is discussed; this term for homosexual and anal intercourse is alleged to have developed from the fact that a king exclaimed "che buco raro" (what a rare hole!) on seeing his catamite's anus. It was claimed that those who maintained

43. Berthomme de Saint-André, 1927.

that, on the contrary, the word was derived from "bucum errare" (to take the wrong hole), were misinformed. This type of etymology was the sort of intellectual word game that was very popular among bisexual writers' circles.

Goethe was also indebted to the libertinism of antiquity when he wrote in his Venetian Epigrams of 1790; "I have also loved boys, but I prefer girls – If I am tired of them as girls, then I can still use them as boys". Was Goethe thinking of the Roman poet Martial?

> I spent the entire night with a girl
> So wanton that no-one could satisfy her.
> I was tired after all sorts of positions, so I asked her
> To give me what boys usually give.
> Almost before I'd made the request she agreed to it.

A girl's "boyish garland"[46] was the ultimate aim of pleasure, and the bottom was an altar on which sacrifices were gladly made.

De Sade's apotheosis of a lovely posterior was really a blasphemous insult to the view taken by Christianity, although he placed great emphasis on examples from Antiquity; "This rare pleasure has nothing to do with age; young Alcibiades was no less susceptible to it than the elderly Socrates; there are many nations who have preferred this exquisite part of the body to all other beauties of the female form; and indeed there is no other that so deserves the voluptuous caresses of a true libertine more than this, due not only to its pallor, curves, and enchanting perfection of form but also to the tender pleasures it promises.

"Unhappy the man who has never fucked a boy or treated his girlfriend as a boy! For anyone who has experienced neither the one nor the other, debauchery is still virgin territory" (*Justine*). In *120 Days*, de Sade writes; "O precious arses, upon your altar I swear never again to stray from you." For writers in classical antiquity, homage to this part of the body was a variation on the theme of sensual pleasure, but de Sade experienced it as "excess", as expressed by Bataille.[76] The blasphemous intention is obvious. Coeur-de-Fer instructs Justine, "Many father confessors have trodden this pilgrims' path, without anyone's parents being aware of it. Do I need to say any more, Justine? If this temple is the most secret, it is also the most pleasurable."

As recently as a century after de Sade and Goethe, the idea had already become anathema. Such pleasures suffocated under bourgeois morality, by which the *Psychopathia Sexualis* was very much influenced. Krafft-Ebing's[77] air stood on end: "One hideous phenomenon is the paedicatio mulierum, in some circumstances even uxorum! Libertines sometimes do it for particular titillation with prostitutes or even with their own wives. There are examples of men who sometimes have anal intercourse with their wives!" All that remains of the breadth of humanistic education is bad schoolboy Latin. What was previously an enjoyable variant of sexual behaviour was now classified as a perversion. The previous condemnation of anal intercourse under Christianity had become a quasi-scientific condemnation, introduced under the cover of *Enlightenment*.

Are we experiencing a new Renaissance today, as far as sexuality is concerned? One of our aims in life, apart from career success, is to have a fulfilling sex life. We have a less rigid upbringing, with the result that anality is no longer so vehemently condemned. The pressure of Christian sexual

44. Jean Morisot, 1925.

45. Jean Morisot, 1925.

46. Marcel Vertés, 1938.

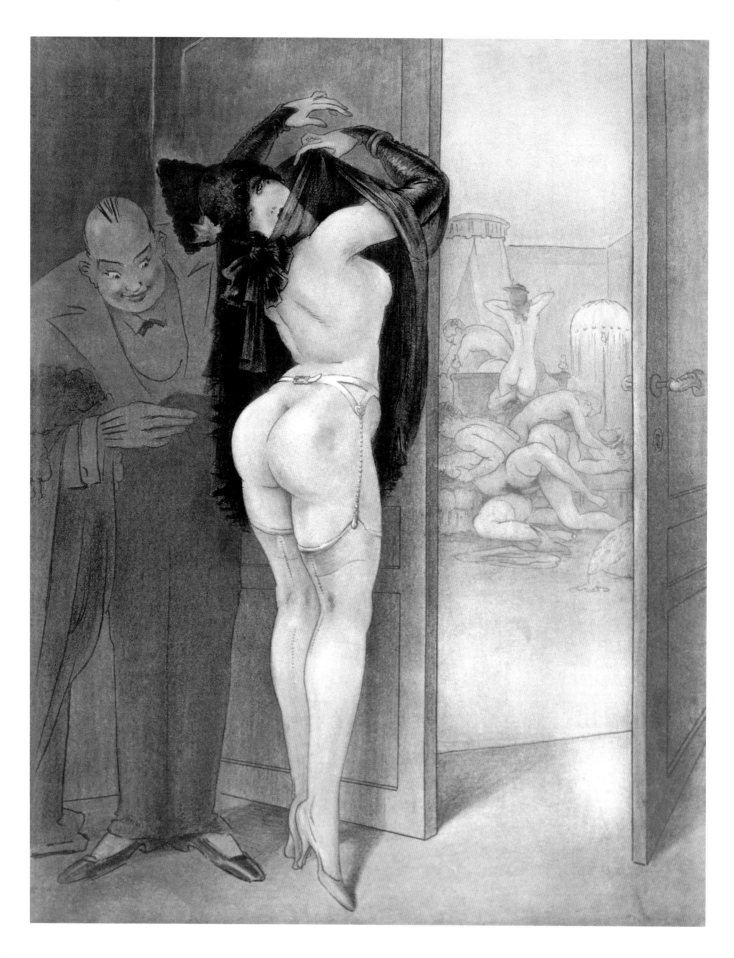

morality has given way to a "morality of negotiation" between partners; whatever gives pleasure is permitted, as long as there is mutual consent.

A culture of bisexuality is developing which is opening up the one-way street of heterosexual intercourse to traffic in the opposite direction. The image of a "boyish" posterior is idealised, at least within European culture, and men and women promise equal pleasures "from behind" – this is reinforced by fashions which minimise the differences between the sexes. Is there going to be a cultural reconciliation with our "part maudite"?[78] This poem by Hans Magnus Enzensberger[79] may be an indication of the future:

> Shit
> I often hear people talk about it
> As though everything were its fault.
> But look how gently and modestly
> It takes its place among us!
> So why do we sully
> Its good name
> And bestow it
> On the President of the USA,
> On the cops, on war
> And on capitalism?
>
> How transitory it is,
> And how permanent
> Everything we give its name to!
> It is yielding,
> But when we talk about it
> We mean exploiters.
> Is this now
> How we express our anger?
>
> Has it not relieved us?
> Soft
> And curiously powerless
> It is probably
> The most peaceful action of humanity.
> What has it ever done to us?
> Or, as Mozart put it, "Our arses should be signs of peace!"

47. Anonymous, 1900.

Une pièce croustillante.

70.

Feet-Ishism

"Find me a ribbon from her bosom,
A Garter of My Lust!"

Every lover is also somewhat of an erotic fetishist. He, or she, loves objects that have been in close or intimate contact with the beloved and thus are especially dear. These objects ensure the proximity and closeness of the beloved. Special physical forms of expression of this desired person can also become a symbol for the significance of the partner as a loved and cherished individual: a way of walking, a way of smiling, "the way you wear your hat, the way you sip your tea." Physical characteristics such as hair colour, shape of eyes and mouth, clothing, etc. can constitute the cause, the movens, of being in love. Today, a value such as youth itself seems to have turned into an overvalued fetish. As long as these concrete and physical symbols represent the totality of the loved individual, one can speak of a "normal fetish".

However, there are forms in which the sexual partner disappears completely behind the symbol, sometimes to the extent that the symbol is stripped of its symbolic character and becomes the sexual trigger and stimulus itself. This is what occurs when items of clothing, especially shoes, stockings, handkerchiefs, and underwear play a significant role.

In classical literature cases are known when handkerchiefs, clothing, money purses, and braids are snatched from their owners through violence and trickery to satisfy a sexual motive, while orgasm occurs in part during the act of purloining, in part through masturbation when subsequently viewing, or handling the fetish.

All of these objects are charged with magical powers similar to the "holy relics" of Christianity and the amulets of so-called "indigenous tribes." The term applied to the phenomenon of fetishism also has its roots in ethnology. During the fifteenth and sixteenth century, when the Portuguese in West Africa noticed the reverence and veneration with which the local natives treated such objects as stones, sticks, and idols, they compared these objects with amulets or talismans and called them "feiticio" [Italian: "fetisso"] or "magic," a word which is derived from the Latin "factitius" [of magic power]. This magical thinking, which also penetrated the cults of Christian religion, corresponds with a deep human need. Those who are aware of the close relationship between religious and erotic sensations and feelings understand that fetishist imagery also occurs frequently in love.

The Frenchman A. Binet was the first to describe sexual fetishism in his 1877 article *Du fétichisme dans l'amour*. The few mentioned examples of fetishist objects already illustrate how much the fetishes themselves depend on current fashions. The braids of old have been cut off a long time ago and a paper Kleenex will hardly become an object feverishly desired by a lover. Shoe and foot fetishism has been influenced by fashion as well. When women still wore long skirts with their feet every so often accidentally peeking out from underneath, it was literally a "fiendish joy" to steal a glance at an ankle and shoe. When calves were still hidden from view, never mind the knees, the

48. Cold-painted bronze dating from the end of the 19th century.

calf fetishists were happy about bad weather: This gave them the opportunity to follow women for long stretches in the hopes that the ladies might be forced to lift their skirts because of the puddles and thus expose their calves to the greedy looks of their pursuers. Concealment, thus, steered the imagination towards calves, feet, and footwear, and promoted the fetishist preference for these body parts and their clothing.

There were shoe fetishists who aroused themselves with the shoes and boots which used to be placed outside the doors of hotel rooms for cleaning. Hirschfeld describes the case of a man who engaged in masturbation when he looked at a pair of large men's boots, preferably a soldier's boots with spurs, next to delicate women's shoes that were placed outside the door; during the cover of night, he would sneak over to where the shoes were to caress, smell, and kiss them.

An expressive example of how both the foot and the shoe can become a fetishist object is provided by the French writer Rétif de la Bretonne (1734 – 1806). He represents the type of a pure shoe fetishist. When looking at women's shoes, he used to quiver lustfully and blush in front of them as if they were the girls themselves. He collected the slippers and shoes of his lover, kissed and smelled them, and sometimes masturbated into them. In his autobiographical novel, *Monsieur Nicolas*, Rétif wrote the following about his shoe fetish: "Dragged away from the stormiest, completely adoring passion for Colette, I imagined seeing and feeling her in body and spirit by caressing the shoes she had worn just a moment ago with my hands. I pressed my lips on one of these jewels while the other substituted as woman during a frenzied fit... This bizarre, mad pleasure seemed to – how should I say? – seemed to lead me straight to Colette herself."

His famous story *Fanchette's Foot* was conceived in 1767. One Sunday morning, at the corner of Montorgueil Street he saw a pretty girl standing in front of a boutique. She was dressed in a white slip, silk stockings, and pink shoes with high stiletto heels. He was enchanted by what he saw, including the charming walk of the girl, and in his mind immediately began writing the first chapter of the above-mentioned work, which starts with the words: "I am the actual historian recording the glorious conquest of the small foot of a beauty." The following day, when his imagination had somewhat cooled, he wanted to see his muse once more but instead noticed a woman on Saint-Denis Street whose foot was a "miracle of daintiness" dressed in a delightful gold-trimmed shoe made by the premier shoemaker of Paris. Full of enthusiasm he hurried home and in two days wrote the first fourteen chapters of *Pied de Fanchette*.

A friend reports about Rétif: "Our dear Nicolas had a rather strange but I believe excusable obsession. No matter how ugly a woman's face was, whether she was hunchbacked or limped, our

49. Series of anonymous watercolours illustrating *Women of the world*, 1940.

50. Series of anonymous watercolours illustrating *Women of the world*, 1940.

dear friend always fell madly in love with her if she had a pretty foot and especially if she wore pretty shoes. He relished a woman's feet more than anything; they were everything for him in terms of bliss and pleasure." The woman herself was viewed as a somewhat insignificant appendix of her foot or her shoes.

In his eyes, the dainty shoe made these women divine: "If one were to show a savage who has never seen a woman wear a shoe, a lady's shoe, crafted by the shoemaker Bourbon who lives on Vieux-Augustins Street, and were to ask this savage what kind of creature would wear this object, he would surely answer: 'An angel, a fairy, a sylph!'" There is nothing worse than the heavy flat foot coming in contact with the dirt of the earth. In *Monsieur Nicolas* he heavily criticised the "low-heeled shoes of the female republicans" and was angry at the newspapers that promoted this ugly fashion trend.

The foot and shoe fetish was Rétif's primary sexual perversion in life. Since he was the first to describe this variation of fetishism in detail, the German sexologist Ivan Bloch suggested calling the shoe and foot fetishism "Retifism" – applying the same logic that derived the term "sadism" from Sade and "masochism" from Sacher-Masoch.

Literature mentions foot fetishism quite early. Brantôme writes in his work *Lives of the Gallant Ladies* (1665) that Lucius Vitellius, father of emperor Vitellius, supposedly was a shoe and foot fetishist. He reports that he asked Empress Messalina one day for her permission to wear her shoes. "After he had worn them, he kept one and always carried it with him under his shirt and kissed it as often as he could and, by adoring the shoe, adored his beloved since neither her natural foot nor her pretty legs was available to him." Brantôme declared this piece of clothing more sensual than nudity itself. "The foot has to be slipped into a pretty, white shoe, a shoe made of black or coloured velvet, or a pretty little shoe with a stiletto heel." He considered an average-sized foot as more beautiful than a very large or very small foot. Such a foot is especially seductive if its wearer "moves and shakes it with small little turns and kicks" and if covered by a "pretty little shoe with stiletto heels, white and pointed at the front, not square." French fashion of the eighteenth century finally picked up this impression and systematically used it while discovering the charms of the female foot.

Was Goethe a foot fetishist? On 14 July, 1803 Goethe wrote to Christiane during his long absence: "Next chance you have, send me your latest new shoes, the ones that are already worn from too much dancing you described to me so that I once again have something of you close to me to press to my heart. Farewell!" This individual case is often cited as proof of Goethe's foot fetishism. The significant role that this fetishism played in his life and work cannot, however, be denied. His work *Wilhelm Meister* is an excellent source for the continuation of this subject. In *Wahlverwandtschaften* [Elective Affinities] he writes: "He threw himself down at her feet and she was unable to prevent him from kissing her shoes and grasping her foot to press it tenderly against his chest." Still, Eisler felt some reservations about Goethe being a shoe fetishist which

51. Anonymous drawing, 1922.

52. Félicien Rops, *Pornocrates*, 1878.

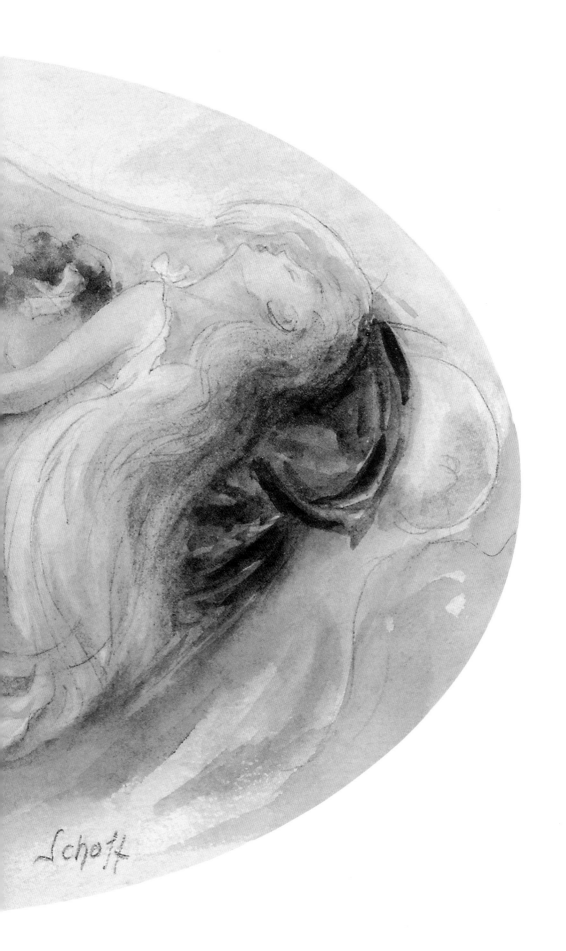

53. Otto Schoff, circa 1930.

Lithograph.

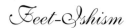

he expressed in his psychoanalytical study of Goethe: "He voiced his request to Christiane only once and that should be a deterrent from assuming with certainty that this perversion was a part of Goethe's life."

Already Rétif was pondering about the causes of this strange inclination. "Does this preference for pretty feet which is so strong in me that it always arouses my lust and let's me forget any other ugliness, have its roots in a psychological or intellectual natural disposition? The passion for pretty footwear I have had since childhood was an acquired inclination based on a natural predisposition."

Sigmund Freud recognised the symbolic significance of the foot and linked it with early childhood. "The fetishistic veneration of the female foot and shoe seems to use the foot only as a substitute symbol for the once venerated, since then sorely missed, penis of the woman; the 'cutter off of braids' play, without knowing it, the role of persons performing the act of castration of the female genitalia." This means it is the fixation on the urgently desired object, the penis of the woman, which leaves indelible tracks in the emotional life of the child.

Freud's essay about W. Jensen's *Gradiva* analyses the interest of the young archaeologist, Norbert Hanold, in the feet and foot positions of female individuals. Hanold had no interest in the living, breathing woman; rather he had shifted this interest to woman made of stone or bronze. "When suitable, our poet imbues his hero with a lively interest in the walk and foot positions of women, which has to lead to him falling into disrepute as a foot fetishist - with science as with the women of his home - which, however, is derived from the memory of this female childhood playmate. Already as a child, this girl exhibits a beautiful walk with an almost vertically placed tip of the foot when walking and by describing this walk, an antique stone relief Norbert Hanold discovers later gains said significance for him.

"We should add that the poet is in full agreement with the sciences when attributing the peculiar phenomenon of fetishism to early childhood. Since A. Binet we have been really trying to link fetishism with erotic childhood events and impressions." This means that fetishism offers a symbolic, mental link leading to the substitution of the object, namely the female penis. Freud mentions the binding and subsequent mutilation of the female foot in ancient China: "First, the foot is mutilated, then it is venerated. One could think that the Chinese man thanks the woman for submitting to castration." The foot is an age-old sexual symbol, already mentioned in myths. The shoe or slipper thus became the symbol of the female genitalia.

In his 1914 book *Marias Jungfräuliche Mutterschaft* [Mary's Virginal Motherhood], A. J. Storfer refers to the fairytale of Cinderella: "The prince sees her shoe (vulva) and is so delighted with its smallness and daintiness that he searches for its owner and marries her." Cinderella, who has a "small shoe," is the proper counterpart to the youngest brother who has a "large sword." The Cinderella motif can already be found in the ancient tales about the beautiful Rodopis. An eagle - the symbolic animal of patriarchal sexuality - stole one of her sandals while she bathed and brought it to Memphis to the king. The king, delighted with the daintiness of the sandal, searched for its owner to marry her.

The soft sandal might also represent the vagina; the shoe with stiletto heel, however, combines vaginal and phallic meaning. The dream reported to us in 1905 by the writer Franciscan Countess of Prevention 1905 is especially illustrative of the phallic significance: "Tonight - dreamed twice of

54. De Monceau, circa 1940.
Watercolour.

55. Egon Schiele, *Woman in Black
Stockings*, 1913. Gouache,
watercolour, pencil, 32.2 x 48 cm.
Private collection.

56. Léon Bakst, *La Sultane Jaune*,
1916.

shoes with stiletto heels – I accompanied myself to a restaurant and did not know how to refer to myself. Thought quite confused: should I say 'my wife" or 'he'?" A confusion of sexual identity. What is interesting about this dream is that it is not the imagination of a man, as it is usually the case, who has to deal with his castration complex. It is also interesting that women have a tendency towards such substitutions. Just look at the vast number of shoes many women own! Has the foot and shoe fetishism lost its potency in our era of short skirts? Certainly not. Early childhood fantasies do not change with the fashions. Only their subsequent execution and costume utilise the store of available options.

The fact that we continue to be born of mothers and must find our sexual identify with, and against, them is cause enough for stumbling long before fashion can exert any influence over us. It is a piece of "recherché due temps Perdue" [*Remembrance of Things Past*, but re-translated recently and more accurately as *In Search of Lost Time*] that is frozen within all variations of fetishism.

Every madam of a bordello can even today tell stories of "shoe johns" and "foot johns." For example, D. – owner-operator of a Frankfurt luxury bordello – told me of a client who always arrived with a suitcase full of different shoes. It was the task of the selected lady to try them on and to parade up and down in front of him until he reached a climax.

The forms and fashions of shoes can differ according to varying inclinations. One person might be especially enchanted by pumps, another by riding boots, a third might react only to lace-up boots, or little button-up booties, others love only dancing shoes or slippers. Hirschfeld mentions a man who was only sexually aroused by the folds around the ankles. The smell of leather is often significant as well.

Masochistic and sadistic notions frequently are part of a shoe fetish: to imagine being stepped on or kicked or to have a foot placed on one's neck. Krafft-Ebing saw in the shoe and foot fetishist a masked masochist. He assumed that foot and shoe are turned into a fetish because they symbolise the wish for being submissive or overpowered. This corresponds, perhaps, to the sign of subjugation practised in history where the winner places his foot on the body of the loser, although, in our case, love would be the motive.

Entering the keyword "foot fetish" into any of the internet search engine yields a surprising number of pages dedicated to this passion. An internal drive, therefore, still exists which keeps this fetish alive and well. Today, however, it has probably lost its societal and legal negative taint. Anybody is permitted to find happiness according to his, or her, inclination without being labelled as "sick" as previous sexology textbooks used to do.

It is an ice-cold Easter, and I am listening to the processions of the "Semana Santa" (Holy Week) in Seville on a Spanish radio station. How much bloody, chain-rattling masochism, medieval terror and naïve worship of relics is hidden in these rituals! The "Hermandades" (brotherhoods) are very popular. Even women establish sisterhoods that participate in the processions. The need for transcendence increases.

As far as that is concerned, the foot and shoe fetish is only a secular variation of a religious ritual of veneration that has slipped completely into the private realm. It guarantees the same passionate impetuses and edifications. Fetishism – an ardent, poetic private religion in an a religious time?

57. Anonymous, circa 1920. Etching.

84.

Sapphic Art

Sappho's Repudiated Love

Are They Women?, the title of a French essay about lesbian love, demonstrates a typically male attitude toward Sapphic love. For centuries men have assumed the right to write about lesbianism and express opinions about it while rarely accepting the phenomenon. The author of this essay is a man who typically writes not so much about lesbian love itself as about the phallocratic view of it.

This attitude began with early opinions of Sappho, the celebrated Greek erotic poet, who was born round about 612 B.C. in Eresos on the island of Lesbos. Her private life was denigrated and, in complete contradiction to the facts, she was ridiculed as a nymphomaniac. Sappho's liaison with the handsome Phaon can be dismissed as a fable as can her supposed suicide by leaping into the sea because he had grown weary of her. (The metaphor of a suicidal plunge from a cliff was merely a current literary image for the attempt to free oneself from the suffering caused by love-madness or the ecstasy of love. It is incorrect to interpret it as historical fact.)

Sappho's life – and her poetry – were completely dedicated to love for her own sex. She can be seen as the incandescent prophetess of womanly love, to the extent that the concept of "lesbianism" already existed in antiquity. Sappho gathered a circle of young girls around her; the names of Anagora, Euneika, Gongyla, Telesippa, Megara and Klais are found in the poetic fragments. Interest in poetry and music were what first of all united her with these friends. In her "House of the Muses", the girls were instructed in all the musical arts – playing instruments, singing, dancing. She loved her girls with fiery passion, and this passionate ardour can still be felt in the scanty remains of her poetry. The attempt, therefore, to "exonerate" Sappho from the "calumny" of having been a lesbian is nothing short of scandalous. Indeed, homo-eroticism in Greek antiquity needed no exoneration; it was not regarded as a vice, nor was it subject to any penalties. Sappho was not spared ridicule only because of the frankness with which she laid bare her heart, but the fact that she broke out of the limits of domestic existence imposed at that time on Greek women. Horace, who took the "Sapphic metre" of the first book of her poems as the model for the metre of many of his odes, calls her "The Masculine Woman". Her masculine nature, he said, explained her love and was the key to the understanding of her poems. "Like an oak-tree in a storm", she was convulsed by the omnipotence of Eros. "She combines all things, however diverse, soul and body, ear, tongue, eyes and colour[80], she unites opposites, freezes and burns simultaneously, loses her wits and finds them again, trembles and is close to death, so that in her not merely one passion is apparent but a conflict of passions." Passion, however, appears to be a male preserve.

Contemporaries noted parallels between Sappho's love for her pupils and the close relationships between Socrates and his disciples. Maximus of Tyros (125-185 B.C.), for instance, observed "The Lesbian Eros – what is it other than the Socratic way of love… what Alcibiades[81], Carmides and Phaedrus were to Socrates, Gyrinna, Atthis and Anaktoria were to Sappho". For both Sappho and Socrates, an extraordinary susceptibility to physical beauty was the basis of same-sex love. But already in Attic comedy, Sappho was

58. Gustav Klimt, *Nude Women*, drawing.

being presented as a nymphomaniac or as a shameless tribade[53]. The poet's sexuality was exaggerated and made to seem ridiculous. Later generations found her heartfelt lyrics rather indelicate. In his *Dialogues of Courtesans*, Lucian gives a detailed description of lesbian love-making. Two women, Klonarion and Leaina, are discussing Megilla, who lives on Lesbos:

Klonarion: "It's said that there are women on Lesbos who look almost like men; they don't let men do it to them, but they behave like men towards women." Leania then tells the inquisitive Klonarion about her experience with the lesbian, Megilla, who said of herself; "I was born a girl just like the rest of you, but my character and my instincts and everything else are distinctly masculine... You'll see that I can give you as much pleasure as men, for I have a member like a man's." Thus a woman who did not identify with the image of the weaker sex, complementary to men, was designated "phallic". The patriarchal point of view saw the lesbian as a would-be man.

The image was anatomically perfected by attributing to her an over-developed clitoris. Hans Licht, an expert on Greek culture, has also succumbed to this masculine projection; "That part of the woman's pudenda known as the clitoris, which is a smaller equivalent of a man's penis, is, in some women, so well-developed that it can fulfil the function of a penis. Women with such a clitoris are quite capable of having penetrative sex with other women; indeed, there have been cases of anal intercourse"[54]. Male erotic certainties, unsettled by female pleasure and passion, are re-established through the paradigm of male sexuality.

In later generations, it was especially the Humanists who emphasised the "immoral" character of Sappho's relationships with her friends. They too were men who could not acknowledge the validity of female sexuality. Hubert Fichte[55], a gay writer who carried out extensive researches into the reception of Sappho's poetry, summarised the practice this way: "Little is known of Sappho's life. None of her poems survive in a complete version. Yet no other female writer in the history of literature has caused so much agitation, especially to the masculine mainstays of literary history, who transformed her into someone elevated, chaste and tender – or used her as a sort of peepshow through which to scrutinise and condemn the love of women for women."

There are two conflicting threads running through European literary history – on one side, "Lesbian Sappho" ("the tenderest sensitivity", "an epoch of timidity") and on the other, "Sappho from Lesbos" (excess, abnormality and perversion). Female sexual pleasure is impugned, re-interpreted, falsified out of existence, and condemned.

"A heterosexual man feels as though he is on a hot tin roof", writes Fichte. "The idea of a lesbian pair in bed excites and degrades him, he peers through the keyhole and if they don't admit him, he ridicules them; in most cases, he does not even consider them worthy of criminalisation... all this may help to elucidate the bizarre reaction that men have shown to the songs of the Lesbian poet." Fichte concludes; "almost all the fragments of Sappho's poetry can be read as descriptions, as metaphors of love – of sexual love, of Eros, because how can leaves, nights of caresses, dew-bedecked shores, violet-coloured laps[56], sorrow, sweat, raging feelings, be separated from the body and its effusions?"

Ovid, who was able to read Sappho's complete poems, found nothing more sensual than her poetry, and urgently encouraged the young girls of his time to read it.

There were many explanations in Antiquity for the origins of same-sex love; the best known is that propounded by Aristophanes in Plato's *Symposium*. According to this theory, there were originally three types of human beings; male/male, female/female and male/female. Zeus then re-fashioned them into their

59. Attila Sassy, circa 1910.

60. *The Fisherman*, circa 1925.

61. Attila Sassy, circa 1910.

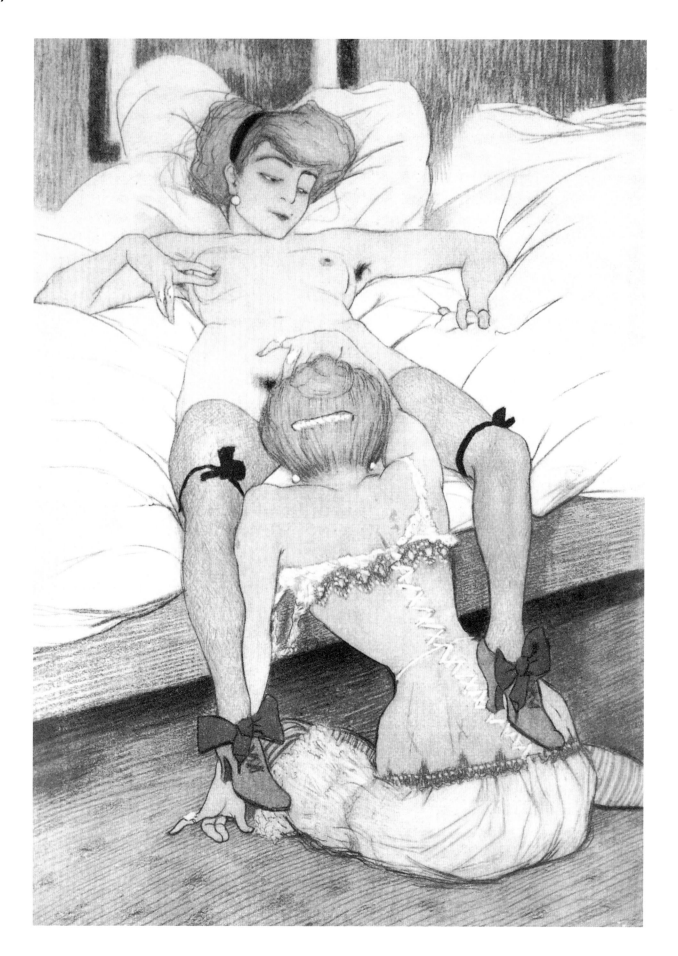

definitive form by bisecting them. The different types of love developed from the original whole from which the individual was separated.

Each of us is, therefore, one half of a spherical being because we have been cut in two. Everyone is continually in search of his, or her, other half. All women who are half of a female/female pairing have little interest in men and are much more drawn to women. This explains "why two seek to become one, since we were once unseparated wholes. The desire and the striving towards wholeness are thus given the name of Eros."

For the Romans, the God, Amor, was the personification of desire. He was the God of heterosexual love and of male homosexual love, whereas the deity, Bona Dea was the goddess of female homosexual love. Even the other deities are powerless against Amor. He is a demiurge and thus has no parent; he is, therefore, not the protector of procreation but of love. He is the representative of sexual love, not of reproduction.

"Tribadism" (lesbianism) was no less common among the Romans than among the Greeks.

If lesbian love is mentioned less often than pederasty in pre-Roman literature, the reason is not that it was less frequent, but that women in antiquity played a very negligible role in public life, and, therefore, writers had little occasion to concern themselves with this subject. This changed under the Roman Empire. The satires of Martial and Juvenal are full of lesbian scenes. Women's mass orgies at the Feast of Bona Dea have become notorious thanks to Juvenal's incomparable descriptions. Seneca reports a man's jealousy of his wife's girlfriend, and Martial makes several references to contemporary lesbian debaucheries.

Naturally the Church Fathers did not overlook the opportunity to rail against lesbianism, as they did against all sexuality, which may not have abolished lesbian love but certainly brought it into disrepute. There is no doubt that the general anti-feminism of countless theologians owed its origin to a latent fear of women. The first derogatory remark about women in Christianity was made by St. Paul, and it is cited by every propagandist for gynophobia. From the earliest origins, the Catholic Church saw women as impediments to perfection, as carnal, inferior beings who seduced men. For Tertullian[57], Woman is "the Devil's gateway". During the Middle Ages women were regarded as "snakes and scorpions", "vessels of sin", and "the damned sex". Chaste veneration of the Virgin Mary was merely the obverse side of the coin of the denigration of women. Simone de Beauvoir wrote; "From the Middle Ages onwards, to have a body meant a sense of shame for women". In accordance with the slogan "tota mulier sexus", women were held to be sexually insatiable. No wonder that the anathema of theological anti-feminism was particularly severe against lesbianism. The punishments that were pronounced against homosexual women in the Middle Ages indicate that lesbianism was not uncommon in convents. For instance, a French court sentenced a nun to seven years' penance for homosexual relations with another nun using a "machinamentum", *i.e.* an artificial penis. The penalties for the laity were less severe and covered shorter time spans.

Lesbianism flourished throughout the Middle Ages and the Early Modern Period but the penalties were dire. If women appeared as "Amazons"[58], their lives often ended on the gallows even though this was less criminal than the actions of a "girl of good family" who was executed in 1515 in Leipzig for a long period of highway robbery and for having followed the army to battle. According to one chronicle, in 1721 a woman was put to the sword. She had served as a soldier in wartime and had deserted, but was pardoned when her sex was discovered.

Then she impersonated a man and married a girl. Shortly thereafter she was apprehended by the authorities, who, first of all, condemned her to be burnt to death – the penalty for same-sex love, which constituted heresy and sodomy – but later mitigated the sentence[59].

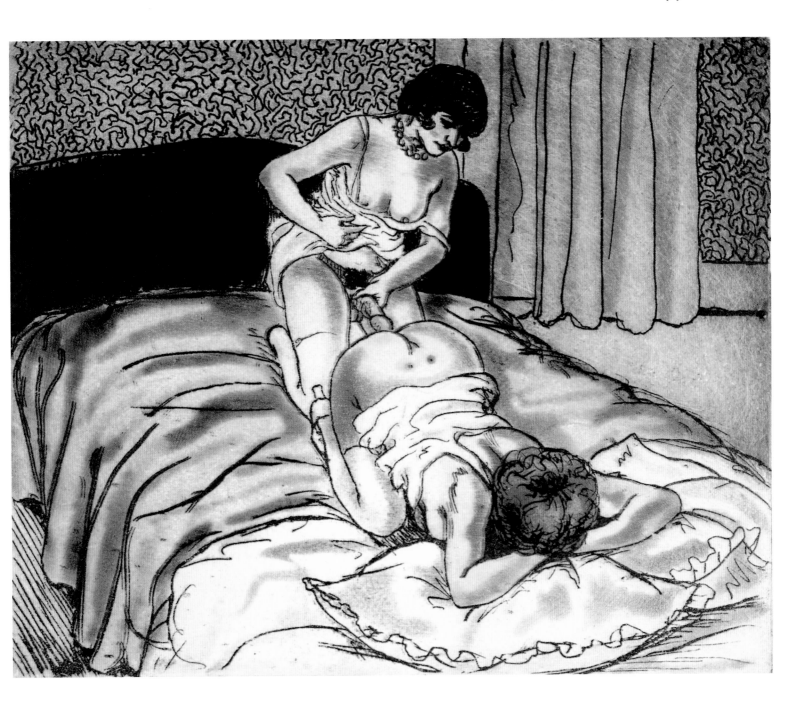

According to a Hamburg chronicle of 1701, a woman called Maria Jürgens was accused of having committed "unnatural acts and sodomy" with one Anna Buncken, "using an instrument designed for the purpose". "In 1544, a woman was condemned to the stake and burnt in men's clothes because she had gone about dressed as a man, claimed to be a man and had taken two women in marriage. She had damaged the health of the first through unnatural intercourse, and betrayed the other through her villainy". There are many similar stories. The death penalty for female homosexuality was in force in Prussia until 1747. The Prussian Common Law of 1794 established imprisonment as the penalty for "tribadism". In view of these drastic penalties, it is hardly surprising that, at least in elevated circles, lesbians withdrew into secret societies.

62. Courbouleix, circa 1935.

In Paris at the period, the most famous was Anandryne, founded in 1770 by Madame de Fleury. The members met in the Rue des Boucheries-Saint-Honoré in a magnificent hall in the centre of which there stood four altars on which the Vestal flame burned continually. Next to the altars were busts of Sappho and the renowned Chevalier d'Eon. The priestesses sat on day beds with the novices ("désirantes") who were to be admitted. At the beginning of her examination, the désirante was disrobed and examined as to her suitability. She had to exhibit at least six attributes of beauty and forswear all intimate relationships with the male sex. Finally she was enclosed in a cabinet containing numerous objects reminding her of male love. The most conspicuous was a statue of Priapus in all his glory. At the foot of the statue was a fire that had the singular characteristic of extinguishing itself if attention was withdrawn from it for a single moment. The novice was not permitted to give free rein to her imagination on beholding these objects of male sensuality because of the risk that the fire might go out. These tests lasted for three days. The sect had many members, including some from aristocratic circles. Eventually there was a split. Another society, also called Anandryne in imitation of the first, was founded in London in 1780.

The legal situation, at least in Germany, did not begin to change until the nineteenth century. The Imperial Penal Code of 1871 is similar to the Prussian Penal Code of 1851 in recognising only the existence of male homosexuality. "Unnatural sexual practices between male persons or between human beings and animals, are punishable by imprisonment; loss of civil rights may also be incurred; section # 175" How had it come about that women who loved women no longer needed to fear the law? M. Pieper[60] explains that women had been 'privatised'. An important pre-requisite for the development

63. Gerda Wegener, 1925.

of bourgeois society was an ideology of the family based on a strict dichotomy between 'man's sphere' and 'woman's sphere', between production and reproduction. "Female sexuality, in so far as it was admitted that it existed at all, belonged in the remotest corner of hearth and home, and was subordinated to the pre-eminence of *children-kitchen-church*."

In 1787 the Bavarian jurist, Johann Jacob Cella, declared himself in favour of exempting homosexual relationships between women from penalties: "It would probably be most natural to assume that a woman cannot practice sodomy with another woman; since, whether it is done with an instrument or not, it is really nothing more than indecent games in which imagination plays a greater part than reality". This shows the extent to which the de-criminalisation of "tribadie" was related to the degrading and trivialisation of lesbianism. The phallocratic fixation of bourgeois-patriarchal society is also expressed precisely in the forms of sexuality considered subject to penal sanctions; only anal intercourse counts as "indecent practices between male persons". Female sexuality is infantilised, indeed negated, as "fooling around".

But a process of pathologisation began at the same time as decriminalisation; it was no longer lawyers, but doctors and psychiatrists, who felt themselves called upon to pronounce judgments upon homosexual men and women. Previously, words of power belonged to religion and the law; now, they were pronounced by medical and anthropological science. Kraft-Ebing[61] saw "perverse sexual feelings in women as a phenomenon of degradation". In his criticism of Section 175 of the penal code which excludes women, there is almost a rehabilitation of female sexuality; he says that the view that "women cannot commit sex crimes with each other" is incorrect. They act, after all, for the sake of pleasure.

64. Gerda Wegener, 1925.

93.

However, he sees the main cause of female homosexuality in the absence of a basis for "the development of normal sexuality." Thus, homosexual relations due to "hyper-sexuality" often take place between prison inmates or between girls of upper-class families, who are only too well protected from seduction by men or who are afraid of pregnancy. It often occurs between "wives of impotent men, who are only able to stimulate, not to satisfy... and ultimately cause their wives to feel disgust at coitus and at all intercourse with men."

Prostitutes of great sensuality, who "are disgusted by their dealings with perverted or impotent men", take refuge with sympathetic members of their own sex and "regress" with them. "Perverse sexual feelings in women" are, therefore, avoidable; it is not the doctor who provides the cure for lesbianism but the potent man. It is not conceded that a genuine desire of woman for woman can exist. Eulenberg[62] expresses a similar opinion. The majority of pseudo-lesbians at the turn of the century were sexually surfeited, sensation-seeking women of the upper classes. They were "idle, wealthy, genteel ladies (the word "women" is actually too good for them) who have exhausted every pleasure, who are blasé about everything, especially men, and only find a certain pleasantly exciting charm in the unnatural and abnormal, precisely because it is unnatural and abnormal". There is a phenomenon of degeneration here too, therefore. Bourgeois sexual research is unable to escape from the shadow of phallocentrism. Ivan Bloch too (*Sexual Life in Our Times*) does not doubt the existence of genuine, primary homosexuality in women but only accords it negligible significance and regards women who love women rather as pseudo-lesbians. They are indulging "an externally influenced, temporary, same-sex attraction, not really based in the nature of the personality". Men know best, it seems, what constitutes the nature of the personality. Lesbian love is insignificant.

According to Bloch, the few cases of genuine homosexuality occur "when a girl even looks different from her heterosexual sisters, and there are suggestions of a masculine build (minimal breast development, a narrow pelvis, growth of a moustache, a deep voice, etc.)". Here again the question: Are they women? (Recent research indicates that very few lesbian women regard themselves as definitely masculine. Furthermore, it has been shown that gender identification is not a determining factor in the development of female homosexuality; many women who define themselves as somewhat masculine are heterosexually oriented.) The phallocratic attempt to masculinise the lesbian woman must be regarded as a failed attempt to re-establish the phallus as the central focus of sexuality.

Only psychoanalysis has been able to elucidate this nebulous discussion, even though Freud only glanced briefly at lesbianism. Freud accorded bisexuality considerable importance as a psychic structure, and was of the opinion that bisexual desires were universal in childhood. "All our libidos oscillate between the male and the female object". It is, however, impossible in his view, to be both sexes; the bisexual longings of childhood must necessarily remain unfulfilled. Thus under a culturally imposed mono-sexuality

65. Peter Fendi, c. 1835.

66. Hans Pellar.

95.

67. Gustave Courbet, *The Sleep*, 1867.
Oil on canvas, 135 x 200 cm.
Petit Palais - Musée des Beaux Art
de la ville de Paris, Paris.

G. Courbet. '66

we only have half our sexuality at our disposal. During love-play we can create the illusion of being both sexes, if only momentarily. Plato's spherical human beings can find their way back to their original wholeness only for the instant when they are freed from their mono-sexuality by projection and identification. Similarly, the individual finds his or her completion in same-sex love. The objects of sexual desire are, therefore, not innate; they have to be discovered.

Certainly after Freud it is no longer possible to speak of "unnatural love". Homosexuality may be contrary to culturally-conditioned norms, but it is one of the basic forms of the possible variations of human love. Freud wrote: "We are accustomed to expect a certain amount of repression of perverse instincts – of anal eroticism, homosexuality, father-complex, mother-complex, and various other complexes, from every human being, just as we hope to demonstrate the existence of the elements carbon, oxygen, hydrogen, nitrogen and sulphur in the chemical analysis of an organic structure. What distinguishes one organic structure from another is the relative proportions of the elements and the constitution of the links they form with one another". One may, therefore, conclude that nothing is less natural than a one-dimensional, limited gender role. We know today that exaggerated masculine, or over-emphasised feminine, demeanour often masks strong tendencies to homosexuality[63]. Both tendencies can exist within the same person.

But these are thoughts that are difficult to accept under patriarchy. The concept of bisexuality is related to the concept of "intermediacy" as developed by the homosexual sexologist Magnus Hirschfeld[64]. Between the ideal types of "total male" and "total female", according to Hirschfeld, there are countless individual combinations, and every human being is a unique androgynous combination of characteristics resembling intermediate stages between the extreme forms. The most successful of his explanatory brochures

68. Paul Avril, circa 1910.

69. Achille Devéria, circa 1830.
    Romantic Lithograph, (detail).

appeared in 1901 under the title, "What People Should Know About The Third Sex". Hirschfeld had a preference for the expression "The Third Sex"; it was a designation applied equally to lesbians and gay men, which was not burdened with a medico-psychiatric, or pejorative, sub-text. Hirschfeld was convinced that lesbians and gay men had common interests and should, therefore, co-operate; "The homosexual man and the homosexual woman have a natural affinity with one another and, in fact, belong to a third sex, which has the same rights as the other two though it is not identical to them".

In 1897, Hirschfeld founded the "Scientific Humanitarian Committee", which initiated a campaign against legal prosecution and social ostracising of same-sex relationships. But in 1909, the "Preliminary Outline for a New German Penal Code" contained an attempt to extend the provisions of Section 175 to lesbians. This attempt was prepared and accompanied by medical and anthropological publications in the name of "Dr. Philos".

"Dr. Philos" thought that one reason that female homosexuality was taken less seriously than its male counterpart was its freedom from prosecution under German law; another was "leniency towards the female sex: but the public was beginning to discover the less innocent basis of many female friendships". "Dr. Philos" repeatedly warned of the dangers that "perverted" women constituted in his opinion. According to him, "Intellectual women are drawn away from men to their own sex and thus to lesbianism. Over-exertion of the female brain is notorious for causing its hypertrophy and this larger brain, which has become more masculine, also alters the rest of the subject's character to a more masculine form, altering the sexual psychology at the same time. Such half-male women also lose all their attraction for men, and this, together with the arrogance of having experienced equal rights – indeed, superior rights – contributes to the instinctive hatred that the remains of their femininity must feel on being disregarded. These half-male females endeavour to draw normal members of their sex into their orbit, not only for the satisfaction of their conscious sexual needs but also because of instinctive cravings for revenge against men, to deprive them of as many objects of sexual desire as possible."

Increasing fears of competition, not only in the professions but in the sexual field, is the reason for the attempt to criminalise lesbian women. If this law had been passed, it would have created the opportunity to prosecute lesbians active in the Women's Movement, and to divide the movement into "normal" heterosexual women and "diseased" lesbians. In a report to the Imperial Judiciary of 1911, Magnus Hirschfeld concluded – "legal penalties against lesbians would lead to denunciations and blackmail – the misdemeanour was uncommon; it consisted merely in masturbation, which was not a criminal offence for men either". The attempt to introduce a law against lesbianism failed completely, not least because of campaigns by the radical wing of the bourgeois Women's Movement and the "Scientific Humanitarian Committee."

After the First World War, especially in the 1920s, a liberal and permissive lesbian culture centred in Paris and Berlin developed in Europe. This emancipated atmosphere was also reflected in erotic art. Women such as Gerda Wegener, Margit Gaal, Susanne Ballivet, Charlotte Behrend-Corinth, and others created works in celebration of love. Male artists too, such as Wilhelm Wagner, Albert Marquet, Jules Pascin, Otto Rudolf Schatz and Otto Schoff devoted themselves to this theme. (It is said of Otto Schoff that he always felt like a woman himself in the presence of a woman. This "lesbian sensitivity" enabled the "painter of Spring", as he was known, to produce the most beautiful representations of lesbian love). Meanwhile, the phallocrats continued to peddle the prejudices of previous centuries but their complaints were largely ignored. As late as 1929, Curt Morek (*Cultural and Moral History of Modern*

70. Achille Devéria, circa 1830.
Romantic Lithograph.

Times) described female homosexuality as primarily a confused heterosexuality. It is worth mentioning the strange case he cites of Princess R.: "*Amor lesbicus* does not occur during the prime of the *vita sexualis*, but rather develops during the years of matronhood[65] and sometimes in extreme old age. After a life rich in heterosexual amours, Princess R. became a lesbian at the age of sixty. This belated change of orientation must be considered a manifestation of a senile sex drive."

In the eyes of ideologues such as this, 1933 must have appeared as the beginning of convalescence; the lights were extinguished in all gay and lesbian clubs. Women were again obliged to seek fulfilment in motherhood – with papal blessing – while men were dedicated to a martial cult of masculinity. Gender roles became rigid moulds which allowed no overlap. The discussion of the unnaturalness of same-sex love continued after the Second World War. It will continue as long as men feel threatened by the autonomy of "the other sex". But it was now mainly women who led this discussion. Simone de Beauvoir, in particular, attempted to present female homosexuality as something authentic. "Women's homosexuality", she wrote in *The Second Sex*, "is an attempt to harmonise her autonomy with the passivity of her body. If one brings Nature into the equation, it can be claimed that Woman is naturally homosexual. A lesbian is characterised by the fact that she rejects men and finds pleasure in the female body. Every young girl feels fear of penetration, of the power of the male, feels a sort of aversion to the male body. In contrast, the female body is an object of desire, for her as well as for the man". But does not this assumption of a basic opposition between man and woman just stand the old order on its head? Heterosexuality is here suddenly presented as the confusion of a basic homosexuality. She has a very low opinion of women who "submit" to men.

At the end of the 1970s, lesbianism was even interpreted as a form of political opposition. In 1979, a German left-wing journal proclaimed, "We understand lesbianism as a psychological response to male power and violence. We must understand lesbianism as a form of political protest; we must live by it and spread the message. It is a non-violent form of protest. We can withdraw from men! Lesbians withdraw their power and their love from men, give both to women. Thus they can strengthen themselves and other women." Is this not the exact reverse of the abstruse theories of a Dr. Philos? Whoever is still committed to the phallus, even while rejecting it, will never achieve authentic and autonomous love, in whatever form. Even in its denial the phallus dominates. Where do we stand today? Have we become more liberal and more tolerant? It appears so. Nancy Friday[37] writes in her book *Women's Sexual Fantasies*, "Bisexuality seems to be currently fashionable. The question is not whether one is or is not, but whether one looks down on those who are". The idea that we all have something of the other sex in us robs conventional gender roles of their rigidity, and especially robs the male role of some of its force. Male violence developed when the feminine had to be oppressed, in the male subject himself as well as in the female object confronting him. Due to the polymorphic character of human sexuality, there is from the biological point of view, nothing more natural and necessary in love of Woman for Man than there is in love of women for other women – "Anything goes!"[38] There are other ways of being male and female than the current ones.

The law of the phallus is no longer secure, and so for the first time there is the historic opportunity to develop authentic forms of lesbian love – authentic forms of love in general. But there are contradictory tendencies: current popularisation, trivialising and commercialising of previously "deviant" sexual behaviours – especially in the media – is accompanied by an increase in auto-erotic behaviour. If the question is finally one of narcissistic self-satisfaction, then it is a matter of indifference whether the choice of partner is bisexual, homosexual or heterosexual.

71. Achille Devéria, circa 1830.
Romantic Lithograph.

Objects of Desire

"SEE ME! - TOUCH ME!" The Eroticism of Touch

"Don't touch!" There is nothing more unnatural than this eternal prohibition which occurs in art exhibitions and forbids all contact with the objects on display. They occupy space, they are three-dimensional, and we experience them with our sense of sight, but we also feel the desire to touch them. Nevertheless, this ban on touching seems to have an unexpected effect on people: under the humorous title "An Evaluation of the Consequences of Contact with Art: The Marble of Love", the Frankfurter Allgemeine Zeitung of 23 June 2001 published the results of an extraordinary poll carried out by the Institute of Psychiatric Psychoanalysis in Rome. They questioned nearly 2,000 museum visitors and discovered that the fact of being exposed to art directly stimulated people's erotic senses. One fifth of visitors admitted to having felt, after their virtual encounter with statues and other sculpted figures, an impressive series of very concrete sensations. Some mentioned "vague but intense experiences", others "a keen feeling of love" or "unexpected feelings." Even the relationship between long-standing couples seems to experience something of a fillip as a result. Thus the sculptures of Canova, Berni and Michelangelo seem to have a kind of aphrodisiacal effect which is difficult to reconcile with those ideals which state that art only stimulates the most disinterested form of pleasure. And yet surely the interiors of Catholic churches with all those languishing virgins and galleries of naked, martyred bodies, are a school of sensuality in themselves? Do we have to conclude that museums and churches are dangerous places because they awaken a desire to touch?

Krafft-Ebing, in his *Psychopathologia Sexualis*, gives us examples of acts of aggression committed against statues. He mentions, for example, the story of a young man who used a Praxiteles' Venus to satisfy his desires; or the ancient story of Clisyphus, who abused a marble goddess in a temple of Samos after having placed a piece of meat on a certain part of her anatomy. He also tells of a gardener who in 1877 fell madly in love with the Venus de Milo and was caught rubbing himself fruitlessly against his beloved. However, Krafft-Ebing does not question the pathological or abnormal nature of these cases. (At this point the author can freely recall his own personal experiences during youthful nocturnal escapades in a park where there was a group of sculptures by Georg Kolbe which initiated him into the pleasures of touch. It was here that he understood for the first time how art can be erotic.)

Our sense of touch is a sexual sense in the most profound sense of the word. That is why Mantegazza describes physical love as the most developed form of the sense of touch. Ivan Bloch, following a similar argument, even speaks of the skin as 'one single sensual organ.' In order to achieve the natural conclusion of desire, one cannot do without touch: looking and touching are generally the two acts which precede the sexual act itself. It is not by chance that Freud mentions that "the sensations of touching the skin of a sexual object first of all create a new source of pleasure and a swelling of excitement." Even if looking remains the normal route to sexual excitement, excitement

72. *Pipe with Nymph,*
    second half of the 19th century.
    Meerschaum pipe with
    practical amber mouthpiece,
    Vienna.

also comes from touching. "Seeing the sexual organs naked gives us the desire to touch them. And as is often the case, looking replaces touching." Kissing forms part of these exciting sensations. Freud writes rather seriously on this subject: "One specific form of contact, that of the mucous membranes of the mouth, has gained amongst many peoples (including the most civilised) its own significance as a kiss, even if the body part involved is not a sexual organ but the entry to the digestive canal."

Indeed, after birth, isn't the mouth the first erogenous zone? Touching and looking are temporary but very exciting sexual pleasures. A useful technical comparison in a book about twentieth century customs can help us to understand better the difference between these two modes of sexual appropriation: "If the eye is in some sort the telegraphic station of love, then touch is nothing less than the electric contact that makes the morse hammer move." Literature is full of examples of caresses between lovers which are far removed from the sexual act itself, but which can provoke states of violent excitation.

"Ah, how the blood rushes through my veins, "exclaims Goethe's young Werther, "when my finger accidentally touches hers, or when our feet meet under the table! I draw back as if from fire, and a secret force pushes me on again – and I feel something like vertigo all through my body. – Oh! Only her innocence and her unprejudiced soul prevent her from realising how these little familiarities drive me to distraction. And if during a conversation she puts her hand on mine and comes closer to me in order to speak more clearly with me, and thus I feel the divine breath from her mouth on my lips, I dream of falling, as if I had been struck down!"

Like Goethe, Rousseau describes in his *Nouvelle Héloïse* the exciting sensations that a simple, light touch can provoke: "As soon as her hand rests on mine, I am overcome with shivering; this game plunges me into a fever, or rather into a kind of madness; I can no longer see or feel anything...!"

The feelings which Voltaire describes in his Pucelle are, by contrast, more overtly sexual:

73. Cigarette Holder,
   second half of the 19th century.
   Made from meerschaum
   and amber, historism,
   Probably from Vienna.

74. *A Monk - and What He Is Thinking
   of,* c. 1900. Bronze. Vienna.

"And gradually, her hand
began to lose control
and to open, trembling with pleasure,
her corset, lace after lace;
Ah, he touched her, looked at her,
Took her in his arms, explored her,
Embraced her and gave her pleasure.
Everything was beautifully round and full,
And pleasant to the touch
And her mouth was quite red
Ready to gather his kisses!
Everything moved in every sense
And both hand and eyes looked
Towards the lovely gardens of pleasure."

The hand follows the eye – as with an infant who wants to grab an apple he has glimpsed. However, touch is not secondary to sight. It is only genetically preceded by it. Kissing and hugging, touching and feeling are the primary experiences of sensuality.

However, tactile stimulations are not limited to the hand, they can also be provoked by the foot and can lead, in some cases, to orgasm. In his books on psycho-sexual infantilism, Stekel mentions such a case: a thirty-four-year-old traveller, who was particularly excited by stimulation of his skin, used to like to go to a brothel and have his body tickled slowly from top to bottom. When the girls who were tickling him reached the soles of his feet, he would have an orgasm. In the light of this story, is it surprising if, as Havelock Ellis wrote, the Patagonians have only one word to describe both sex and tickling?

In the eighteenth century at the court of the Russian Tsar, it even appears that there was an official post of 'foot-tickler' whose sole duty was to tickle her master's feet. Anna Ivanova created this post, as B. Stern reports in his *History of Russian Customs*, and it was a prestigious position at court. The Princess Regent, Anna Leopoldovna, having obtained the guardianship of the infant Ivan VI after the death of Anna Ivanova, used to keep up to six official foot-ticklers in her private salons, and their delicate art was organised in the form of a competition. During the tickling sessions, the women told each other bawdy stories and sang obscene songs. Whilst the erotic value of reading has been rediscovered with the release of the film *La Lectrice*, tickling as an erotic activity has yet to enjoy a renaissance.

The skin is doubtless the most sensual organ of the body, but it is also something on which all sorts of punishments can be inflicted: flagellation, stigmatisation in various forms, and sometimes even torture to the death, as the Greek god Apollo inflicted on the satyr, Marsyas. The skin is thus the organ both of pleasure and of pain.

In his seminal study *Bodily Contact*, Ashley Montagu examines the significance of the skin in terms of human development. Contrary to established opinion which holds that the process of learning is carried out by the eyes and ears, he demonstrates that knowledge is also passed on via the skin. The embryo develops a sense of touch long before it can see or hear. In the mother's body, the principal organ of perception is the skin. For the infant it remains the basis of all contact and of all communication with the world. Thus he can tell the difference between being picked up by someone who loves him or someone who is indifferent to him. Even as adults we still have this power of discernment. Through the different experiences of touch, the infant slowly learns the importance of each instance of contact: tenderness and warmth, consolation and caresses.

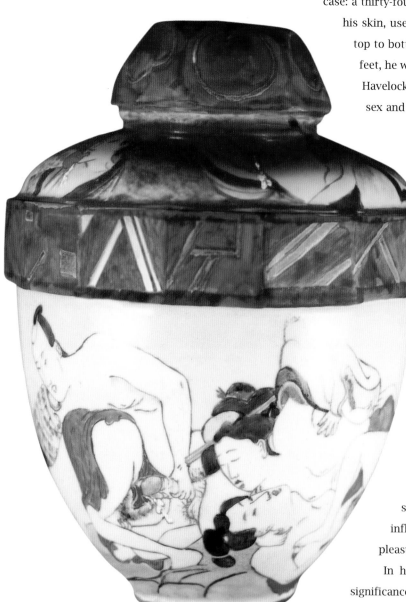

75. Japanese vase with erotic decoration.

Even linguistically, 'tender' and 'consoling' have their origins in tactile sensations without which they would have no meaning. Thus the language of touch is the first language. There are so many words and expressions that express our most important feelings, and if one considers the varied uses of the word 'touch' in every language, it is clear that they are all variations on the same theme: touching with a hand, a finger, or all one's fingers. It is hardly surprising that there are a huge number of entries under the heading 'touch' in an English dictionary.

The idea of the embrace was a central preoccupation of German romantic poetry. At the same time the theme of the pain of abstraction also emerged. According to Kleist, communication can only be successful if one does not exchange words but only gestures; the establishment of physical contact is a fundamental condition for this communication. In the short text *Letter from One Poet to Another*, he writes: "If by writing I could seize the thoughts in my heart, if I could hold them in my hands alone, unassisted, and if I could put them into your heart: then, to tell you the truth, I would have achieved everything I could have wished for." Kleist develops a theory according to which true poetry makes words superficial by becoming a language of gesture rather than a language of words.

Thus the hand is truly both a passive and active organ of communication. People who use it in this way understand each other less through the use of reason than through 'feeling', not only in an emotional sense but also in a process which is genuinely tactile.

> "The feelings in this heart, o young man,
> Are like hands, and they caress you." (Penthesileus)

These words remind us that language in its beginnings was a language of gestures and body. The close connection between tactile sensations and a person's inner feelings is expressed very clearly in the French language. Chamfort claimed "that love is nothing more than the manifestation of touch." And another Frenchman, going beyond both materialism and idealism, wrote:

> "Love is the harmony between two minds and the contact
> between two bodies."

Experiments with animals (for example, the famous one with Harlow's monkey) have demonstrated that limiting bodily contact can cause serious developmental problems in individuals. These problems do not only concern their behavioural development, but also their physical growth, their capacity to defend themselves and their general state of health. Moreover, neglecting tactile sensations in the early years of life can lead to significant retardation of both emotional and intellectual development.

"It is probable," wrote Montagu, "that tactile stimulation represents for man a decisive factor in the development of his emotional and affective capabilities; that the act of 'licking' is in a textual sense connected even with the possibility of love; that one cannot teach love to someone by explaining it to them, but only by loving them."

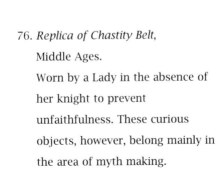

76. *Replica of Chastity Belt*,
Middle Ages.
Worn by a Lady in the absence of her knight to prevent unfaithfulness. These curious objects, however, belong mainly in the area of myth making.

77. Bergman, *Satyr and Nymph on
Arabian Rug Performing
Cunnilingus.* Bronze. Vienna.

Tactile communication represents the first and most primitive language of the child on which verbal language is later built. This is why people refer to the sense of touch as 'the mother of all senses.' Thus our verbal language is just a continuation of our physical language. They both have the same purpose: to establish a relationship with other human beings. Love and hate are feelings. The real significance of the word 'feeling' is connected with the first tactile experiences. (Thus the German word "Gefühl" (feeling) also designates the sense of touching something). If we like something, we want to touch it – or to 'feel' it in a sexual sense. In the sexual act, as Montagu explains, human beings experience a sensation through their skin that is so strong it can almost equal the sensation of birth itself. Often, he says, women "use the sexual act in order to be held in someone's arms. What they desire above all else is to be close to someone; the sexual act is only the price that they agree to pay. The satisfaction of the orgy is forbidden them."

Contrary to the indirect experiences of the eyes and ears, the sense of touch allows us to experience things directly in our bodies. Touch is different from the other senses "because it requires the direct and unshared presence of the body we are touching, as well as the participation of our own body with the one we are touching." Finally, we believe in the reality of an object only when we can touch it. Even religious belief demands some kind of substance and cannot be satisfied without objects to touch: thus the relics and other objects of veneration of saints are made up of parts of bodies, bones or ashes,

78. *Nude Acrobat.*

clothes or an object of daily use. This veneration of relics is explained by the idea that the remains of saints have preserved a specific power, so much so that the fact of touching or embracing them can affect a transfer of this specific and amazing power to the person who touches them. Tactile contact establishes a relationship between man and saint. For a believer, a relic is like a fetish.

This similarity between a saint and a fetishist is not totally far-fetched, because just like the believer, a fetishist finds the satisfaction of his desires in a piece of clothing. For the fetishist, the sense of touch is completely separated from the image of woman as a sexual object, as a piece of clothing can sublimate all desire in his eyes. Krafft-Ebing gives us an impressive number of examples:

"Observation 110: Z, thirty-six years old, university student, has until now only been interested in the 'outer wrapping' of woman, never in the woman herself, and he has never had sexual relations with one. Under the general 'chic' and elegance of female dress, his preferred fetishes are underclothes, embroidered cambric blouses, corsets, delicate and silk-embroidered petticoats, as well as silk stockings. His pleasure consists of looking at and touching these garments on the shelves of department stores."

Other examples mention fetishists of petticoats, handkerchiefs and shoes. However, an object can become a fetish without being in any direct way related to a woman's body, manifested, for example, in the desire for a certain type of material which can create erotic sensations in itself. Fur, velvet and silk are well-known examples in this category. Krafft-Ebing cites the case of one man, "who was known in a brothel under the name 'Velvet' because he would dress up one of the girls in a black velvet dress and would excite and satisfy his sexual desires just by caressing his face with the edge of the dress, but he never had any contact with the girl herself."

Another fetishist confesses: "From as early on as I can remember, I was always absolutely crazy about all kinds of fur and velvet, and the mere sight of these materials would create a state of sexual arousal in me, contact with them gave me a feeling of pleasure... I have a strong desire to feel these materials on a woman's body, to caress them and embrace them, then to cover my whole face with them. In the same way, fur or velvet alone have the same effect on me... Even more, just the word 'fur' possesses in my eyes magical qualities and stimulates my erotic imagination."

In other words, states of sexual development which in normal people are intermediate and temporary – that is, touch and sight – in fetishists come to hold a particular significance; they have, in some sense, 'gone up a grade.' Touchable material has replaced a real human being. Nevertheless, there is one conventional erotic object which lies at the base of fetishism: the soft skin of a mother, with all its attendant pleasures and delights.

However, not all fetishists are lucky enough to experience the pleasure of Pygmalion, whose fetish was transformed into a living goddess. Pygmalion was King of Cyprus, and didn't want to marry because his heart and senses were completely absorbed by a snow-white ivory statue which he had created himself with such love and passion that the marble seemed alive to him. His hand, as it caressed the statue, could not differentiate what it was feeling: was it flesh or was it ivory? Pygmalion embraced and hugged the statue, firmly believing that his love was reciprocated. By night, he lay down next to her, by day he dressed her up in costly clothes and precious jewels. Then there came the day of a festival which is very important in Cyprus, that of the goddess Aphrodite. Pygmalion went up to the altar, made his devotions and showed his respect, and prayed to the gods to give him a woman who resembled the one he had created with his own hands. Aphrodite, who was present at the festival, heard his prayer and gave life to the statue.

79. *Snake charming.*

Ebony, contemporary work. Africa

113.

The artist Oskar Kokoschka is a sort of inverse Pygmalion. After he separated from his lover Alma, he ordered the Munich doll maker, Hermine Moos, to make a life-sized copy of her. In his letters to her, he explained in detail how his fetish should be made. Thus, the skin should be made from soft cotton because its tactile quality was particularly important to him. "Finally, the surface of the skin should be as soft as a peach, without visible seams which would remind (him) that this fetish is nothing more than a vulgar doll made up of rags." He added: "Please differentiate between the tactile sensations of soft and hard, especially in the places where muscular tissue and soft tissue move under a covering which is rather similar to leather." The "shameful parts" should be made with the same attention to detail, with hair, "because otherwise it will not be a woman but a monster." Because for him, "this is something that he should be able to embrace." By looking at and embracing his fetish, his lost lover would reappear, living, before him.

What he received in the end was a monstrosity. Kokoschka did not want to believe that he had asked for the impossible: the magic of a living being. Soon afterwards, the doll suffered a decadent and ignominious end: at the end of a heavy night's drinking, she was doused in wine, decapitated and thrown in the garbage.

Just as in psycho-sexual development the genitals finally become the executive organ of desire, so the hand becomes the executive organ of touch. It is the active party in the appropriation of the world, the medium of knowledge between subject and object. And what is cherished by the infant is not derided by the philosopher: for Hegel, knowledge cannot be acquired by splitting subject and object, in which the object is understood as something different from the thinker who is contemplating it.

In order to understand the world, man must first appropriate it. For him, as for Spinoza, Goethe and Marx, man is only alive if he is productive, if he captures the world outside himself by expressing his own human predispositions to form a sort of bridge between inner and outer worlds." Man," says Goethe, "can only know himself by knowing the world that can only be perceived inside himself, as he cannot reflect himself except within himself. Every object, properly contemplated, opens a new organ to us."

In today's world, in which our experiences are first and foremost transmitted virtually by various media, there is a palpable decrease in our sense of reality. From the point of view of the sense of touch, our urban life is sadly monotonous: the smooth surfaces of synthetic materials offer little in the way of tactile experiences. The anonymous mediation of the outside world, whether it is via television or internet chat rooms, makes personal contact less frequent and less substantial. In the shadow of the hysterical debates around sexual abuse of minors, the tiniest sign of affection becomes suspect. The 'confession' of a mother who said she had felt pleasure in breastfeeding her child, so an article from the US tells us, led to formal charges being made against her.

Children spend most of their time in front of the television, and those who live in large cities suffer particularly from this lack of reality. Not being able to experience the world concretely through the sense of touch, they must, of necessity, appreciate it as unreal. Sexuality is subjected to the same process of alienation. In these days when AIDS is such a danger, a German medical professor in all seriousness recommended using erotic telephone lines as the only method of sexual contact that was risk-free. Physical contact is dangerous even today!

In any case, experiencing those things that are near to us through the sensual act of touch remains something that is neglected in the West and is often treated as a taboo. Thus a trend which has been

developing for a long time in our civilisation comes to its conclusion. The sixteenth century could still be seen as a period of real, palpable smells, fragrances, sounds and bodies. But the Christian denigration of the body has gradually and inexorably silenced this reality. Body and soul are, in the mind of the public, two completely separate things. Herbert Marcuse wrote that civilisation demanded the suppression of any feeling of closeness, thus guaranteeing the de-sexualisation of our organism by mutating it into an 'instrument of work.' "Our bodies as bodies are less and less useful," wrote Rudolf zur Lippe. "Our limbs serve more and more to operate systems that are more or less autonomous. Our bodies, in contrast, are no more than the carriers of our head, which works in isolation, or other trained systems that function automatically, such as arms or hands."

One of the great negative successes of Christianity has been the association of the pleasure of touch with the idea of sin. In contrast to Asian or African cultures, in Europe we have rarely proposed the 'physis' of man as a means of development. This lack creates a hunger to touch whose echoes are found in contemporary pop music. "Touch me," sing the Doors, and 'touch' is surely the most commonly used notion in our pop hits. "Songs that Touch your Heart!" In the title "I Hungered for Your Touch," sung by Nat King Cole, the tactile desire is even mixed with the primary oral desire.

Montagu sees in the rock and pop music of today, with its deafening rhythms and its audiences of swaying youths, an aural substitution for basic tactile experiences; he thinks that it is a reaction to a lack of tactile stimulation in childhood. One cannot emphasise too strongly the importance of stimulation for man. The most important relationship one can have with an object can only be had by touching it. That is why the hand of a collector who has found an erotic object should be called a lucky hand.

80. *Erotic Jewel Box,*
second half of the 19th century.
Three ivory dildos and a small
ivory cream bowl. England.

Sadomasochism

On the Ecstasies of the Whip

A diagnosis of contemporary sexual behaviour would reveal a paradox. On the one hand there are increasing complaints of a lack of excitement and enthusiasm in the sexual sphere, something also encountered in psychoanalytical practice. After a long period of permissiveness a return to the "new prudery" appears to be in vogue. This was already beginning to emerge before the subject of AIDS provided an additional chill in the bedroom. The flesh is sad. (Here we are speaking of the behaviour of the consumers of sex and those who practise it, not of the spheres of state or clergy; these always distinguished themselves by their old-fashioned ideas and prudery and still have not reached the stage of genital maturity after all this time, as the discussion on the policy concerning brothels in the old West Germany proved). On the other hand, an increase in clubs of a fetishistic nature and their corresponding magazines is to be noted. Films such as *Baise-Moi* make violence between the sexes their only subject. S&M and flagellation appear to have become lifestyle elements. A search for "S&M" using the Google search engine currently produces about 171,000 hits! While, on the one hand, it appears as if all energy is being withdrawn from eroticism, apparent aggressiveness is attracting the attention of the entire libido in a way that is full of excitement and power.

Through the Sade exhibition which opened in Zurich in December 2001 under the title of *Sade/Surreal*, the notorious Marquis has been accorded the venerable status of a classic at a time when sexuality itself appears to have forfeited its explosive power. It would be reasonable to ask whether there is a connection between the increase in sado-masochistic subjects and the increasing brutalisation of life in the community. But above all what we are concerned with here is the fate of the compulsive desires of individuals, in which something which has until now been concealed, demands expression. Is this not a widespread phenomenon that implies a widespread dilemma where desire is concerned?

The moment of violence, to whatever degree it might be diluted, is probably one of the ingredients of erotic experience. However, what was once regarded as illegal or immoral in sexual matters is rehabilitated, disinfected, hygienically packaged and dragged up to a legally acceptable level when a contract is entered into. Discussions concerning violence against women and child abuse have created a climate in which every accompanying erotic fantasy which contained even the slightest hint of violence had to evaporate. But as Bataille well knew, violence and pain remain inseparable from the experience of pleasure.

Let us listen to the words of a Portuguese nun (Maria Alcoforado — *Love Letter of a Portuguese Nun*), which still sound relevant today: "It is from feelings of pain that we give birth to ourselves. We want to avoid the feelings of pain. And that is how we kill ourselves. If we do not want to feel the pain, we mortify our feelings. We have no separate organs with which to experience feelings of pain and

81. Gerda Wegener, 1925.

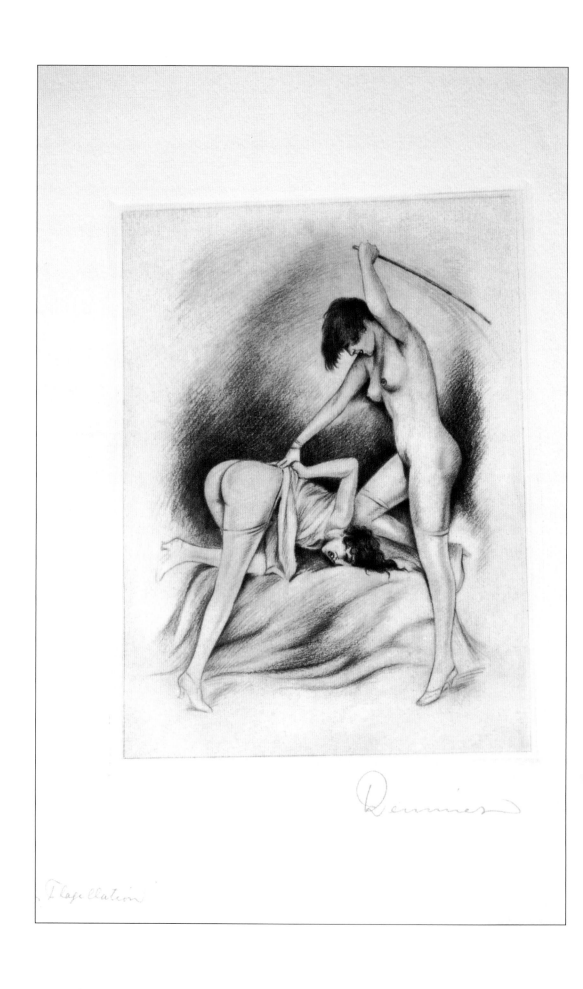

82. Reunier (pseudonym of
    Breuer-Courth), 1925.

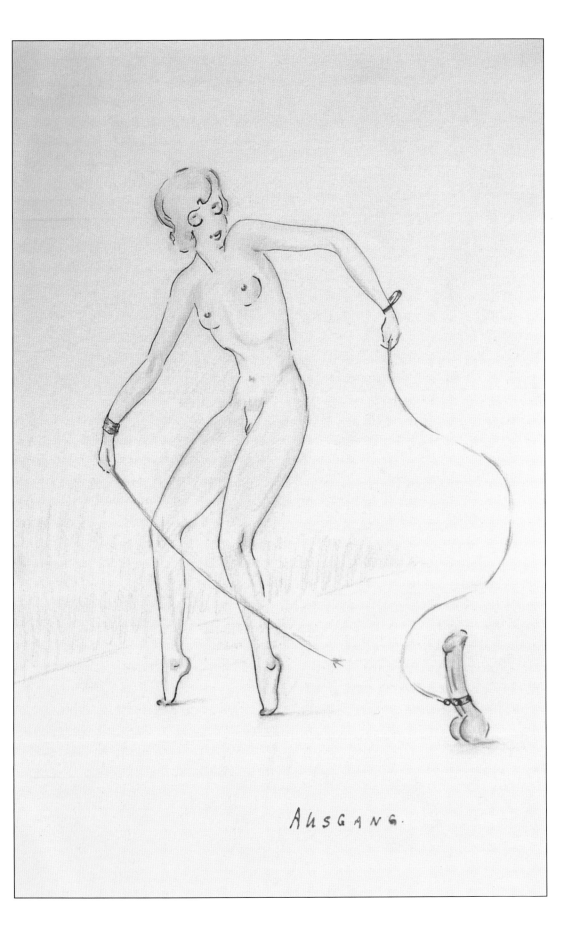

AUSGANG.

83. Campa (pseudonym), 1936.

happiness. The person who wears armour as a protection against feelings of pain also does so against happiness or pleasant feelings. What is important is not a particular kind of feeling. It is the question of being able to perceive at all, to feel at all. To be alive."

In the Middle Ages it was the eye of God that gained pleasure from the nuns and monks who scourged themselves. Here it was less a matter of "sexuality" than of the arousal of religious imagination which was connected with ecstatic experience. This can be both erotic and spiritual in nature, or, as with the Marquis de Sade, erotic and sensual. Both experiences should converge.

If the scenes of self-flagellation which were staged by monks and nuns were a matter of ritual "imagining" in which the relationship between human beings and God was grasped, we can equally interpret the ritual as the "imagining" of human beings in pain. A successful understanding of the opposite pole in the relationship of man to God was only achieved by the discipline of psychology in the twentieth century. It was not only a sense of the unmediated presence of God that was being created, but primarily an unmediated experience of oneself. We shall return to this subject later.

The practice of flagellation was present throughout the Middle Ages. It was not only considered to be a gesture of repentance, the *imitatio Christi*, but also a therapeutic agent to excite tired passions. Flagellation, so people thought, would stimulate the flow of juices and thereby also the mood of the soul. It was thought to be an effective therapeutic agent against melancholy which takes the soul prisoner and paralyses it, as it is not only arouses the flow of juices but simultaneously excites the imagination and the production of fantasies, which are able to free the soul from the embrace of melancholy. The term 'disciplina' was used of scourging in monastic life. From the twelfth century onwards disciplina was also used to describe the instrument itself, the scourge, cane or switch. In his book, *Praise of the Whip* (*Lob der Peitsche*), Nikolaus Largier sees in these practices a simultaneous affirmation and rejection of the body. "One can quite reasonably speak of a radical individualisation that is taking place here.

Every gesture is at the same time affirmation and rejection but if it torments the body in the name of a spiritual freedom whose ultimate aim is the absolute affirmation of the body, the overcoming of the duality of body and spirit in the moment of resurrection and the victory over death." To the same extent that flagellation appears to be the negation of the body it is also its radical affirmation. There is no salvation without the body, although it is the latter which supposedly stands in the way of all freedom.

In the middle of the fourteenth century at the same time as the plague appeared, processions of people scourging themselves took place almost all over Central Europe. Priests and counts, knights and vassals, burghers, peasants and professors took part in them. The angry God who was threatening to destroy sinful mankind would supposedly be appeased with the help of the Virgin Mary and by means of lashes of the scourge. It seems as if human beings were afraid that "the power of God wanted to consume them or swallow them up by means of a cleft in the earth or destroy them with a powerful earthquake and other plagues," as can be read in a work of the time. It is possible to speak here of a fashion for scourging as an epidemic mass phenomenon. Above all the processions of flagellants consisted of men, although occasionally men and women would also allow themselves to be scourged together in public. What was always striking about such occasions was the theatrical and ritual quality of the scourgings. It is curious that this movement coincided with the beginnings of the formation of the bourgeois individual in Europe.

84. Otto Schoff, 1925.

85. Engravings for the illustration of
Sade's *Justine and Juliette*, 1797.

The Italian Renaissance in particular was very important and the form that the flagellant movement took in Italy was a particularly urban, early-modern phenomenon, more than was the case to the north of the Alps. "Penance as an urban practice," records Largier, "has created a form here which goes hand in hand with the development of new ways of urban living and in which self-flagellation also retains its status at least until the eighteenth century". During their scourgings and processions through the cities most of the brotherhoods of flagellants bore hoods and crosses, such as those which can still be seen today in Spain during Semana Santa.

The Age of Enlightenment replaced the discourse of salvation history with that of psychology and medicine. So the Lübeck doctor, Johann Heinrich Meibom, implied in 1639 that the imagined nearness to God and the spiritual sensuality which is portrayed in pictures of scourging was nothing more than the covert and sublimated fulfilment of a desire which is in truth always erotic and which by its linking of pleasure and pain is also perverse. "This curious ceremony of the lashes of the cane," writes Meibom, "fans the flames of lust in these people in such a way that they froth at the mouth and every member that bears testimony to their masculinity looks upwards towards heaven". And he quotes Pico della Mirandola: "I know a man with a very sweet temperament who nevertheless is unable to caress a woman without being scourged beforehand. It is in vain that his reason tells him that the delight that he takes which is so refined is a criminal act; indeed he even reproaches the man scourging him because he is not hitting him hard enough, when weariness or compassion causes his exertions to slacken. The patient does not reach the summit of his sensual feelings until he sees the blood dripping from the wounds." "Susceptible persons," continues Meibom, "believe that they knew a man, who with the coldest of temperaments, which made him quite incapable of serving Venus, possessed the liveliest imaginative powers which always tortured him with erotic images. He lacked natural warmth and physical strength for the contest of love, and so he had to excite himself violently with lashes of the cane. It is difficult to decide whether this manipulation, or sexual intercourse itself, afforded him the greater pleasure. He even allowed himself to come down to the level of requests against those whom he used to select to become his tormentors. He always left the canes soaking in vinegar one day beforehand. If someone did not hit him hard enough he would bandy about swear words and the strongest reproaches. He regarded the work as unfinished until the blood began to flow. This man was perhaps the only person who experienced pain and pleasure at the same time, while being unable to obtain any feeling of delight without the former. Currents of blood were the portents of his greatest pleasure."

This new point of view engendered mistrust towards the supposedly lascivious monks and depraved nuns, who merely found complete expression erotically in such superficially pious practices. Nothing could, therefore, be more offensive, lecherous, and piquant than the monk and the sinner, the nun and her sisters. Satyrs and nymphs concealed themselves beneath their habits. The scandalous story of Cathérine Cadière and Father Girard, the records of whose trials were published in 1731 with the first literary adaptation appearing in 1748 under the title of *Thérèse philosophe*, is a prime example of this.

However, it is England that is regarded as the classic country for flagellation. Writing under the pseudonym of Ivan Bloch, Eugen Dühren claimed in *Flagellomania* ('Die Flagellomanie'), his essay of 1902, that: "in no other country has the passion for the cane been so systematically practised and cultivated as in England, in no other country is the entire literature from the seventeenth century onwards, be it poetry or prose, respectable or pornographic, so greatly preoccupied with this subject as it is here. Likewise nowhere else have the theatre and daily newspapers treated the same subject so much in public, which is doubly conspicuous given the prudery that otherwise prevails among the English in sexual matters. Finally, there can scarcely be another nation that can lay claim to so many artists who have dedicated their talent to this peculiar subject, as is the case in England". England is the country in which the bourgeois character came into existence very early on. What violence must the subject inflict upon itself in order to constitute itself as a – masculine – identity?

Has the "vice" of flagellation put down deeper roots in England than elsewhere? Or is it more conspicuous there, since by contrast with those countries which are both Latin and Roman Catholic it is not dressed up in religion? While flagellation remains restricted to the religious sphere there, its secular character in England by contrast allows it to be more widespread.

There were brothels for example that were entirely reserved for prostitution involving flagellation. From the end of the eighteenth century and throughout the whole of the nineteenth century they were a characteristic feature of prostitution in London. Eugen Dühren writes of them: "These brothels, which appeared in ever greater numbers from 1800 onwards in London, were exclusively devoted to flagellation, for which reason the name 'flagellation brothels' is an accurate one. They were mostly magnificently furnished and not only served as places where men could submit themselves to passive flagellation to their heart's content, but also as educational establishments (*sit venia verbo*) for those girls and women, who wanted to learn the 'art' of the gracious and effective application of the cane."

The *ars flagellandi* also developed into a high art in England's famous public schools. It was here that the English élite was reared: clergymen, professors, industrialists and government officials were educated here. Corporal punishment was regarded as an indestructible tradition. Often the "discipline" lay in the hands of the pupils themselves. But "the headmaster was the key to the whole, at once inimitable ideal, fair-minded judge, and supreme enforcer." Peter Gay summarises the situation thus in *The Cultivation of Hatred* (*The Bourgeois Experience: Victoria to Freud*, vol 3, 1993). The headmasters were true democrats in administering beatings. An ex-pupil recalls John Keate, the popular headmaster of Eton, saying that he had "no favourites and flogged the son of a duke and the son of a grocer with perfect impartiality". Beatings were dished out — with every confidence in the blissful relief of the cane. Even if the secondary, erotic aspects did not become conscious, they nonetheless showed through here and there. This was also the case with Dickens, who appeared to approve of corporal punishment. In *Our Mutual Friend,* he describes the angelic Mr. Wilfer as being so "boyish [...] in his curves and proportions, that his old schoolmaster meeting him in Cheapside, might have been unable to withstand the temptation of caning him on the spot".

Canings were not only a form of castigation of which one was afraid but were also, at the same time, a stimulant for which one yearned. Swinburne, a pupil at Eton, who made his masochistic leanings immortal in candid novels and poems, was only the most famous among the many boarders at public schools, who, as Gay describes, "grew to lust after corporal punishment and to need it in their adult sexual life as an addict needs a daily dose". Corporal punishment has survived in England until today.

Towards the end of the nineteenth century French writers called this desire for the cane "the English vice". And it was only towards the end of the same century that educated citizens had at their disposal terms for the desires of those for whom inflicting pain and receiving it aroused pleasure:

86. Zéllé, 1930.

87. Illustration by Carlo, 1930s.

88. Anonymous, 1930.

sadism and masochism. It was the famous Austrian psychiatrist Richard von Krafft-Ebing who coined the terms, referring to two noted authors. In this century of the bourgeois, Sade was almost entirely unknown. The most famous of his numerous works were the pair of novels that appeared in the 1790s, *Justine* and *Juliette*. Flagellation is of considerable importance in these works. Clairwil, who procures four women for Juliette, explains the heroine's cravings to her as follows: "Now then, send me your four women and canes as well, if you want to see me in a frenzy". – "Canes? Do you then beat people, my love?"– "Certainly, until the blood runs, ... I allow the same thing to be done to me as well. For me there exists no more delightful pleasure; nothing inflames my entire being more ... The feeling of the pain in the parts of the body that have been exhausted by whipping set the blood circulating more quickly and stimulate the spirits, while creating an extraordinary heat in the sexual organs. Finally it creates the possibility for the seeker of lust to go on and complete the act of pleasure for himself, if nature will no longer oblige, and the joys of illicit sex which go beyond the limits that poor nature has set for him.

"But as far as active flagellation is concerned, can there be a greater pleasure for toughened creatures such as us in the world? Is there a pleasure that would better mirror the cruelty, that in one word would satisfy more completely this inclination to blood-lust that nature has endowed us with? ... Oh, Juliette! To humiliate to the depths an interesting, young, sweet creature, that is our soul mate as far as is possible, to allow her cruelly to feel this kind of torture, to be delighted by her tears, to be excited by her annoyance, to become aroused with her movements, to be inflamed with the throes of lust, which pain elicits from the tormented victim, to allow her blood and tears to flow, gloating over the agonisingly distorted features and rejoicing in the muscular spasms of her pretty face caused by despair, — oh, Juliette, what furious joy!"

Masochism, like Sadism, also had a living model, that of the Austrian nobleman Leopold von Sacher-Masoch. The fact that he had to give his name to a perversion which was available to all was a source of much annoyance to him. In Sacher-Masoch's novel *Venus in Furs,* the hero, Severin, signs a contract which ties him to his beloved, Wanda von Dunajew. She despises Severin because of his feminine desires and would prefer to him a man who could dominate her. By means of the contract, Severin delivers himself over to her completely: "Frau von Dunajew is not only allowed to punish her slave for the slightest oversight or offence at her discretion, but she also has the right to mistreat him according to her mood or to pass the time, as she pleases, even to the point of killing him if she likes, in short, he is her absolute property."

The man's wish to be a submissive, humiliated woman, can – through the identification with the inferior person – similarly be expressed in a concealed fashion in a sadistic scenario. It is for this reason that many couples who participate in sado-masochistic performances are often also prepared to exchange roles, even if there are preferences for this role or that in the *mis en scène*. It is the totality of the sado-masochistic undertaking that is more important than the question of who is master and who is slave.

The perception of the phenomenon changed with Krafft-Ebing with sado-masochism turning into a pathological condition. It now constituted an interesting pathological model because it described the most extreme paradox in sexuality, namely a relationship in which pain gives the most intense erotic pleasure. However, it soon became clear in Krafft-Ebing's case histories that pain is more the condition than the source of the pleasure. One of his patients, Case number fifty, twenty-nine years old, recognised that "scourging was incidental to the principal idea of being subjected to the will of the

89. Godal (pseudonym), circa 1925.

woman". And Herr X., Case number fifty-one, twenty-six years old, "draws attention to the fact that humiliation is the principal factor and that the ecstasy of inflicting pain never occurs". Being subordinate to the woman is also the highest joy for Case number fifty-eight, Herr Z., fifty years old: "A voluptuous lady beautifully shaped, with especially pretty feet, could arouse him greatly by sitting down. He felt that he had to offer himself to her as a chair, in order 'to be allowed to carry so much splendour'. The thought of having coitus with her horrified him. He felt the need to serve the woman. It occurred to him that ladies liked riding. He revelled in the thought of how marvellous it must be to struggle beneath the burden of a beautiful woman in order to experience pleasure. He pictured the situation to himself in its every aspect, imagined her beautiful feet, the splendid calves, the soft, full thighs. Every beautifully-proportioned lady, every pretty foot belonging to a lady provided a powerful stimulus for his imagination, but he never betrayed his strange feelings which appeared to him to be abnormal; he knew how to control himself. However, neither did he feel the need to fight against it — on the contrary, he would have been sorry to have to surrender these feelings which have become so dear to him." So we can see that in the beginning masochism was not the deed, but the fantasy. An attempt is made to prolong the excitement and to avoid the "final pleasure". Its appearance is experienced as "horror".

Krafft-Ebing also recognised that most, if not all, cases of shoe fetishism are based on acts of self-humiliation which are more or less conscious. A quotation from Goethe's poem *Lili's Park* ought to show us that such moods are also ingredients in normal love:

> She runs her feet over his back;
> He thinks he is in heaven.
> How his every sense is itching!
> Her composed look his heart's leaven [...]
> I kiss her shoes, chew at the soles,
> As demure as is only the bear's way,
> Quite gently I rise, so furtive my leap,
> Softly to her knee. — On the happy day
> She will wave me on, and tickle my ears,
> And cuff me wilfully with her soft hand;
> I growl, and new-born shed joy's tears [...]

Sadism and masochism almost never occur separately. "A sadist," according to Freud, who was one of the pioneers in research into this phenomenon, "is always a masochist as well at the same time". But it is possible that "the active or passive side of the perversion is more strongly developed in him and can represent his predominantly sexual activity". In sadists as well as in masochists there is concealed an unconscious tendency in the opposite direction; however, one of the two compulsive orientations mostly has the upper hand. At the same time, Freud dispelled the notion that there was anything odd about this perversion, believing that it was only those sexual conflicts which all "normal" human beings concealed in their unconscious that are visible in it in an intensified form.

If Krafft-Ebing understood sadism as "a pathological intensification of the male sexual character" and masochism as a "rather pathological degeneration of specifically feminine psychological peculiarities,"

90. Anonymous, 1930.

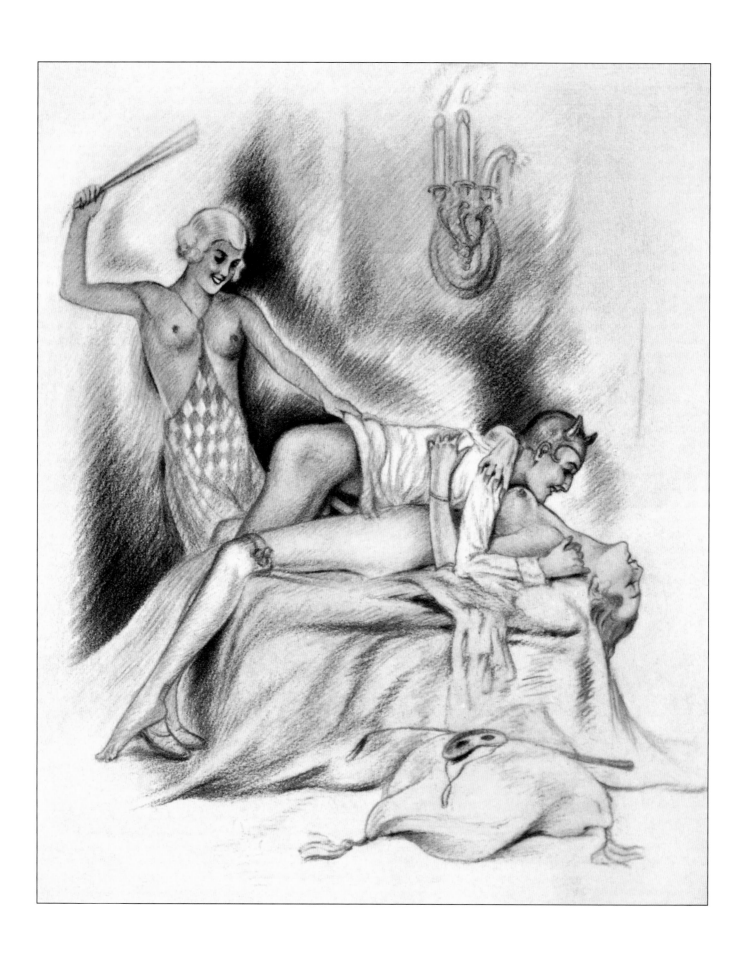

91. Reunier (pseudonym of
    Breuer-Courth), 1925.

92. Aroldo Bonzagni, circa 1910.

93. Martin Van Maele, 1907.

this was not simply an expression of the understanding of the roles of the sexes of his time. According to Freud's theory these two opposing characteristics are to be found in every man and in every woman as a confusion of their identity. It is the eternally feminine in us as men that drags us down.

Nothing seems to contradict the pleasure principle more strongly than masochism. While human beings generally tend towards avoiding pain, it appears that the latter is sought after by masochists, even giving them pleasure. Masochistic fantasies as an accompaniment to sexual intercourse and masturbation are very common. In contrast to fetishism and transvestism, which occur almost exclusively among men, masochism is to be found among both sexes. As Louise J. Kaplan states in her book *Female Perversions: The Temptations of Madame Bovary* (1991), contrary to popular belief sexual masochism is much more widespread among men than among women (in a ratio of approximately twenty men to one woman!), above all among homosexual men. It is typical for a woman in a sado-masochistic scenario which has been thought up and led by a man to take over the role of the sadist as a remunerated or voluntarily participant. The male partner demands that she ties him up, beats him on the backside, sits astride him, and urinates or defecates upon him. If it is also the woman who is issuing the orders, they will have been imposed upon her beforehand by the man. The key to understanding this phenomenon lies in the realisation that an important aspect of this strategy consists in giving expression to the "feminine" desires of the man without taking away his position of power as a man in the process. Freud was referring precisely to these feminine desires on the part of men with his phrase "feminine masochism."

Masochistic traits, as well as the tendency towards self-harm which is closely related, are to be found in almost all human beings to a lesser or greater extent. These masochistic elements can be located on a broad spectrum between self-destruction and its apogee, suicide, and the enjoyment of pain in sexual perversion. Freud stated that erogenous masochism was one of the primary compulsions. It was a part of the death instinct which had remained in the organism and which stays there bound to the libido by means of sexual arousal. Freud saw in primary masochism the actual "enjoyment of pain", "a connection of the destruction which is turned inwards with sexuality."

As far as the sado-masochistic *mis en scène* is concerned, is it less a question of increasing the "erotic desire" and far more a question of restraining destructive impulses? These would then be concealed in a script which places erotic motifs in the foreground. "Sexualisation of destructiveness" would be the motto of this mask. The key to the understanding of masochism for Theodor Reik (1941) is the imagination. According to him human beings with a poor imagination have no appetite for masochism. The imagination has the role of preparing the sexual tension. "Masochistic actions are merely the acting out of pre-existing fantasies." The masochist thereby seeks to prolong the pleasure of anticipation with the help of the moment of suspense, that is to say of an unconscious, floating tension which brings about a delay. Masochists appear to prefer the pleasure of anticipation to pleasure and the fantasy to reality.

Nancy Friday collected such fantasies in her book *My Secret Garden: Women's Sexual Fantasies* (1975). She makes the distinction between masochists who long for pain and the "rape fantasists" who fantasise more about being overpowered, as in the case of Rose Ann: "These fantasies or dreams usually begin with my body being stretched, one brutal man on each limb, pulling me in opposite directions, literally spreading me wide open so that some immensely huge penis — there is no one or nothing on the end of it — begins to enter me, stretching me, ripping me, my vagina, wide open as it pushes its

way deeper into me. The men twist my arms painfully as well as pull them, and I can hear my bones breaking and cracking, while the sound of my skin, around my vagina, also rips audibly. I cry out in reality even as I cry out in my fantasy. But I love it, even though my intelligence and logic tell me that I am being ghoulish, that this is not a normal way to enjoy sex. And I do enjoy it. I hate what is happening to me in my fantasies but it is inextricably involved with my very real pleasure." There is therefore a clear difference between fantasy and reality. What in reality she would never long for or endure is wished for here. Where does the experience of pleasure come from, one asks oneself, that is connected with this torment?

This hiatus between fantasy and reality is also apparent in Barbara's account:

"I cannot tell you why, but my fantasy has always been that I like to imagine myself as a naughty girl of about seventeen, hauled up in front of the headmistress for a caning, and that I am wearing the old-fashioned type of gym tunic and Directoire knickers down to my knees. From this stage I like to be told to bend over, after a lecturing, and then get caned with my gym tunic raised, the cane coming on my knickers. Therefore I told my lesbian friend just how far she could go and the date and scene were agreed upon. Naturally I found that the whipping I got with the cane wasn't half so thrilling as the fantasy and while I had no heart in masturbation with the lesbian woman, it came easily after the punishment. ... All my fantasies are concerned with various methods of being caned and various methods of me giving the cane to someone else. For instance, I would like to be tied hand and foot and then given twelve strokes of the birch but, if this happened, I would probably faint with the awful pain."

It is also striking that the number and strength of the blows are negotiated. The masochistic situation is one that is staged and controlled. The masochistic position can easily give way to the sadistic one: "being caned and ... various methods of me giving the cane to someone else". What is important is the situation of power and submission. The positions which are adopted here often seem to be interchangeable.

It would be premature to conclude that the desire for domination is to be ascribed to the yearning for the traditional role of the woman towards the dominant male. A paradox is to be noted here insofar as the more women grow accustomed to their newly won sexual freedom and leave behind their historical role, the more they indulge in fantasies of domination. This is very clearly expressed in Natalie's account:

"I'm totally at his mercy. I keep saying, 'What are you going to do with me?' and he just sits there. Then the fantasy takes one of several courses. Sometimes he loves me all over with his mouth, until I beg him to enter me. Sometimes he enters me without foreplay and seemingly just takes me as if I'm nothing ... Whatever he does, the fantasy ends with him releasing me and hugging me and massaging my sore muscles and my sobbing with relief and thanking him — not for letting me go, but for tying me up! ... I've just recently added this [fantasy] to my repertoire but it isn't quite as powerful as the other. It goes as follows: I manage to tie him to the bed, spread-eagled exactly as I was. This is done by some sort of 'innocent' playfulness, like, 'Darling, show me how to tie that knot. Oh, I see. Let me try...' and so on. When he realises he has been tricked, he reacts with rage and fear, much as I did in my second fantasy. As a matter of fact, we pretty much change roles — he's helpless and scared, while I'm cool and matter of fact ... I am sure there are other women like me, who having emerged from being under male domination, crave to return to it in bed."

94. Anonymous, 1925.

Disciplina scholae. Anonymes Aquarell. Um 1900

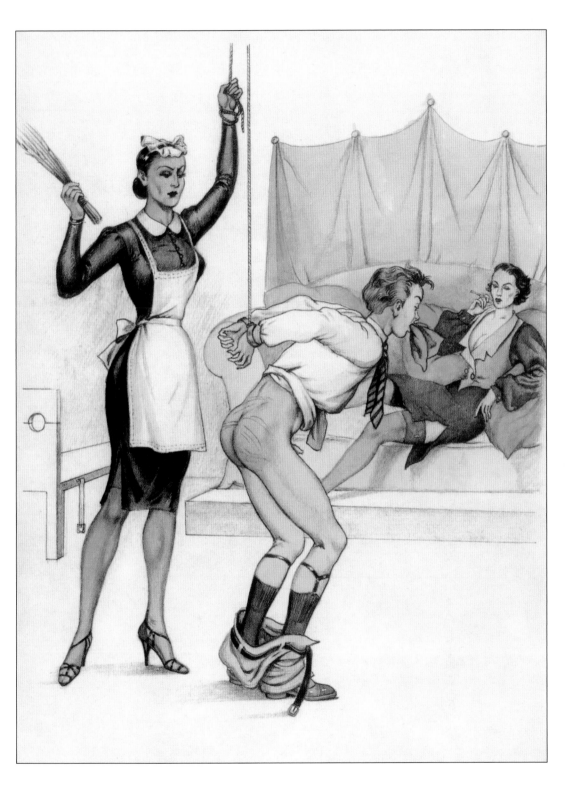

95. Anonymous, watercolour, 1900.

96. Unknown fetish drawing.

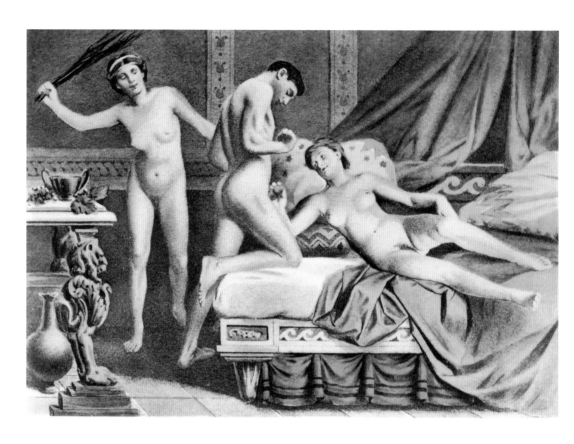

Dominating or dominated: what is crucial is becoming involved in these erotic desires of one's own free will. There is a feminist moral stance which would have it that women who use themselves in relationships and allow themselves to become an object, are the prisoners of a "false consciousness" which can be traced back to "brainwashing". However, it is more the case that "autonomous" erotic desires — which go back to forms of experience in early childhood — allow women to enter into such relationships. "Free will" is an entirely contradictory issue, as erotic passion is often experienced as overpowering energy and we believe that we can decide of our own accord where we are overwhelmed by this energy. According to Jessica Benjamin sado-masochism is merely the intensified expression of moments that are fundamentally present in sexual excitement. Our culture is shaped by the conflict between our needs to assert ourselves and to go out of ourselves. ("Transgression and violation of boundaries", Bataille would say here.) This conflict constitutes the core of the fantasy of erotic submission.

Jessica Benjamin advances the theory that the individualistic overstressing between one's own self and the other brings about a feeling of unreality and isolation. It is precisely the individualism which is the hallmark of our culture that makes it difficult to accept others as independent beings. As a result, it is difficult for us to relate to others as living erotic beings. Hence Benjamin asserts that violence plays such an important role in erotic fantasies because it is the expression of the desire to force open this rigid casing. That fantasies of violence are so widespread today can, therefore, at least in part be attributed to the increasing importance of rationality and individualism in our culture. Benjamin bases her observations on the study of a story, *The Story of O* by Pauline Réage. Dependence and power are interwoven here inseparably; the conflict between the need for autonomy and that of

97. Paul Avril, 1910.

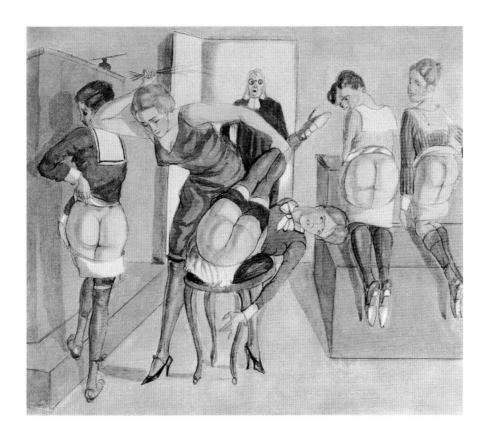

confirmation can only be overcome by means of complete self-abandonment. This book illustrates Benjamin's thesis that the root of the problem of power and dependence in the erotic sphere lies in the failure of the process of establishing boundaries.

Some feminist critics do not see an allegory of the desire for recognition in the masochism of O but merely the sad story of a woman who becomes the victim of male violence. What sort of gratification is being sought and found in submission remains open. There is an equal lack of explanation as to why fantasies of submission play an important role in the inner life of many people who in reality would not act out such fantasies. *The Story of O* "confronts us boldly with the idea that people often submit not merely out of fear but in complicity with their own deepest desires". According to Benjamin a strange distortion of the desire for recognition is evident in the desire for submission. The masochism of O represents an effort to be recognised by another, in her case a man – but by another who is powerful enough to become aware of such recognition. This other has the power that the woman desires for herself. The men who preside over O find more pleasure in their power over her than in the erotic services she provides. Their sadistic pleasure does not lie directly in enjoying O's torment, much rather in the knowledge of their power over her. In the course of the novel, O's desire for attachment increasingly assumes the character of religious devotion. Her lover is like a god and the desire for him is only to be satisfied through obedience. While she becomes the tool of the superior will, she retains a transcendence which is reminiscent of the humiliations of the saints. At the end of the novel, O is ready to risk her complete destruction in order to continue to be the object of the desire of her lover and thereby to find recognition. As a masochist, O does not derive her pleasure from pain. Her pain only arouses pleasure if it is connected with submitting to a

98. Hegemann, circa 1925.

powerful person. The pleasure of the female masochist, as is confirmed by recent psychoanalytical studies, is not to be understood as the direct enjoyment of suffering.

"She liked the idea of torture but when she was being tortured herself she would have betrayed the whole world to escape it and yet when it was over she was happy to have gone through it." The physical pain takes the place of the psychological pain, which loss and being left entail. Physical suffering can conceal psychological suffering. While O is being wounded by others, according to Jessica Benjamin, she has the feeling of being touched and reached. She puts it thus: "... she is able to experience another living presence. O's pleasure, so to speak, lies in her sense of her own survival and her connection to her powerful lover. Thus as long as O can transpose her fear of loss into submission, as long as she remains the object and manifestation of his power, she is safe."

The forcible violation of physical integrity represents a breaking through the feeling of separation in the other. This violation of boundaries is described by Benjamin as the innermost secret of all eroticism; it becomes most clearly visible in erotic violence.

The paradox of free will, which we discussed at the beginning, also becomes clear here. One takes part in a masochistic situation voluntarily, the aim of which is to strive for recognition of one's own self by means of another; this striving, however, is alienated insofar as the moment of violence takes the place of the moment of freedom. True freedom, according to Benjamin, should consist in giving oneself of one's own accord to a mutual relationship.

But O's striving to be free of boundaries, her striving for real union, assumes the form of submission because she is not an independent person and cannot stand being alone. However, if the psyche has become deaf and dumb, can the physical pain of detachment only find its reflection in the physical pain of violent submission? The dissolution of the structure of the self in physical union is always painful and beset with anxiety. However, physical pain is a compensation, it is a violent breakthrough into the structure of the self. In the meantime Freud's conception of masochism as "pleasure in pain" has been improved upon by some modern psychoanalysts, who interpret masochism with reference to the ego or the self and its relationships with objects. They understand masochism as the desire for submission to an idealised other in order to protect oneself from overwhelming psychological suffering, loss of the love object, and fragmentation. These are above all narcissistic problems which can be "solved" by the infliction of pain.

For Robert D. Stolorow (1975), masochistic activities frequently have as their goal the reconstitution and stabilisation of structural cohesion, where self-representation is uncertain and fragile. "The inference to be drawn, then, is that masochistic activities, as one of their multiple functions, may serve as abortive efforts to restore, repair, buttress, and sustain a self-representation that had been damaged and rendered precarious by injurious experiences during the early pre-oedipal era, when the self-representation is developmentally most vulnerable." In an individual with diffuse or fragmented self-representation, the masochistic search for real experiences of pain can be understood as a means of acquiring a false feeling of being real and alive thereby reconstituting the feeling of existing as a differentiated being and as a coherent self. In his *Regulatory Functions of Masochism* (*Regulierungsfunktionen des Masochismus*), J. Grunert found among patients with a premature experience of separation "an almost insatiable yearning for fusion with the primary object, a need for the object. But almost as regularly we come upon fears of fusion which are just as strong behind these desires, resulting from the original undermining of the

99. Erotic Photograph.

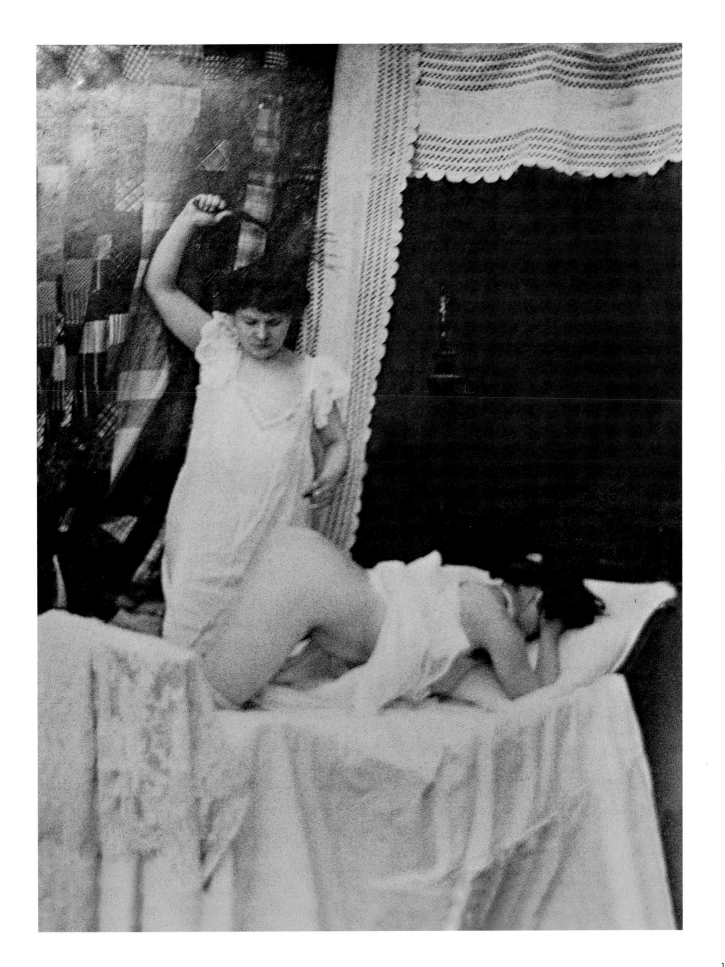

100. Erotic Photograph.

101. Erotic Photograph.

behaviour of the self-object, that behaviour not being optimal and experienced as life-threatening, thus allowing a premature separation." The correlative of overcoming both the isolation which resulted from the early separation and the threat of the loss of the self is the fear of being destroyed by this very desire. The sado-masochistic situation offers here a mechanism for regulation to manoeuvre the weak self between the Scylla of self-fragmentation and the Charybdis of the fear of destruction.

It is a fact that an elementary need for physical contact as a way of fending off a depression resulting from isolation or desolation often plays a role in the desire to be beaten. The wish to be struck repeatedly is one of the ways people adopt in an attempt to escape the fear of being alone, of non-existence, the fear of disintegration. It is one of those "forced acts" that halt self-fragmentation. In their analysis of a dream and a series of perverse fantasies of the Marquis de Sade, Bach and Schwarz (1972) come to the conclusion that the masochistic fantasies of the marquis which arose while he was imprisoned represented an attempt on his part to overcome acute narcissistic decompensations – the other possibility being by way of sadistic fantasies. The authors described Sade's masochistic fantasies as regressive attempts to reconstitute and bring back to life archaic, idealized self-objects and interpreted the sexualisation of these fantasies as a despairing effort to fend off experiences of total self-fragmentation and self-dissolution.

The breakdown of the tension between self-assertion and self-abandonment, which in reality takes place within the individual, appears in the sado-masochistic couple as a relationship between two people. One person keeps their boundaries intact, the other allows their boundaries to be violated. If self-abandonment and loss of control were mutual, the result would be complete self-dissolution. It is for that reason that the sado-masochistic *mis en scène* allows for a controlled loss in which the ego of the masochistic part identifies itself with the controlling part. In this way the desire can be pursued "without risk."

The drawing of boundaries between self and other is the central problem of the sado-masochistic situation. This is also expressed in the artistic representations of this subject. Of all the works of erotic art, the fetishistic portrayals from the milieu of sado-masochism are among the least lively. The outlines of the figures are clear and stiff, as if everyone has to save his own skin. Despite the dramatic content of the action the characters remain separate from each other. The situations that are portrayed appear stiff and frozen. Spontaneity and liveliness are lacking. In general it is reasonable to assume that there is a connection between artistic style and personal psychodynamics. So the fetishistic graphic artist acts out the same dynamics on paper that otherwise determine his fantasies or fetishistic acts as well. It is here that we find the diagnostic value of many works of art. (On seeing sado-masochistic works by Japanese artists I was astonished that there was so little to distinguish them from those of European artists, since they were frozen and rigid in character.)

Apart from a few exceptions, sado-masochistic literature is also of little interest as a rule in its redundancy to anyone who is not an aficionado – indeed it is almost a torture. These are texts in which one notices a void, which again points to a deficit in human empathy. As in sado-masochistic pornography, the literature also finds its most important topoi predominantly in homes, boarding-schools, and institutions in which sadistic action is favoured by a difference in power. Power and powerlessness in these institutions determine the relationships between people, and doubtlessly scandalous things do often happen here.

102. Erotic Photograph.

But sadism as it really exists is not under discussion here. What we are concerned with here is imagination and fictitious play. According to traditional models of explanation, authoritarian structures are supposed to produce precisely sado-masochistic tendencies in the individual. However, it would appear presently that the tendencies have only been liberated by the fall of old power structures. It is early wounds and fears, which themselves belong to the *conditio humana,* that now have free rein for endless dramatisation. Power thus becomes a game in a space that is free of power, though not free of unconscious compulsions. In playing with violence, an earlier, unsuccessful attempt to draw a boundary is repeated once more, as well as over and over again.

It was the dilemma between "fear of destruction and rescue in salvation" that drove the processions of flagellants in the Middle Ages. The same dilemma is expressed subjectively in the conflict between "narcissistic decompensation and rescue of the self". "Death and resurrection": the oscillating basic theme of staged violence? In our secularised society, sexual eroticism has taken over the function of religious eroticism.

It is important to stress the fact of the game here. Sado-masochism is a dramaturgy with fixed rules, a ritualised masquerade, bizarre and grotesque to the outsider, but usually quite harmless. According to Eberhard Schorsch, this fictitious game is the "fending off, canalisation and ritualisation of neurotic mechanisms with the result that social interaction remains free from them." If at the outset we inquired into the connection between sado-masochism and the brutalisation of life in the community, the connection can now be more subtly differentiated. Authoritarian societies want to attach themselves to the unconscious, sado-masochistic strivings in each of us and to instrumentalize and misuse them in maintaining inhuman relationships. Liberal societies, on the other hand, allow this dark, violent side of our sexuality to remain as a fantasy and to be acted out in fictitious play, without social interaction being endangered by it.

An observation made in the study, *The Ordinary Homosexual* (*Der gewöhnliche Homosexuelle*), by M. Dannecker and R. Reiche (1974) is revealing in this respect. It suggests that sexual crimes with a fatal outcome – in other words murders of a sadistic kind – are especially untypical of homosexuals precisely because in these relationships violence hardly ever appears outside of the "reciprocal" sado-masochistic *mis en scène*. Deviant instinctual impulses are ritually absorbed in this subculture and made less harmful. Conversely, it is known that as a rule among sadistically deviant criminals that there is no access to the sado-masochistic subculture.

"Sexual offenders" are only to be found outside of this subculture. "The deviants," Schorsch writes, attempting thereby to circumvent the concept of the perverse, "know this destructiveness and have formed and administered it; those who are not deviants are either not aware of it or much less so. For this reason the controls can be less reliable, the behaviour can be less foreseeable, the threat possibly greater."

Let us accept that aggressiveness is an inherent aspect of the sexual, which cannot be removed from it, and that it is no strange, "perverse" ingredient! Eroticism and passion suffocate beneath the prescribed image of a sexuality that is harmonious, equal, considerate towards partners, and gentle. However, the contemporary trend of removing the drama from sexuality by no means leads to gratification. The ostracised part, the violent element that was split off and forced into the unconscious will always find a way of expressing itself in unpredictable ways comparable to volcanic eruptions. The impulse to cross boundaries will only allow itself to be tamed and cultivated if it remains a playful part of our culture.

103. Erotic Photograph.

148.

Ecstasy

"Beauty should lead to a paroxysm of emotion:
if it doesn't, it isn't beauty."
André Breton

There is nothing more exciting for a man than the face of a beautiful woman in the throes of passion. For a red-blooded male, after all, beauty represents the ultimate lure, an irresistible attraction. Conveyed by the eyes, beauty can inflame his desire and arouse him to the very depths of his being. "Beauty," said Bataille, "is that aspect of the beheld that arouses desire." In his *Satyricon*, Petronius describes the subtle devices considered essential to stimulate the libido in ancient Rome. Even a goddess might not be able to relight the dying embers of passion –"Her hair fell in natural ringlets over her shoulders. Her high forehead was bespotted with drops of gold. Beneath, her eyebrows extended to the line of her cheeks, which became finer and finer until it disappeared altogether. And from between her eyes – which shone with a clarity never otherwise seen in a sky without a moon – her nose sloped down from her forehead at a superb gradient. Her mouth was such as the sculptor Praxiteles might have conjured up as his dream for the face of the goddess of the tree-nymphs in ecstasy. Her chin, her neckline, her hand, and her foot surpassed in all respects the most beautiful of all sculpted marble."

What is considered the epitome of beauty has been seriously influenced by the passage of time. The ideal of beauty in the Middle Ages reposed in the figure of the Blessed Virgin. One of the Fathers of the Church in the fourth century strikingly described what he imagined as the beauty of the Mother of Christ: "Most well-made in body, she was the most beautiful of women. Fair, not too short but of excellent height. Her skin was pale but of a pleasant hue, and unblemished. Her hair was of the colour of gold, its tresses long and lissome. Her mouth was gentle, and pleasing to behold. Her lips were red, rose-coloured, and without fault. Her teeth were perfectly aligned, white and spotless like new-fallen snow. Her cheeks radiated the colour of valerian, combining the hues of a red rose and of pure white snow – indeed, just as if her cheeks had actually been decorated with a lilac flower and a sweet-smelling rose. Her throat was white and smooth, her neck neither heavy nor long, but just right."

For a holy man to imagine the charms of the Virgin Mary in such a way - both profane and pious – and for him then to describe them with "all the internal passion of a troubadour" is simply astonishing. This image of the Blessed Virgin prefigures the ideal of beauty for an entire epoch. Most cultures agree on what makes a mouth beautiful. Already by the Middle Ages the consensus was that lips had to be "soft, dainty, small, and quick to smile, pleasant to caress, and of a rosy red colour."

In medieval French poetry, the ideal was depicted by the rogue troubadour, François Villon, in his *Grand Testament*. The wife of a helmet-smith bemoans the fading of her former good looks and sings of her delight in her erstwhile beauty.

104. Jules Duboscq, *Second Empire*. Daguerreotype.

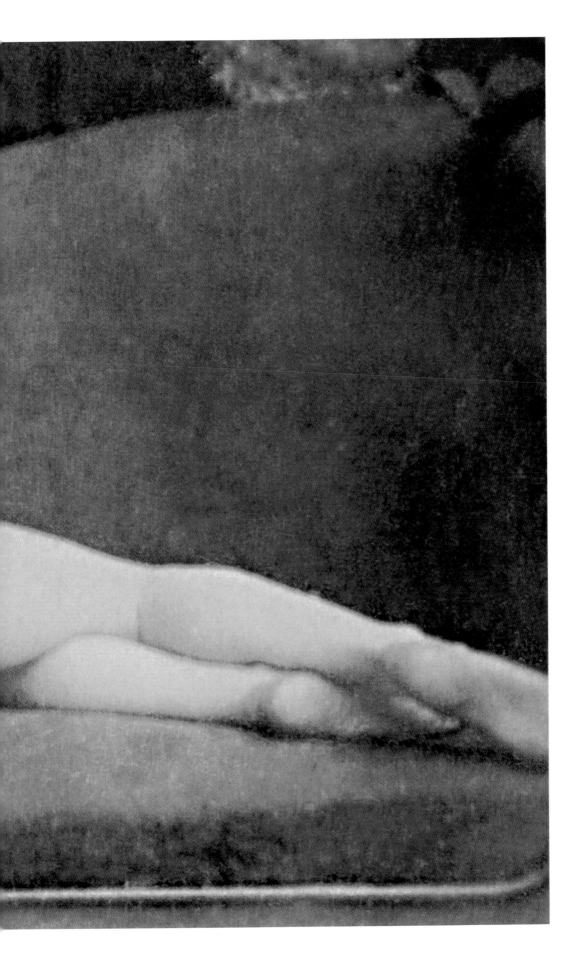

105. Félix-Jacques Antoine Moulin,
1851–1854.
Coloured daguerreotype.

106. French postcard,
     end of the 19th century.

107. Giovanni Zuin, *Seated Nude.*

52

Where now is that smooth forehead,

The blonde hair, those arched eyebrows,

. . . , that pretty look

Which so subtly betokened so much,

That fine nose, straight if not small,

Those daintily aligned ears,

The dimpled chin, . . .

And those beautiful scarlet lips?

53

Those gracefully slender shoulders,

Those long arms and those tapering hands,

Small breasts, shapely hips,

Held high, and quite perfectly made

For use in the lists of love,

Those wide loins, that honeypot

Set between large, firm thighs

Inside its own little bower?

Why do some faces seem more beautiful to us than others? Georges Bataille stated that a man or woman might be thought handsome according to how far removed their overall shape seemed to be from that of a mere animal. For a human being, there cannot be but a certain distaste for anything that in any way resembles the animal-like. Particularly disliked is any characteristic that suggests something of the simian. The erotic quality of the female form, it appears to me, is linked to a toning down of the naturally heavy awkwardness rendered inevitable through the purely evolutionary and logistical assemblage of the bones that make up the skeleton. When vital statistics are distanced from physical and animal realities, from the evolutionary requirements of the human body, they depart from perceptions of reality to correspond more or less to the universal image of the desirable woman.

It is thus the neat, the trimly pretty aspect of a woman that affords her greatest charms. The German poet, Johann Georg Scheffner, in his *Catalogue of Dora's Charms*, describes beauty in terms of hearty ancient Greek verse – a nose that is "mildly retroussé", eyes "as blue as violets", small "dimples in the cheeks", teeth "like a string of pearls", a "springy bosom", "rounded knees" and thighs that are "soft and lissome". But then, rather than the act of love, his pleasure was a lively enjoyment of the female nude.

Yet the image of a desirable woman was not simply of one who aroused that desire, but of one who at the same time also betrayed some hidden animal quality. As Georges Bataille wrote in his major work on erotic philosophy, *Eroticism* (1957): "The perceived beauty of a woman who is desired centres on the genital areas – notably the areas that have hair, the "animal" areas. It is instinct that arouses our desire for such parts of the body... Beauty that rejects the animal and awakens desire releases a surge in excitement and heat in "animal" parts of the body!" We do not desire beauty for itself, therefore, but for the extreme pleasure it gives us to foresee its approaching profanation. Beauty that manages somehow to reduce its animal aspect to a minimum is the focus of intense desire that it should be well and truly "sullied" by the animal instinct at the moment of possession. Beauty seems to be desired in order to be "dirtied." Specifically, it is the animal that manifests itself violently at the moment of orgasm.

Everyone knows of people renowned for their beauty who nonetheless do not arouse in them any form of sexual passion. Even those described as the most gorgeous models may seem sculpted from utterly sterile clay. Their beauty has no actual being, is entirely superficial. They have no erotic mystique whatever. This is why women photographed by Helmut Newton are often described as "ice maidens" – perfect, but occasioning no emotional reaction at all.

What makes a woman alluring? Is it knowing something special, something secret about her? Such knowledge of her may be revealed subtly, in a single instant – but enough to activate the instincts. The hidden purpose of beauty is disclosed within a mutual liking that, according to Franz von Baader's celebrated description, is "silver-plated" – meaning a liking that simultaneously has both internal and external elements. A "silver-plated" mutual regard of this kind turns the spark of beauty into a brilliant flame. A man who experiences it is irresistibly attracted by it – attracted by desiring it.

It was the surrealists who were especially sensitive to expressing notions of beauty in "emotional" terms. In his novel *Nadja*, André Breton defined beauty within such parameters: "Beauty should lead to a paroxysm of emotion; if it doesn't, it isn't beauty." The key term here is

108. Anonymous photograph.
Erotic Museum of Amsterdam.

"paroxysm of emotion" which suggests a psychological condition equivalent to a physical attack of cramp. Such beauty "in the service of desire", directly linking passion, emotions, and physical reactions, could be described in psychological terms as tantamount to actual sexual activity. In Breton's *L'Amour Fou*, the author expands on his central theme of beauty, love, and madness: "Beauty that leads to a paroxysm of emotion must be experienced as erotic but kept private, must be explosive but lasting, and must be magical but based in reality – or it isn't beauty." The notion that beauty should at the same time be "explosive but lasting" not only recalls the "paroxysm of emotion" but also suggests something like a grand mal epileptic seizure. The stiffening as body muscles tauten is followed, in the final stages of such an episode, by jerky movements, and by shuddering and trembling of the whole body.

Part of the paradox of an epileptic attack, however, is that it comprises both specific movements and an absence of movement. An "attack" of beauty, on the other hand – as described in *Nadja* – is neither dynamic nor static.

No work of sculpture expresses the paroxysm of emotion that is desire more powerfully than *The Ecstasy of St. Theresa*, by Gianlorenzo Bernini (Sta Maria della Vittoria). It represents being "pierced by a golden arrow" – feelings exactly those of sexual congress, even if the Roman Catholic Church has always insisted on believing that its themes and observances incorporate no sexual connotations whatsoever.

The moment of ecstasy is difficult to describe. It defies verbal representation. It is beyond telling in words. To try to give a detailed account of the instant of sexual climax is like trying to catch a lizard. At best, you end up with its tail while the lizard makes a rapid escape. Yet we ought to have a go at least at listing the personal events and feelings experienced during this "petit mal seizure" that is orgasm. It is the precise moment when the antagonism between "beauty" and the "animal" or the "beast" breaks down. The effects on the body of the flows of mental energy are set free and given sway. These mental currents have themselves become themes of representational art. In the most subtle works, representation of bodily gestures enables an observer, almost through mimetic intuition, to perceive in them "movements of the soul". Changes in facial expression are well-known to be produced by the involuntary contraction and relaxation of specific muscle groups. Such changes can certainly result from sexual stimulation – and of course from fear, grief, or rage.

Before the investigations of Masters and Johnson, bodily reactions during such sexual activities as masturbation and intercourse were never systematically observed, described or studied. As a direct measure of sexual tension in a woman, the scientists established the "sex flush", the reddening of the skin surface, which peaked in intensity at the point of orgasm. In a man, such a flush manifests itself during the "plateau phase" and not in the stages of initial excitement or when approaching climax. That is why a woman's face strained and taut expresses, as an image, by itself, the muscular tension that is active over her whole body.

Unlike a man, a woman can sustain this state of orgasm for a long duration. A strong and accelerated heartbeat – described as a "vaginal pulse" – is often an apparent effect of sexual climax.

Sexual desire, and its satisfying, may be accompanied by various feelings and emotions. But in order to study how sexual stimulation really works, we must stop looking at the matter from a coldly scientific, analytical point of view and bring in the scope of the imagination.

109. John Collier, *Lilith*, 1887.
Oil on canvas. The Atkinson
Gallery, Southport, Lancs.

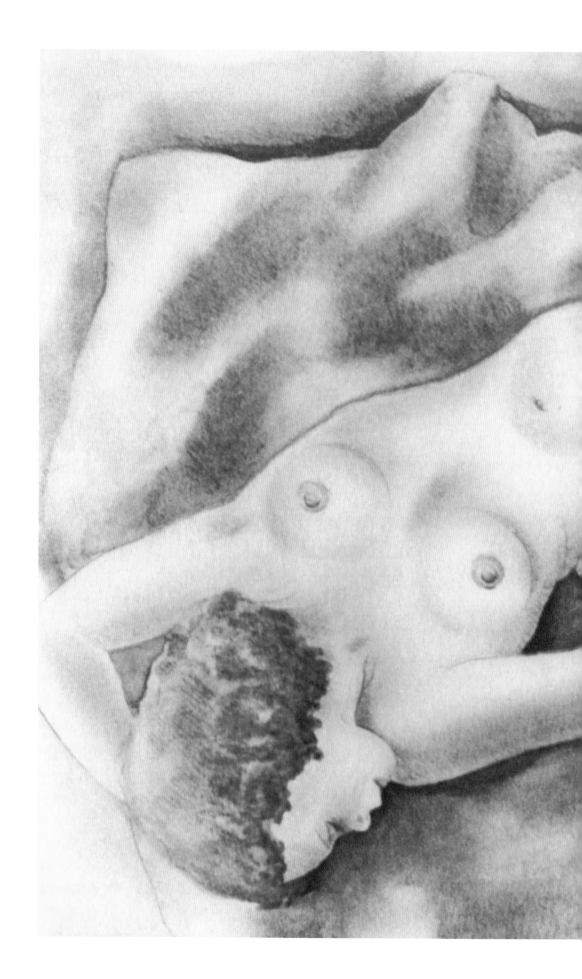

110. Léon Bakst, *Erotic Scene*, 1920.

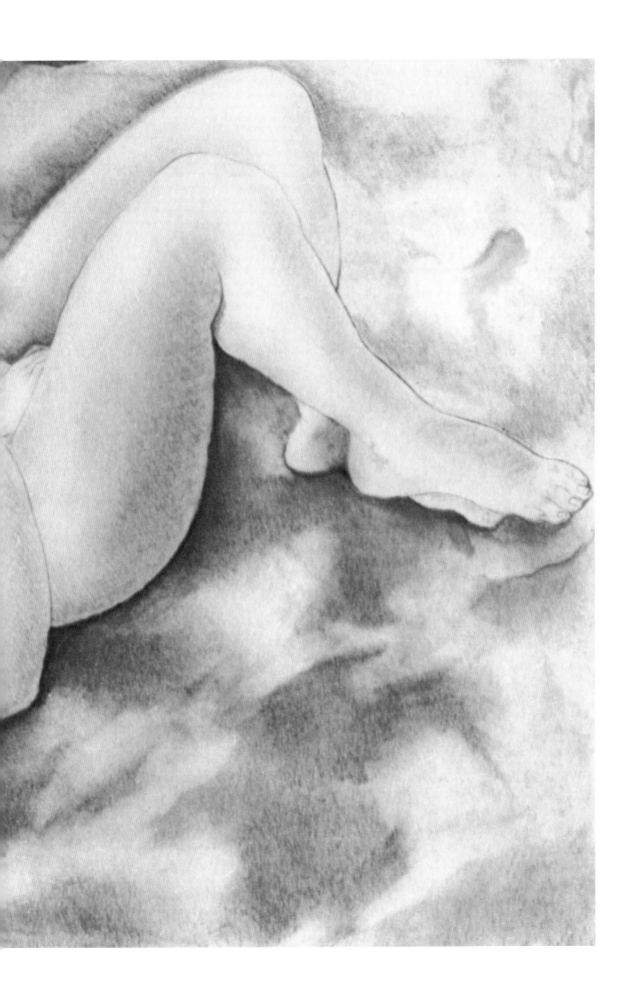

In her book *The Sexual Fantasies of Women* (1973), Nancy Friday notes that many of the longer fantasies are in fact made up of lots of little fantasies, which all contribute to the build-up of excitement. At the same time she rejects the notion that the fantasies themselves represent a sublimated form of frustration. Some women who are perfectly happy and sexually-fulfilled nonetheless enjoy fantasies. And the fantasies may even afford them more satisfaction than do their sexual partners ... It is not only a lack of sex that may inspire such fantasies, but the sex itself. For certain women there is even a sort of chain reaction between real-life sex and the fantasies they create for themselves. One fosters the other. It would seem that the imagination can attribute a sort of "extra interest" to even the most banal objects of everyday life. It is not only dildos that are used as phallic substitutes for masturbation, according to Nancy Friday, but cucumbers, vacuum-cleaner tubes, electric toothbrushes, the silver-plated handles of hairbrushes, or no more or less than running water. Total unfamiliarity with a sexual partner would seem to constitute a stimulus of comparable potency.

The significance of fantasies of violence in evoking excitement is demonstrated in a study by Isabelle Azoulay called *Abîmes Fantastiques*: *La violence dans l'imaginaire sexuel féminin* ("*The Abysses of Fantasy: Violence in the Sexual Imaginations of Women*"). Desire can be associated with pain, and so increase the intensity of the sexual act. But remember – violence in fantasy need have nothing to do with violence in real life. Specific scenes tend to be integrated into such fantasies. Every depiction of a sexual act tells a story, and every sexual act has its own dynamic. Every woman sees the sexual act in an entirely personal context that also naturally involves her own problems and aspirations. Mind you, men do that too. The central focus for this introspection is the orgasm. All the fantasies that have led up to it pale beside this "paradisiacal" instant. The entire fantasy-construction built up so carefully with different tools and techniques, gradually putting together a unique assemblage of factors for excitement and tension, abruptly unravels at the moment of the "petit mal seizure."

To some, sex may seem a means to combine intimacy with an easy-going familiarity in relation to the sexual partner. Skin-on-skin contact is an experience that has calming propensities, reducing fears about coming together more closely still. For most people, it is above all the orgasm that is the premier experience – and an almost hallucinatory one at that. Together with the momentary sensation of un-being, of losing one's personality and one's identity, it may even feel like a religious or mystical experience.

The inability of language to keep pace with understanding, however, prompts us to turn again to reference sources in literature. There is a delightful passage in the works of the ancient Greek poetess Sappho (c.612–550 BC).

> I love a pretty girl.
> She knows nothing of it yet,
> and I strongly want to tell her;
> but when I see her
> and I want to go and talk to her,
> looking at her face
> I feel a tautening of my senses

111. Anonymous. Etching.

that I have no control over.

A blazing fire lights under my skin.

My eyes no longer see anything.

There is a buzzing in my ears.

From my heart to my arms and legs

pounds a frantic throbbing.

My breathing is rapid and rough,

and I collapse to the ground,

for in my infatuation

I am close to swooning away.

The momentary experience of un-being, even of the non-existence of the world, is to be found also in *La Légende de Tristan et Iseult* ("*The Legend of Tristan and Isolde*").

O bring sleep,

night of love:

make me forget

that I live.

Take me

in your arms,

and remove me

from the world!

The sexual fantasies of quite ordinary women, as collected and published by Seymour Fisher in his book *The Female Orgasm* (1973), demonstrate the same elements. The question he put to the women in his survey was: "Could you describe to us precisely how you reach orgasm, including bodily sensations and the thoughts that come into your head, your feelings, your overall sense of well-being, and any problems or distractions you experience at the time?" In this way he managed to establish impressively objective descriptions of subjective states of excitement.

"I was soaring above a field with flowers. I felt quite light, as if I need never again come down to earth. In a way I felt like a goddess. It was as if there was only one single body – as if the whole world was just that one body."

"I imagined myself as the most notorious whore in the whole of history."

"I have no conscious knowledge of my body movements or even of orgasm. I feel as if I am directed solely by desire. The only description I can give as to how I feel during these moments, during orgasm, is of a blurred darkness in which red or white points of light sparkle. ... Orgasm gives me a feeling of vertigo. I lose all sensation. It's almost as if I no longer existed in bodily form, but only as an emotion."

"Lightness and being able to fly, the impression of immortality, of great size, of the disappearance of the conscious self, of the loss of both self and the world, the feeling of merging and becoming one with the world – this is almost as much as to suggest that "the end is no more or less than the beginning."

112. Franz von Stuck, *Salome*, 1906.
    Oil on canvas.
    Municipal Gallery of
    Lenbachhaus, Munich.

113. Amedeo Modigliani, *Nude*.
Oil on canvas, 92.4 x 59.8 cm.
Samuel Courtauld Trust,
Courtauld Institute of Art Gallery.

Such impressions seem to put us right back into the intra-uterine state before our birth – a state that first gave us such impressions as an inheritance we might make use of for the rest of our lives. It was surely to get away from such narcissistic sentiments that religions were developed. Life after birth requires everybody to do what they can to resist tension. The sexual impulse tends thus to re-establish a situation from an earlier existence in which a guaranteed absence of tension reigned. From the beginning of time, humankind has looked to the sexual act to find "an ephemeral instant of happiness."

Ferenczi, the *enfant terrible* of psychoanalysis, suggests a parallel between our human origins in amniotic fluid within the womb and the beginning of all life on earth in the sea. Organic biological development thus mirrors the cataclysmic events of evolution, and gives us reason to believe that our sexual maturity, at puberty, represents an endeavour to re-establish not only intra-uterine life but palaeontological marine life. According to Ferenczi, the goal of the sexual act is nothing other than an attempt that is at first tentative and awkward, then more and more assured, and finally partly successful in reintegrating the self with the maternal body – the maternal body inside which, yet to come out into the world, there did not yet exist this painful division between the self and the world. In this "thalassic" retrogression we express a nostalgia for the marine world we left in the dark aeons of prehistory. The goal of the sexual act thus becomes the elimination of the difference, the reconstruction of an environment in which there are very few stimuli or inconveniences.

Ferenczi refers, then, to a force of narcissistic desires that is not entirely accounted for by the psychoanalytical doctrine of "sexual pulses." Sexuality during the genital stage is influenced by a double desire: for the satisfying of the sexual pulses and for narcissistic union. So sexual ecstasy is at the same time the entrance to and the exit from a divine world. At the point that is the culmination of the sexual climax, all fixations projected onto the external world are abandoned. They sink back into the "night of love" that is perceptible only with eyes closed. That certain statues portray the saints with their eyes turned instead towards the sky might then suggest an expression of eroticism that has been repressed. Let us venture to interpret the instinctual cry of joy uttered by women at orgasm as a "threshold phenomenon." To the cry of the new-born at leaving the comfort of its maternal place of peaceful security responds the cry of the mature, adult woman at the instant – and for the instant – she regains the paradisal world from whence she came.

In refuting the hypothesis that women's sexual fantasies represent a sublimated form of frustration, Nancy Friday also rejects the notion that every human being is subject to the opposition between satisfaction and denial that constitutes the formational process of individuation. It is in this problematical context that "nostalgia for paradise lost" makes its appearance. Without equivalent "retrogressions serving the interests of my secret self," life for a human would be unbearable. No joy without denial or delay. "Nature has no true understanding of joy; it stops short at doing simply what has to be done," write Adorno and Horkheimer. "Joy is a social phenomenon, as indeed are all feelings and emotions, whether sublimated or not. Essentially, joy derives from alienation."

After an orgasm I feel much less tense, much more at peace, more relaxed," declared one of Seymour Fisher's respondents. "I almost always fall asleep." Another admitted, "When we've

114. Egon Schiele, *Sapphic Couple,*
1911. Gouache, watercolour and
pencil, 48.3 x 30.5 cm.
Private collection.

115. Egon Schiele,
Scene in a Dream, 1911.
Watercolour and pencil.
Museum of Modern Art,
New York.

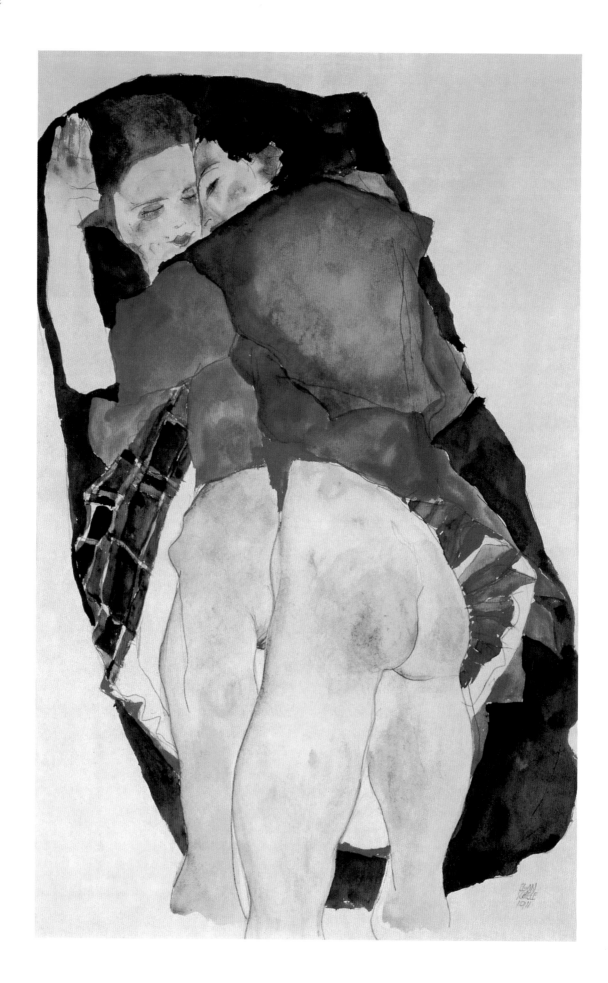

finished, I stretch out in his arms. I am so much less tense, in such a good mood, and so full of love for my man – but not in a passionate way, not with desire or lust." We may again discern in these words the echo of an older mode of fulfilment. The first joy of the infant is the nipple of its mother when being nursed at the breast. As Freud noted, sexual activity is primarily based on a function that ensures survival. Only much later has it freed itself and become independent. To see a babe at the maternal breast give up sucking, sated, and fall back, with red cheeks and a placidly content smile, and begin snoozing, is surely to remark how comparable such a scene is with the sexual satisfaction experienced by an adult. The loving kiss represents a vestigial form of the archaic reflex that causes a baby to suck at its mother's nipple. In this way even the action of sucking familiarises an infant with joy, with ecstasy.

Up to now, we have been little concerned with sexual reactivity – the capacity to reach orgasm. It is, therefore, appropriate here to inquire why women's sexual excitement has been "stretched", extended over time. After all, for most men, reaching orgasm is a progressive development of tensions and stimulations. The climax is a unique experience represented by a momentary loss of the conscious will, a momentary lack of the awareness of *self*. Seymour Fisher in his book *The Female Orgasm* has utterly discounted all the standard contemporary explanations of an incapacity to reach orgasm. Religion, education, even traumatic experiences during puberty and adolescence – none of these factors has any genuine effect on *the ability to successfully achieve* orgasm. Yet the ability to reach orgasm is nonetheless considerably reduced in women who have personal histories of being left, being rejected, or being separated from a loved one. We note that all those women who found difficulty in achieving orgasm spoke to us frequently of deprivations they had suffered during their childhood. Conversely, those women who had no problem at all in reaching orgasm often referred specifically to the consistent presence of their fathers during their childhood. It would seem that for a woman the capacity to reach orgasm is seriously influenced by how secure she feels in the constancy of her environment. The retaining around her of people and objects she loves is an additional factor in favour of orgasm. If these background elements are not there for a woman having sex, and if she is already fearful of failure or loss, the overall experience may become so upsetting that sexual excitement thereafter may become altogether impossible. Anxiety over the failure or loss may increase to the point of mental disturbance.

We ought also to look at the possible consequences, for certain adults, of a parent-child relationship that is not constant – and at the gap in a child's emotional development that may result. A lack of balance resulting from inconstancy is surely what the Greek *ecstasis*, our word *ecstasy*, is all about – not by any means the prerogative only of neurotics and saints. Sexual intimacy means taking a risk. It is an adventure that presupposes a personality strong enough for it. Only a person who has conquered the fear of possibly losing his or her identity can dare to let go entirely and drift freely. But sexual intimacy can also reinforce identity. As E. H. Erikson wrote, "The fact that two human beings united in sexual congress undergo at the same moment of orgasm a mutual experience of a uniform kind can additionally soften or reduce antagonisms and the potential for anger inherent in the ever-continuous opposition of male-and-female, real-and-imagined, love-and-hate." Intimacy thus reduces destructive potential, even if it threatens the unity of the individual or the cohesion of a society. The lover thus uses intimacy as a means of overcoming isolation and alienation.

116. Armand Petitjean, 1946-1947.
Pastel drawings.

Ultimately, then, every instance of participation in the sexual act is equivalent to a rebellion against pain or separation or, at the extreme, against death. This may explain the facial expression of pain at the moment of climax. On the face of an aroused woman we perceive not desire, joy or happiness, but effort, labour, and pain.

So what we once saw as *beauty* we might now see as an invitation to a game that swallows and destroys everything. In that instant of emotional paroxysm that is the orgasm, everything is both beautiful and ugly at the same time! For a microsecond, actual reality triumphs over learned conceptions of reality - "nature" triumphs over "nurture."

However, as we know from paintings and sculptures in Europe, even the facial expression of passion has an aspect to it of the cultural, of the way people in the area have been brought up to behave. Of course, the people of the area firmly believe that their expression is the "natural" expression of passion, just as *we* believe *our* expression of passion is the natural one. This is quite different from oriental art, in which - in both religious art and erotic art (and especially in the Japanese *shunga*, or "Images of Springtime") - faces tend to remain as expressionless as masks. Their unique method of depicting internal agitation is for a person to be biting a handkerchief, or for his or her toes to be tightly clenched together. The Tibetan and Nepalese peoples are excellent at portraying the sexual act in art. The eyes are opened very wide, suggesting the opening wide of the consciousness. Far from sex being an instinctual animal practice, it thus becomes the mark of a much more highly developed culture.

But let's go back to Bataille. For him, the beauty of a woman may be likened to a display of the animal elements of a sexual act. "There is nothing more depressing to a man than the ugliness of a woman who no longer allows the ugliness either of her genital area or of the whole act to be seen. The primary function of beauty is to be there to be dirtied, while ugliness prevents what is the actual core substance of eroticism from the possibility of being dirtied. ... The more dazzling the beauty, the greater the opportunity for dirtying." Modern sex therapy endeavours to enable certain women to come to terms with bodies they think of as ugly and "dirty." It teaches also that nothing should obstruct the image of the sexual exchange. But all that is no more than a therapeutic exorcism service designed to facilitate the continued denial of the fundamental antagonism inherent in the tension between the sexes. Have sex, and be fit for life! It might then possibly prove that those who regard sexuality as something distinctly "dirty" do in fact understand sexuality rather more accurately. But what these women are simply incapable of accepting, deep down, is precisely that paradoxical experience to which they surrender themselves.

Central to Bataille's understanding of eroticism is the notion of "transgression." According to him, the very neutrality of a reasoned and reasonable sexuality such as is practised today is suspect because there are no longer any limits to burst free from. There is - as much for women as for men - an "economic" position in relation to sex, when the sexual act becomes a routine thing, an event that may certainly produce pleasure but that is merely one activity among many others. As "recreation" pure and simple, it takes second place to work. Once the act has become so clinical, there can be no transgressions, no ugliness or dirtiness - just as there can be no face beautiful enough to provoke a paroxysm of emotion.

117. Peter Fendi, *Sequence of Erotic Scenes*, 1835.

174.

The Kiss

Oral Pleasures

Oh, tell me: whoever invented the kiss? His lips were aglow with rapture like this!
He kissed and never once troubled his head. The beauty of May was burning red ...!
Heinrich Heine[39]

What moves two civilised human beings to press the upper ends of their digestive tracts together like flatfish while making a smacking sound of the lips and to avow afterwards how heartfelt and romantic this damp contact was? The phenomenon of kissing is so widespread in our culture that it is regarded as quite natural and not worthy of any detailed consideration. The kiss is something fleeting, lightweight – and yet at the same time something profoundly irrational.

Our lips form a sensitive border between the skin and the mucous membrane. Apart from contact with the genitals and the breasts there is no stimulus that arouses sexual desire more than the kiss on the mouth. For that reason it belongs to the preliminaries of coitus. During coitus the kiss, therefore, undergoes a transformation. What begins as tentative, apparently chaste contact, turns with increasing passion into an ardent marriage of the lips. If the tips of the tongues are still touching at this point, there ensues an embrace of internal organs; an event which is analogous to the act of copulation. Thinking about kissing? We associate kissing so closely with the term, "romantic" that one might be forgiven for not thinking about this phenomenon any further.

Philosophers of evolution have considered the origin of this behaviour which is apparently so difficult to explain. According to Bölsche[40] the loving act of sucking in the kiss is an atavism, a reminiscence of the early animal form that man took when, in the absence of a sexual organ, the mating couple held on to each other by means of the kiss. The art of kissing, like that of love, then developed gradually with the higher stages of culture keeping pace with it. That so-called savage peoples know nothing of the kiss is thought to demonstrate that fact. Müller-Lyer thinks "that the custom of kissing is quite unknown in the first epoch of the primitive feeling of love". Darwin[41] is of the view that the kiss is nothing more than the enjoyment of the pleasure of the closest possible contact with the beloved; this would be supported by the fact that the kiss is substituted in various parts of the world by the rubbing together of noses. According to Havelock-Ellis, kissing by bringing the lips into contact certainly has a very old, primitive origin. He argues that the lovers' kiss has developed from the primitive mother's kiss and from the sucking of the child at the mother's breast.

So which came "first"? Another view would have it that the kiss was originally a form of sexual contact, which having been refined and sublimated then became a symbol of friendship and respect. According to this view the kiss developed out of the "love bite", which in turn probably sprang from the effort to guarantee the complete performance of the act of copulation by means of fixing together both bodies in a way that was as intimate and firm as possible. Is it our animal inheritance, since many

118. Auguste Rodin,
The Kiss, 1888-1889.
Marble, 138.6 x 110.5 x 118.3 cm.
Musée Rodin, Paris.

119. Berthomme de Saint-André, 1930.

120. Berthomme de Saint-André, 1930.

animals bite each other when they mate? Other authors have derived a connection with the instinct for food from these violent concomitants. Or was the sniffing of animals the precursor of the kiss, something hinted at by the "Eskimo kiss"?

For Eibl-Eibesfeldt[71] it is certain that many forms of behaviour such as kissing and caressing, which are typically regarded as sexual, have their origin in actions that actually concerned the care of the brood, and are probably forms of behaviour that were innate. Kissing with the lips and the tongue is, in his view, "probably derived from feeding behaviour". His basis for saying this is the habit of feeding by mouth, which is not common only to anthropoids, but also occurs in various human cultural contexts.

The British ethnologist Desmond Morris[72] also regards kissing precisely as a gesture which is a relic, something which developed from feeding habits among societies of early man and which comes from a time when small children were being weaned from breast-feeding by mothers who chewed food into a pulp before passing it on to their children by mouth. It is Morris's view that lovers today do something when they engage in a French kiss that feeding by mouth did with another purpose in the dim and distant past. However, none of these theories concerning the origin of the kiss explain why the kiss is so sexually arousing.

If we look back at the phylogenetic development of mankind we are likely to overlook the fact that each individual carries within him his own "dim and distant past". Kissing, so to speak, has been laid alongside us in the cradle. The amorous kiss between adults is always a symbol of sexual union. Goethe[73] has portrayed this union in the kiss very graphically: "Greedily she sucks the flames of his mouth. The one only exists in the other."

It is pleasant to describe this union as one of the souls, a description that the materialist observer would want to repudiate as "taking away the sensuality of the kiss". And yet this mode of expression is justified if something floating and delightful is felt in this condition because of experience which is far removed from the genital stage. Being at one with the other finds its early model in that dim and distant time that was actually more of a rosy one, that of the child being at one with its mother. The fusion with her is enjoyed as "bathing in an oceanic feeling". That attempts are made to achieve this goal during sexual maturation by way of other contacts as well, even coitus, has the effect that "all the bells ring", even if only one of the erogenous zones is touched. And the mouth is such a zone.

One might classify kisses according to their sensual content. The most Platonic and the "purest" would be the one that symbolises nothing. Georg Simmel[74] differentiates as follows: "There are two cases where the kiss is symbolic: in friendship and in pure sensuality. The first symbolises the spiritual and sociable relationship, the latter the conclusive sexual state. However, the kiss of love does not symbolise anything, it is the thing itself — like music, its entire meaning is immediate". But "pure love" would be the one prevailing before the Fall of Man. The mouth is sinful from the beginning for it is an organ which purely contributes ecstasy. In the beginning was the mouth. "From the beginning the first organ to appear as an erogenous zone and to make a libidinous demand on the soul was the mouth," according to Sigmund Freud.

The desire for a pleasurable sucking activity shapes the small human creature. (The word 'kiss' is based on the Sanskrit word *cusati*: *cusati* means 'to suck' - as the infant does at his mother's breast.) Sucking is the first expression of sexuality, and the mother's breast is the original object of the feelings

121. Berthomme de Saint-André, 1930.

Au bois

of love. Even when during the course of sexual development and maturation other areas of pleasure are developed, the pleasure of the first oral experience always accompanies it. The oral factor will accompany the entire development of the maturation of the instincts up until genitality. The diffuse sensuality of the first, almost incestuous embrace still remains in the adult embrace of sexual intercourse. But the desire of the adult overlays the childlike desire; the adult wants motherly tenderness and genitality. It is for this reason that Roland Barthes[75] is able to define the lover as a "child, who becomes erect: that was precisely the young Eros."

In the early oral phase the striving after pleasure is centred in the mucous membrane of the mouth and the skin on the surface of the body. During breast-feeding, mouth and skin bring the child into pleasurable contact with the mother, with whom it still forms a unity of experience at the outset. This relationship can possess a strongly erotic character. Wilhelm Stekel writes as follows in his book *Psychosexual Infantilism* (*Psychosexueller Infantilismus*): "The intake of food is a pleasure-orientated act, which Havelock-Ellis rightly compares with an instance of coitus. The nipple replaces the penis (like the penis it also possesses erectile tissue), the mouth is a vulva, the milk is like semen ... Sucking and drinking happens accompanied by a constant orgasm."

Few doctors are aware that mothers also repeatedly achieve orgasm during breast-feeding. But such self-revelation is not to be recommended to such mothers in a cultural climate in which pleasure is immediately associated with "child abuse". Even Freud emphasised the sexual relationship of the infant to the mother's breast: "Whoever sees a child sink back in satisfaction from the breast, sinking into sleep with reddened cheeks and a blissful smile, would have to say to himself that this image also remains indicative of the expression of sexual satisfaction in later life." Once the original unity of mother and child has been broken, the child constantly strives to seize the maternal object and to possess it. In this "cannibalistic" stage the infant sinks its teeth firmly into the mother's breast in order to keep it or even to annex it. Does this tendency not find expression later in the phrase "I would like to eat you"?

It is widely known that the tendency to "eat" the breast, to "annex" oneself become stronger the more lasting the refusals to which an infant is exposed are. Are such early experiences of denial renewed later in the "love bite"? Lust, in whatever form, is a characteristic that is shaped by the fate of the original erogenous zone of the mouth. There is an" insatiability" about the genitals in the course of love, which it would be equally appropriate to trace back to early oral refusals. Thus certain forms of nymphomania have their roots in the withdrawal of the oral stimulus in early childhood. In this respect, orality can be a phase which determines one's entire behaviour towards the world, an attempt is made through all of one's sensory organs to absorb the world into oneself.

The belief that the vagina experiences hunger and must be satisfied points to an analogy between vagina and mouth. The physical similarity is obvious. The vagina is also a "boundary organ" which passes from the outer skin to the inner mucous membrane. Like the mouth it is also moist, but it can also become unpleasantly dry. Oral sexuality can in this way not only be a re-experiencing of the childlike experience of sucking but it can also be an analogy for genital sexuality. The woman feels herself to be "loved in her mouth" while practising fellatio. And if one experiences the vagina as a mouth, so even the act of kissing it becomes "natural". Someone who is being stimulated passively by fellatio or cunnilingus also experiences these practices as engendering so much pleasure that they are the equal of the experience of coitus. "A woman who is an artist with her mouth," lauds Paul Ableman,

122. Jean Morisot, 1925.

181.

"can elicit in a man a large number of the most refined responses that can never be attained in coitus." The mouth is a highly agile organ, which is equipped with an excellent instrument for tactile stimulation; it is located in a part of the body that is likewise very mobile, the head. But passive fellatio excludes the possibility of complete physical intimacy between two bodies; it does not allow one to hold the beloved in one's arms. It is only the mutual kissing of the genitals in *soixante-neuf* that again allows a greater proximity.

While fellatio today appears to be one of society's party games, it was primarily widespread in the past among older men, whose potency was understood to be in decline. Even among the Romans it was regarded as the final "means of help for the old and impotent". Martial[47] wrote in an epigram:

"Why, Thais, do you call me old man now and then?
To be an old man, Thais, is not to violate anyone's mouth."

The scornful view that cunnilingus was only practised by impotent and old men as a substitute for the spent power of the penis was also widespread. Here is Martial again on the subject:

"Linus, who is known to not a few girls as a lover,
Were his virility to go, tongue, now be careful."

123. Paul-Emile Becat, 1932.

In the case of passive cunnilingus the pleasure factor is even more decisive, as sexual excitement in the woman is concentrated in the clitoris. In coitus by contrast the shaft of the penis scarcely comes into direct contact with it.

Every sexual act is determined by a number of factors. So it should not be overlooked that in passive fellatio and passive cunnilingus the desire for the subjugation of the other can be of importance. The active participant can in turn derive a masochistic pleasure from this constellation. The case of a nurse who was forced to satisfy a ward doctor is worthy of note in this respect. He used to "squeeze his penis into her mouth", and she "did not possess the strength to defend herself against this". However, the man in this situation can also be in the subordinate position: in the eventuality that the woman takes possession of "him" so actively and attempts to make him into her object. What is always decisive is the fantasy that accompanies a scene. And Stekel describes the case of a man with marked masochistic tendencies: "Anastasia treated me as I wanted to be treated. She used to receive me with every possible reproach, made scenes in fits of jealousy and boxed my ears. I had to undress her and then to lay down beneath the bed so that only my head was visible, and then she placed her bare foot on my mouth and ordered me to lick her toes... Then I had to lick her vagina, something that she liked very much; she squatted over me for this and brought her genitals close to my face..."

The wish to taste the object of one's affection and the smell of their genitals are also important in cunnilingus and fellatio. At the end of the nineteenth century it was still not unusual for bourgeois

124. Paul Avril, circa 1910.

125. Lobel-Riche, 1936.

126. Achille Devéria, circa 1830.
    Romantic lithograph, (detail).

sexologists to express themselves contemptuously concerning cunnilingus. Most of them regarded this act as revolting and unnatural. In 1891 Albert Moll became heated over the "men of so-called high society" because they performed cunnilingus upon women "extremely frequently" and regarded it as natural that one could do this without being punished! A crime against masculinity? It is not irrelevant that cunnilingus is practised by women who feel themselves united by lesbian love.

Smell, taste, and touch: all of these components find their place in the genital kiss. These impressions crowd in during the description of a scene by Oscar Wilde[48] from his novel *Teleny*: "I quietly drew near the bed on the tip of my toes, just like a cat about to spring on a mouse, and then slowly crawled between her legs. My heart was beating fast, I was eager to gaze upon the sight I so longed to see. As I approached on all fours, head foremost, a strong smell of white heliotrope mounted up to my head, intoxicating me. Trembling with excitement, opening my eyes wide and straining my sight, my glances dived between her thighs. At first nothing could be seen but a mass of crisp auburn hair, all curling in tiny ringlets, and growing there as if to hide the entrance of that well of pleasure. First I lightly lifted up her chemise, then I gently brushed the hair aside, and parted the two lovely lips ....

"This done, I fed my greedy eyes upon that dainty pink flesh that looked like the ripe and luscious pulp of some savoury fruit appetising to behold, and within those cherry lips there nestled a tiny bud – a living flower of flesh and blood. I had evidently tickled it with the tip of my finger, for, as I looked upon it, it shivered as if endowed with a life of its own .... At its beck I longed to taste it, to fondle it, and therefore, unable to resist, I bent down and pressed my tongue upon it, over it, within it, seeking every nook and corner around it, darting into every chink and cranny ...."

When Shere Hite[49] established in her survey from the 1970s that many women declined cunnilingus since they were afraid that their vulvas could be repugnant because of their smell or appearance, it was understood as a consequence of an inner moral proscription. The passing of judgment on hygienic and aesthetic grounds is often derived from attitudes of sexual morality, which are, however, not recognised as such. Under Puritanism, people spoke more freely and easily of "cleanliness" rather than of sexual fears.

If a kiss on the buttocks is the most improper of all kisses, then the strongest taboo is against kissing the anus. We have known since Freud's studies that the anal region already belongs to one of the most highly treasured erotic zones of the child in the pre-genital phase. Through his empirical studies Kinsey[50] came to the conclusion that more than half of all human beings are susceptible to being aroused erotically by means of a stimulus to the anus. Evidently the greatest stimulus to the mucous membrane of the anus derives from licking. Stekel even maintains that analingus was once highly regarded as the highest form of demonstrating love, something suggested by certain idiomatic expressions of which "Kiss my arse!" is but a pale shadow. Evidently analingus is the most absolute of all kisses of submission. However, submission is always a form of homage at the same time. So followers of the devil show their respect for him by means of kissing the anus. And at the witches' sabbath — in Goethe's *Faust* as well — the devil's anus is kissed on the Blocksberg, which he acknowledges with a mighty breaking of wind. All of the devil's celebrations end in a wild orgy. During the persecution of heretics and witches, analingus became the quintessence of devil worship.

There have also been examples of analingus in our day as a form of sexual self-abasement. Masters[51] maintains that conversations with former soldiers in the Allied army of occupation in Germany revealed that immediately after the end of the Second World War many wives of the defeated licked the anuses of the victors on their own initiative.

127. Javier Gil, 1999.

In his novel, *Teleny*, Wilde also describes a scene involving analingus:

> "At last, the consumptive girl, clasping with her hands the backside of the other one, and thus opening the huge pulpy buttocks, called out, — 'Une feuille de rose.' Of course I greatly wondered what she meant, and I asked myself where she could find a rose-leaf, for there was not a flower to be seen in the house, and then I said to myself — having got one what will she do with it? I was not left to wonder long, for the cantinière did to her friend what she had done to her. Thereupon two other whores came and knelt down before the backsides that were thus held open for them, put their tongues in the little black holes of the anuses, and began to lick them, to the pleasure of the active and passive prostitutes, and to that of all the lookers-on."

At another point in the novel anal penetration is supposed to be made possible by means of analingus: "... bending down his head, he began first to kiss, and then to dart his pointed tongue in the hole of my bum, thrilling me with an ineffable pleasure. Then rising when he had deftly prepared the hole by lubricating it well all round, he tried to press the tip of his phallus into it ...." The fact that these variations on the kiss are regarded as being particularly disgusting suggests that something has occurred during the course of the anal phase, which has induced neuroses.

Disgust is not only engendered by the norms of society, it is also the result of the instinctual development of the individual. We are repelled by the idea of drinking from the same glass as a

128. Aroldo Bonzagni, circa 1910.

stranger. Two lovers by contrast suck on one and the same sweet. Paul Ableman recalls a vulgar expression which circulated among male high school students in the United States in the middle of the nineteenth century and that indicated that a girl was so sweet that her admirer could clean his teeth with her faeces. In the transport of love the polymorphously perverse child that we all once were often reawakens. Our innate tendency to coprophilia finds expression in the mouth kissing its exact opposites — the beginning and end of the digestive tract. Pure love embraces the entire body of the other, in all of its functions: "I don't want a woman as couldna shit nor piss", as a character puts it in *Lady Chatterley's Lover* by D. H. Lawrence[52].

Nancy Friday[82] investigated the sexual fantasies of men and women. She discovered that women feel the tendency to analingus less whereas men, by contrast, positively love to touch the anus with the mouth and to insert their tongues into it.

Is the act of kissing the genitals and the anus to be regarded as "perverse"? From the standpoint of the morality of reproduction, it certainly is. But then to be consistent the normal kiss between lovers must be described as perverse, something which Freud also indicated: "Even the kiss is entitled to be called a perverse act because it consists of the union of two oral erogenous zones in place of both sets of genitals. Yet no one dismisses it as perverse; on the contrary, it is allowed in theatrical performances as a mild hint at the sexual act. However, kissing can easily become a fully-fledged perversion, namely if it is so intensive that it is directly followed by genital discharge and orgasm, something which happens not so infrequently." Also of importance for Freud was whether final genital pleasure is thereby circumvented and avoided.

We come full circle with the anus, which excretes the waste products of the digestive system. In the beginning there was the tendency to take in the love object by means of the kiss, to "eat it out of love".

129. Aroldo Bonzagni, circa 1910.

"For this reason," warned Ivan Bloch, "the frenzy of wild kisses, of passionate love can lead to anthropophagy". Last year the news magazine *Der Spiegel* carried a report about a tribe of Brazilian Indians. Only forty years ago the Wari Indians were still placing their beloved dead on a grill, in order to consume them together. As side dishes the women served freshly baked maize bread...

Kissing and eating: both activities can be subsumed under the heading of "Oral Pleasures". How people kiss can perhaps already be inferred from their cooking and eating habits. What importance oral eroticism possesses for a culture is nowhere more clear than in its gastronomy. Octavio Paz[83] explored the connection between the love of food and eroticism and draws conclusions about sexual attitudes from eating habits. "Desire, in gastronomy as in eroticism, arouses the ingredients, the bodies and the sensations: it is the force that governs the connections, the mixtures and the transformations. A cuisine of reason, in which every ingredient is what it is, and in which not only variations but also contrasts are avoided, is a cuisine which has excluded desire". However, pleasure is a concept which is missing from American cuisine according to Paz: "Not pleasure but health, not the correspondences between the flavours but the gratification of a need: these are the two values". Gastronomy and eroticism share the notion of the importance of "fusing", the latter that of bodies and sensations, the former that of ingredients and tastes. But in the North American tradition the body is not a source of joy but one of health and work, materially and morally. Kissing — in the name of health! There is also evidence of this in a story that was widely reported in the German press in 1994:

Sexology: Kisses Better Than Valium

Hamburg, 17 August (dpa) Are you not feeling well? Why not kiss your partner! Kissing and stroking strengthen the immune system so that much medication can be made superfluous by doing so. The sexologist Professor E. B. reports this in the latest edition of the magazine *Für Sie*. He writes that the body produces so many positive hormones during a gentle caress or a tender kiss, that human beings can become really "high" from them .... Above all, exciting and passionate kisses worked wonders. When the hormones thunder through the body, the skin tightens, the complexion becomes rosy, the oxygen supply optimal — the wrinkle cream unnecessary. The cell metabolism, which is running at full speed, washes the pollutants out of the tissue more quickly. And the weight you put on by eating a bar of chocolate is shed in greater relaxation: an "intimate love game" uses up to 400 calories.

Poor misused Eros!

But there were also movements that sought to fight strictly against kissing even in the name of health. "Cities large and small, North and South start the fight against the 'danger of kissing'", is how an observer describes the "Anti-Kissing-Movement" which started in Russia at the time of the Soviet government. In the year 1924 the people's commissariat for hygiene issued a general ban on kissing for the whole of the Soviet Union, a ban which was directed above all against the old peasant custom of greeting each other at every meeting by kissing, and it was also intended to bring to an end the unhygienic Easter kiss. "On the streets of Charkov there are now posters bearing a call to the people to refrain from this 'dangerous and harmful habit', as far as is possible. The Kazan city council informs

130. Achille Devéria, circa 1830.
Romantic lithography.

Le Rapide de Nice.

131. Anonymous, 1900.

the inhabitants of the Tatarstan Republic that the habit of kissing, which is so widespread within the borders of the most revolutionary state on the earth, contributes to a great extent to the propagation of bacteria and to the swift transmission of contagious diseases. In Moscow, one of the leaders of the Soviet movement explains at a meeting that while the Soviet Union certainly has to deal with other important tasks, hygiene was certainly making progress. The meeting passed the resolution: "Away with the kiss!" In Kiev the young were referred to "Anti-Kiss-Propaganda". In Odessa the postal administration provides an envelope with the message: 'Every kiss contributes to the passing on of 4,000 bacteria! Long live hygiene!'"

And this in a country of which Alexandre Dumas père[84] once wrote: "I have not seen so many people kiss each other in any other country as they do in Russia. One would think that the Russians wanted to make their ice-fields melt with the warmth of their feelings!"

Despite all of the differences between communism and capitalism there was agreement on one thing – in fighting the danger of the kiss. At the same time an invention was actually propagated in American newspapers, which guaranteed the "pure, bacillus-free kiss": a device that resembled a small racket or sieve. Readers of the magazine *Popular Science Monthly* learned of the unhygienic nature of the kiss and the virtues of the invention, the use of which was quite simple and above all highly practical. The device, they were told, consisted of a fine, elastic net that was impregnated with an antiseptic fluid, which immediately killed all dangerous bacteria. The claim was made for the product that using it removed the danger of transmitting bacilli from kissing and it also represented a token of love that satisfied all of the demands of modern hygiene.

"Away with the kiss!" has emerged again as a watchword today in Europe and America under altered conditions. The more liberal sexual behaviour of the West has experienced a chill in the last fifteen years because of AIDS, a condition that provoked anxieties on a scale that was socially pathological. Even amorous kisses dried up with the warning that this illness was transmitted by means of the most intimate contact. All of the desires for spontaneous closeness and union, which were focused on the kiss, were withdrawn and had to pass before a health check.

The mindset of safer sex leads to a physical distance from sexual partners and requires a constant control of one's emotions during sexual encounters. The hunger for strong feelings remains unsatisfied. Aseptic, dry kisses are regarded as risk-free. Rather like mutual masturbation in front of a video recorder while watching an old Hollywood film together, in which people were still allowed to kiss passionately — and to smoke… For centuries churches and other moral authorities have fought what they called "unnatural deviations" of the sexual. Yet nothing is more unnatural than many safer sex recommendations in the age of AIDS. The more distanced from the other, the more risk-free is sexual behaviour, and so the advice goes. It is a sexuality without passion that receives approval; a pleasure without love, for the other has become a possible source of infection. The only sense of mutuality is illusory: that of the solitary orgasm.

These are bad times for frenzy, as Franz Grillparzer[85] still called it:

> "The hands receive kisses of respect, While friendships belong to the brow,
> Pleasure homes in upon the cheek, Blissful love upon the mouth; Yearning
> is paired with the eyelid, Desire with the hollow hand, Arm and neck with
> amour fou; And frenzy takes everywhere else!"

194.

Priapus

The Damned God

"The beginning was anxiety, anxiety and pleasure and a terrible curiosity about what would come. Night reigned and his senses listened, from far away, a din was approaching, a hubbub, a blend of noises: a rattling, a blaring and a muffled thundering, along with shrill shouts of jubilation and an articulated howl on a prolonged *u*-sound – all of this interspersed with, and capped by, the eerily sweet tones of a deeply cooing, brutally insistent flute, which bewitched the body in a shamelessly importunate manner. Yet he was aware of a phrase, obscure, but characterising all that followed: '*The foreign god!*' A smoky glow flickered up, and he recognised mountainous country like that around his summer house. And in the uneven light, from the wooded heights, between tree trunks and moss-covered boulders, there they came rolling and plunging down in a whirlwind: human beings, animals, a swarm, a raving horde – and flooded the mountain slope with bodies, flames, tumult and a reeling round-dance. Women, stumbling over the long skin garments that hung from their belts, shook tambourines above their heads, which were thrown back in a groan; they brandished torches, which emitted a spray of sparks, and naked daggers; they held hissing snakes, grasping them by the middle of their bodies, or held their breasts with both hands as they advanced screaming.

"Fur-girdled shaggy-haired men, with horns above their brows, bowed their necks and lifted their arms and thighs, sounded bronze cymbals and beat furiously on drums, while smooth-skinned boys goaded he-goats with foliage-encircled staffs, holding tight to their horns and letting themselves be dragged along by their leaps, shouting. And the god-possessed people howled out the call that consisted of soft consonants with a prolonged *u*-sound at the end, a call sweet and savage at the same time, like no other ever heard: it resounded in one place, bellowed into the air as if by stags, and was taken up in another, by many voices, in riotous triumph; with this call they incited one another to dance and fling about their limbs, and they never let it die away. But the deep luring flute tone penetrated and dominated it all.

"Was it not luring him, too, as he experienced this through his resistance, summoning him with shameless persistence to the festival and enormity of the utmost sacrifice? Great was his dread, great his fear, honest his endeavor to defend the world to the last against the stranger, the enemy of the sedate and dignified intellect. But the noise, the howling, multiplied by the echoing mountainside, grew, took control, escalated into overpowering madness. Odours befuddled his mind: the biting smell of the goats, the scent of the gasping bodies, a smell like that of stagnant waters and still another, familiar one – sores and rampant sickness. His heart rumbled to the drumbeats, his brain was in a whirl, anger seized him, delusion, numbing lust; and his soul desired to join in the dance of the god. The obscene wooden symbol, gigantic, was unveiled and held up: they howled their watchword with even less restraint.

132. *Multi-phallus Mercury*,
     Pompeii, 100 B.C.

133. *Faun*, Pompeii, 100 B.C.

134. *Tintinnabulum*,
     Herculaneum, 100 B.C.

"Foam on their lips, they raged, stimulated one another with lascivious gestures and groping hands, laughing and moaning; they poked the goads into one another's flesh and licked the blood from their limbs. But the dreamer was now with them, one of them, a slave of the foreign god. Yes, they were his own self as they flung themselves upon the animals, tearing and killing, swallowing scraps of flesh that were still smoking, while an unbridled coupling began on the trampled, mossy ground, as an offering to the god. And his soul tasted the lewdness and frenzy of extinction. The afflicted man awakened from this dream enervated, shaken and without strength; he was now completely under the power of the demon."

In the novella *Death in Venice*, Thomas Mann describes the last months in the life of Aschenbach, who is held captive by his passion for Tadzio, the fourteen year old son of a Polish family, in whom he had seen a perfect, God-like image of beauty. Dionysius appears to him in a dream as "the foreign god" represented by "the obscene symbol, enormous, out of wood": the phallus. Aschenbach succumbs, gripped by passion and blinded, and finds himself amidst unrestrained madness: "And his soul tasted the lewdness and frenzy of extinction." Thomas Mann recreated a world with this Dionysian dream that has long since disappeared and now only exists in the subconscious. Below the surface of consciousness a god continues to exist that once found expression in symbols and was worshipped in phallus celebrations: Priapus.

For modern Europeans and North Americans, this god no longer has a voice or an expression, although it continues to exist as a spiritual force. Deep spiritual conflicts are the result. When Dionysian creatures do appear, even if only on the stage, which is not dissimilar to the world of dreams, there is an immediate, centuries-old, excessively moral, defensive reaction. The Spanish director Calixto Bieito, for example, staged Massenet's *Manon* for the Frankfurt Opera in June 2003. He turns a society that has been seduced by vices into a "literally vomiting, copulating, masturbating, constantly hysterically dancing recreational society" (*Frankfurter Allgemeine Zeitung*, 6.23.03), much to the outrage of the reviewer. "The director is incapable of giving satisfaction," read the title in the features section of this venerable newspaper. And the tabloid press wallows in voyeurism while pretending outrage: "fucking, vomiting, jerking off, fixing" (*BILD*, 6.23.03). They all fail to realise that the figure of Guillot is a humorously exaggerated embodiment of the satyr and that the entire scene resembles a bacchanalia of antiquity. Priapus – incapable of giving satisfaction! The phallus has been considered the image of the creation principle since earliest times. It stands for the *tre Supreme*, the Supreme Being that creates the universe. Worship of the phallus forms the source of all religions. Traces of phallus worship, its symbols and elements, can be found in all Mesopotamian cultures, the Middle East, Egypt and the Aegean, Greece, Italy and the entire pre-Celtic world as far as Ireland. Everywhere where phallic worship spread was marked by large upright stones. We find them in India, Greece and Mesopotamia, Thrace, Egypt, Crete, Malta and Corsica as well as in Brittany and the British Isles. The Egyptian obelisk was a phallic symbol, and, according to Daniélou, the bell towers and minarets of succeeding religions originally had the same symbolism. But the only region where worship of the phallus or lingam with all of the accompanying rituals and mythic tales has been preserved, from earliest times to the present day, is India. "Thanks to the evidence from India," Daniélou concludes, "we can understand the basis of phallus worship, the philosophical views that explain it as well as the myths we will repeatedly encounter everywhere in various forms."

The lingam is considered the origin and source of life. It is the form through which absolute life can be sensed and from which the world was created. We find the following in a Hindu text: "We worship the sun as the giver of light, the sum of all eyes; in the same way we worship Shiva in the phallus, who is present in all procreation." An old Sanskrit text says: "Shiva says: I cannot be distinguished from the phallus. The phallus is identical with me. It brings my followers to me and that is why it must be worshipped. My beloved ones! Wherever an erect organ is to be found, that is where I am, even if there is no other representation of me." In the sacred shrine where it is worshipped, the lingam is represented surrounded by the Yoni, the female organ. The lingam is more than just a symbol of the male organ of reproduction. In creative communion with Yoni ("lap of motherhood"), both create life. The lingam in the Yoni symbolises the original act of reproduction and creation, the dissolution of the polarity of the sexes, the return of the divided to the original state of shared absoluteness.

Without wanting to create a parallel between the historical change of meaning of the phallus with human psychosexual development as described by psychoanalysis, it can be said that in the Shiva cult the phallus functions as a symbol that is not tied to one sex. This would correspond to the meaning of the phallus in the early narcissistic phase of childhood development, about which Béla Grunberger writes: "The phallus is a bridge, it realises narcissist perfection and unites both partners in coitus. It represents the possibility of uniting as well as the realisation of narcissist integrity, of which it is symbol and image." Every satisfaction of an urge or ego enhancement of the child that contributes to strengthening a sense of self-worth assumes a phallic character in the child's unconscious, while in the opposite case the lack of confirmation is experienced as castration.

When the phallus symbol is later associated not only with fertility but also in a broader sense with success and power, this notion has its basis in this early narcissistic phase. Even if the cult of Shiva sees the phallus as the giver of semen and the lap of motherhood as nature and the origin of life, one cannot yet speak of a dominance of the phallus over the female. The two principles, the male and the female, still seem to be of equal value. With the expansion of cultic worship, however, the phallus was accorded greater weight and eventually comes to be seen as the symbol of male patriarchal power. Shivaism, according to Alain Daniélou, is the oldest religion; it was founded in the New Stone Age (10,000 - 8,000 B.C.) among the Dravidian peoples of India. They brought the religion to the Mediterranean as well, whence came the Greek cult of Dionysius.

135. Bronze statue, Athens, 470 B.C.

Everywhere in Greek art and culture one notices the great significance and worship of the male organ. Many archaeological findings prove that one can speak of a cult of the phallus. Above all, in the mythical-religious world of Aphrodite and Dionysius, the erect phallus became the symbol of sensuality and fertility. "This is certain," notes Jean Marcade in his study *Eros Kalos*, "sexual excitement is part of the Dionysian framework, as is the act of intercourse itself and that is why it is nothing shameful ... It remains that erotic arousal even in its animal form, whether among humans or animals themselves, is part of Dionysian arousal and is part of the healing drive of the mysterious forces of fertility and fertilisation. Among the Greeks it has nearly a sacred character."

The Greeks differentiated clearly between the "phallos" as a symbol and the anatomical organ, for which they had their own terms. "Phallos" was used only in a religious sense. In an anatomical sense, the male organ is named "peos," "penis," for example. Phallos processions and phallos consecrations took place in Greece beginning in archaic times, always in connections with Dionysian celebrations. In the sixth century, Heracles of Ephesus noted that it was shameful when phallus processions and songs did not take place in honour of Dionysius. In Attica, the popular Dionysius celebration consisted primarily of carrying around a huge phallos with a procession and a rite of sacrifice. On Delos, Karystios gave gifts of consecration to Dionysius in the form of freestanding phalli on square bases. They frame a 7.50 by 3.20 metre large building that French excavators called "Chapelle de Dionysius" (Chapel of Dionysius). The marble sculptures were created at the end of the fourth or the beginning of the third century B.C. The base construction is decorated with reliefs on three sides, on the front can be found a chicken with throat and head in the shape of a phallos, while on the sides one recognizes Dionysius accompanied by a maenad and a small satyr. The nature of the maenads is expressed in their Greek name: it can be translated as "the raging ones" or "the enraptured ones." In the proximity of the god, the maenads went into a frenzy. Their dance, stimulated by musical instruments in praise of Dionysius, is orgasmic.

In Aschenbach's dream, Dionysius is not only the god of ecstasy: he is also the god of extinction. Walter F. Otto characterises him as the "suffering god": "The ecstasy that he evokes corresponds to the innermost impulses of the living. Where these depths are reached, however, terror and destruction are revealed together with joys and births." What breaks down is Apollonian, reason-based human identity as well as a set sexual identity that is based on explicitness.

Aeschylus called Dionysius "the female-like one." Euripides said he was the "woman-like stranger." Occasionally he is described as "mannish-female." During rituals and celebrations he was honoured by women who went into a frenzy before the phallic symbols included in the processions. The men accompanying him were satyrs, centaurs and silenes, forest spirits similar to satyrs, all known for their lasciviousness. Dionysius represents a world that, as Otto expresses it "comes from the depths of the living." In his view, the chthonic male (phallus) and the chthonic female are linked and jointly give expression to the irrational and the orgasmic. Dionysius is not a human, but rather both animal and god. Thus he expresses the contrasts that lie within humans themselves: his "crazy" characteristics and those of his followers are part of psychic reality. This internal Dionysian reality found its expression in orgies.

Priapus was the result of a liaison between Dionysius and Aphrodite. He was an ugly child because he was equipped with an overlarge organ. It was said of him that he came from Lampsakos

136. *Priapus*, mural painting, Pompeii, 100 B.C.

137. *Phallus*, Delos, 300 B.C.

Priapus

201.

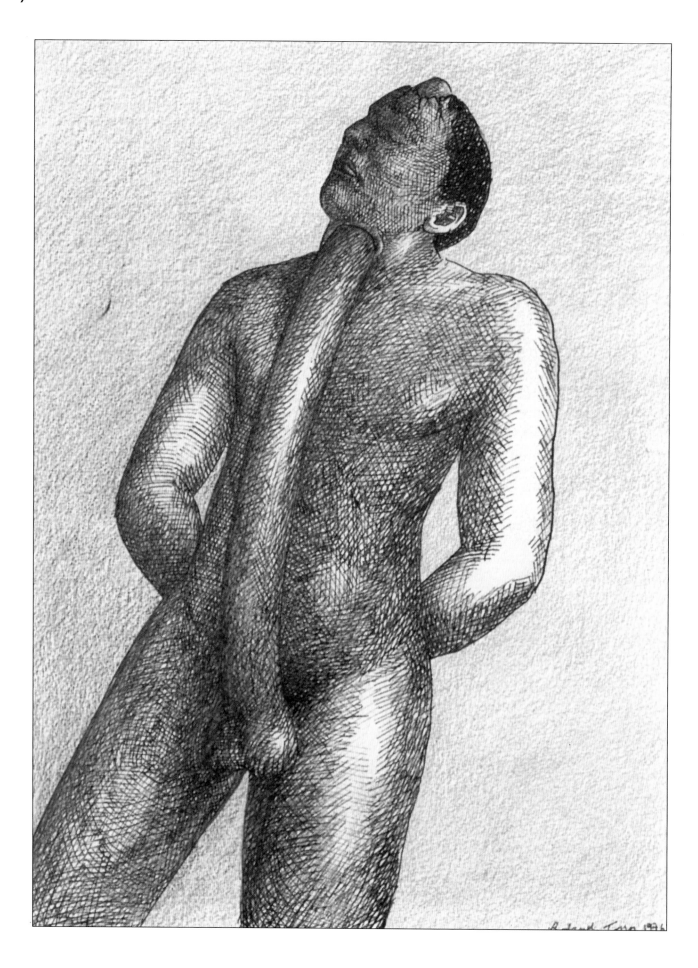

in Mysien. The cult of Priapus expanded across the Aegean islands and as far as Rome and merged with the old Etruscan gods Mutinus-Tutinus, whose names go back to "muto," "the male organ." Priapus, the protector of vineyards and fruit orchards, was always portrayed ritually with an erect penis, with which he protected the harvest. His organ was also supposed to possess magic powers that had positive effects on the bushes where he was placed. He also restored fertility to infertile women. Thus, Priapus is not only the god of the garden, but also of the conception of progeny. Like Pan, he belongs to the followers of Dionysius.

Pan is the god of herders and flocks. His name means "everything." His club-foot points to the truth that humans are half-animals. "He embodies the totality of all begetting energy, all gods, all aspects of life," according to Daniélou. Worship of Pan soon grew far beyond the borders of the Hellenic world. The god loved forests and springs. Daniélou describes him as "carefree, free of burdens and lazy." "It is dangerous to disturb his sleep, however. Half human, half goat, horned, hairy, a light sleeper, well disguised and fleet of foot, he is constantly on the hunt for nymphets and young boys, who are also objects of his desire. His hunger for sex is so insatiable that he also makes a practice of masturbation."

Hermes columns, on the other hand, were marble pillars that ended in a head and had an erect penis at about the middle of the column. Like the rural Priapus figures that warded off evil looks, they were said to have the power to repel evil, or they had a positive effect. In Athens there was a sacred Hermes column on every corner. Passers-by who touched the column were sure to have luck on that day.

Daniélou points out that following the popular belief that is still alive in the Mediterranean countries, men grab their penises to ward off evil looks. To each his own Hermes! Or they used the expressive gesture of *mano impudico* to bring luck. The genitals themselves had magical powers and because they were able to ward off misfortune, they were often found as phallic amulets.

Angelika Dierichs points to a peculiar creation in her book *Erotik in der Kunst Griechenlands* (*Eroticism in Greek Art*): the phallus bird, which one also finds in reduced form as a winged penis; a motif that one finds again and again throughout erotic art of the next two thousand years. Phallic birds, in the form of geese and cocks, also play an important role in European folk art. Is that the source of the English word "cock" for penis? In German, the common term for intercourse is *vögeln*; the Italians call the male organ by the direct term *l'uccello*. And isn't it a big bird, a stork, that brings babies?

Dierichs says "it is very likely that behind such iconographic discoveries stands the attempt to portray the begetting organ with its magic powers as demonic." But psychoanalytic interpretation of dreams teaches us that the image of the winged phallus is based less on a "daemonisation" than on the expression of a physical act. "The close connection between flying and the idea of the bird," writes Sigmund Freud, "makes it understandable that the dream of flying with men usually has a coarse sensual meaning." And he notes the decisive suspicion on the part of Paul Federn "that a good part of these dreams of flying are erection dreams, since the peculiar phantom of the erection, that has continued to occupy human fantasy, impresses as an example of overcoming gravity." Freud specifically points to the winged phalli of antiquity. In this example of varying interpretations, one can see the tendency of human thought to too-quickly demonise anything that appears alien instead of looking for its source in the body's own processes, as psychoanalysis does.

138. Roland Topor, *Self-experiment*, 1976.

One finds these wonderful winged creations particularly in the Dionysius celebrations or in the world of the haloa. Winged phalli can also be seen among the sacred objects of Delos. As some vase images show, phallus birds or winged phalli were also often found on the shields of warriors. As Dierichs describes it, they were considered "signs that warded off misfortune and protected the bearer of the shield from enemy attacks." *Haloa* was the name of the rural festival that honoured the goddesses Demeter and Kore to promote the fertility of plants and vegetables. During the haloa, large clay phalli were set out, but smaller clay phallus formations also seem to have been common. Dierichs describes a vase image that illustrates a kind of fertilisation magic: among the tender germinating seeds are four phalli stuck into the earth, which are watered by a clothed woman. Haloa festival customs were marked by the predominance of sex-related symbols, the joys of eating and the pleasure of wine. Supposedly priestesses of the goddesses secretly encouraged forbidden love. Courtesans also took part in the celebrations.

The phallos could be found in a multitude of forms not only at celebrations but also in everyday Greek life. Vases with sculpted phallos parts were used to drink from at feasts; consecrated oil was kept in phallus containers. Oil lamps showed obscene pictures that suggested the intimacy of the bed and also protected it. Penis imitations were beloved props for the erotic dances that courtesans provided for their customers.

Eros was everywhere. "He was a wild boy who respected neither age nor rank," Robert von Ranke-Graves writes in his *Greek Mythology*. "He flew around with his golden wings and shot his arrows aimlessly or set hearts aflame with his horrible torches." Like all passion, Eros had something anarchistic. The fact that Aphrodite was his mother and Zeus his father is an indication that physical passion does not stop at incest. His most famous shrine was in Thespiai, where he was worshipped in the form of a phallic column – the herder-Hermes or Priapus under another name.

Homosexuality was closely tied to worship of the phallos in Greece. According to Vanggaard, it was a "phenomenon supported by social institutions" that "was deeply rooted in their culture and stood in the service of childrearing in order to promote the highest good, as the Dorians saw it." In this context, the phallos symbolised areas that went beyond sexuality, fertility and reproduction. The graphic depiction of the male organ was the embodiment of male strength, size, independence, courage, cleverness, knowledge, influence upon other men and the possession of desirable women. In paedophile relationships, the man gave his *arete*, his virility, to the boy, for whom the phallos symbolises what a boy admires in men and desires for himself. But the gift was not one-sided: the men participated in the life of youth as well and drew from their creative strength.

"However important the thought of fertility may have been," writes Danish psychiatrist Vanggaard, "it is only one of many possible meanings and in many areas with which the phallos symbol is associated, such as strength for fighting or hunting or skill in sailing, there is no room for a sexual component." But is the function of the phallus of warding off misfortune not linked to the sexual, in the sense that it wards off everything that might prevent the "success" of the fertility of action? Vanggaard's point that Greek men potentially engaged in homosexual acts although married is an important one. Following chemical binding processes, he speaks of a "homosexual radical" that is present in all men. Under the sign of the phallus, Greek culture allowed free men to live these tendencies.

139. Troyen, Illustration for Sade's *Justine*, 1932.

140. Ornikleion, *Priapus Coppice II*, 1921.

141. Ornikleion, *Priapus Coppice V*, 1921.

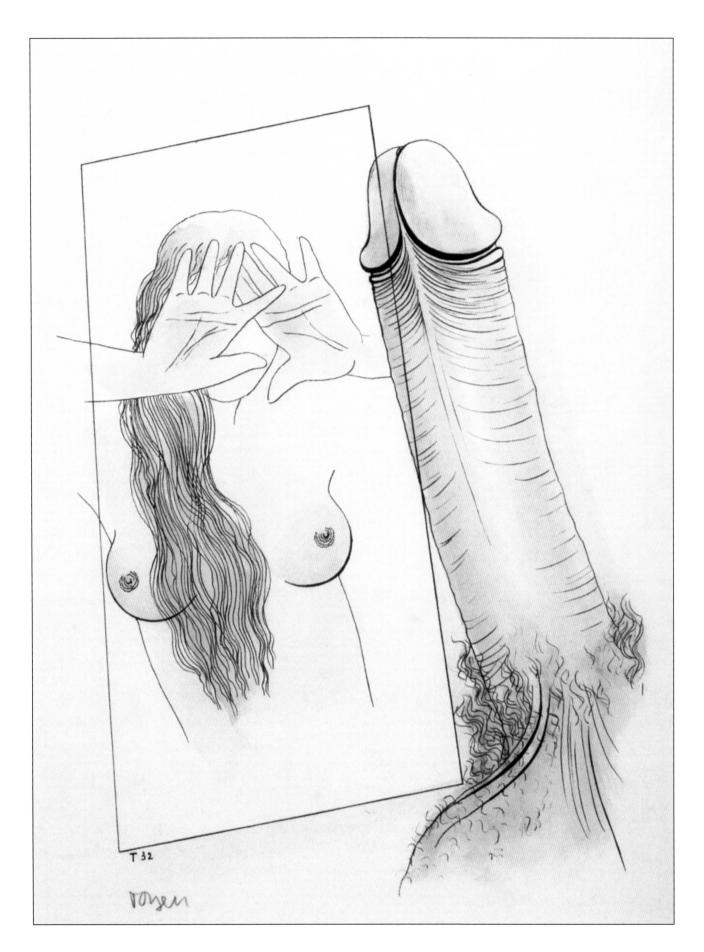

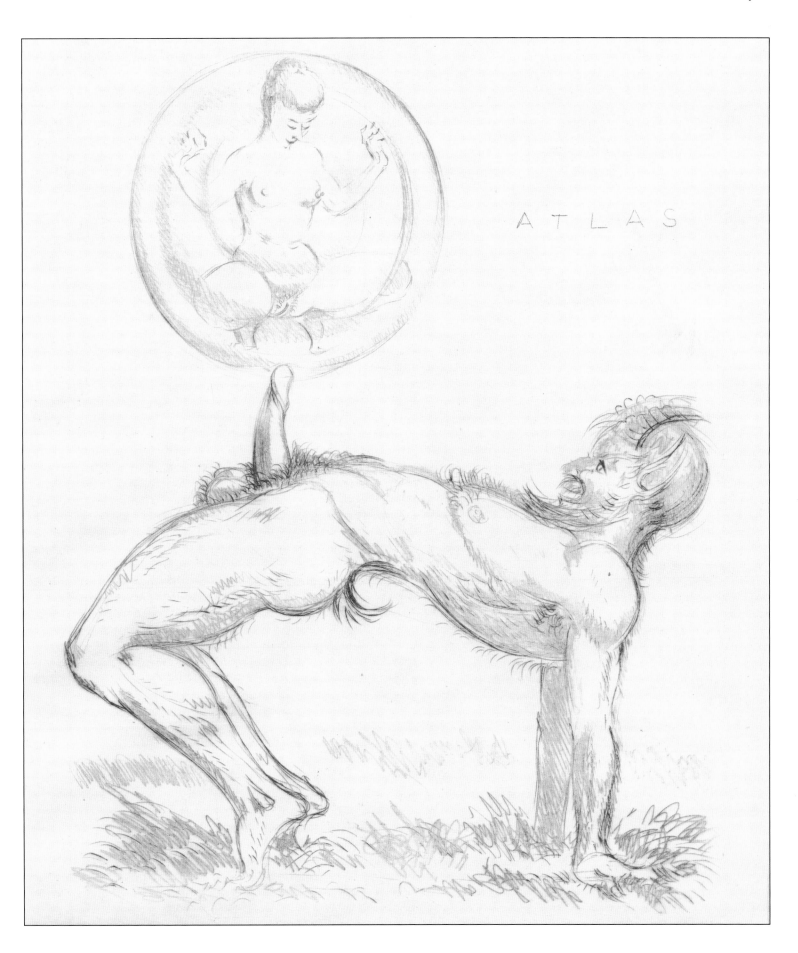

ATLAS

A comparison between the Doric Greeks and today's men in European-American culture shows the difference between the open and the hidden presence of this radical. Vanggaard points to historic developments that have repressed this homosexual radical in our consciousness, whereby the active sense of the phallus symbol was also lost. As Aschenbach's dream shows, it lives on in the unconscious. In Doric society, the erotic aspect of society played a decisive role in worship. In the case of the Ionic Athenians, its significance was considerably more personal, aesthetic and ethical in nature. In Rome, the focus was primarily on the erotic. In Christian Europe, however, sensual and open homosexuality was completely rejected for centuries.

The Romans also held Priapus in high favour. Like Hermes, he was represented by a square column, crowned by a head and decorated with an erect penis. One finds phallus depictions everywhere in Roman areas and they can still be seen today in Pompeii. As in Greece, Priapus was the protector of borders between properties. In fields, gardens, vineyards and sacred places, he acted as a strict but benevolent guard. He is the one who "frightens away thieves with his organ," as Ovid wrote in the *Metamorphoses*. The *Priapea* are an inexhaustible source.

A. Dierichs notes that most of the Priapus evidence comes from the time of the Roman Empire. This suggests that having a Priapus image in the garden or among the sacred objects of the household was considered *de rigeur* or that it underscored the prosperity of the household. In the main, followers of the phallus cult were people who appreciated an enjoyable life filled with erotic-sexual pleasures. Jean Marcadé points to the great Hellenic influence in the lives of the wealthy in Pompeii and notes that much of the luxury that surrounded them was Greek. The most desirable courtesans were also Greek. It is also scarcely in doubt that the recovered paintings – found in bordellos, the *lupanars,* as well as in private homes – were painted by Greek artists or by artists who had been influenced by the Greeks and were able to create a depiction of human passions worthy of the sacred loves of mythology, even if it was only to illustrate the verses of Ovid's *Ars Amatoria*.

It is understandable that Italians were most eager to adopt Priapus when one recognises in him the existence of a much older phallus god. Augustus demonstrates the large difference in the relationship to the male sexual organ between us and the Romans of antiquity. He jokingly called Horace, whom he greatly admired, his "purissimum penem," his very best penis. The penis was nothing to be ashamed of.

The power over evil ascribed to the phallus led to the widespread custom among the Romans of carrying small phallus amulets as protection against hardship and damaging influences, a custom that continued into the Middle Ages and, as the superstition proves, never died out completely. Occasionally, the penis was replaced by a horn. Children, who were in particular need of protection, carried phallus amulets and rings with miniature replicas of penises and testicles. Hundreds of such amulets in the form of penises have been preserved. The "tintinnabulum" was a very specific form of amulet in bronze. Its name comes from the corresponding Latin word, which could be translated as "bell." Many tintinnabula have small bells attached with thin chains to a phallus that could be hung from the ceiling of a room. Such tintinnabula were especially beloved in stores: their sound when the door opened was considered a sign of fortunate business dealings.

When the Greek phallus cult was taken over by the Romans, however, an essential dimension was lost. Together with the male-female Dionysius, a sense of the bliss of creation, one that also

142. Erler, *The Holy Priapus II,* 1927.

honoured the feminine, was worshipped. As a masculine and warlike people, however, the Romans had a weaker sense of the organic and the religious. The Dionysian gods suffocated in the forced adherence to standards of the Roman Empire. "Under the pressure of the Roman nature, human development moved from woman to man, from nature to history, from Eros to law, from religion to the statehood," Walter Schubart summarises. "With Rome's victories, the female epoch closes." The phallus lost the religious dimension that included both sexes and became a symbol of the power of patriarchy. The man had conquered the woman. "Where Rome gave the orders, there was no matriarchy, no mother religion, no idolisation of nature and no experience of the bliss of creation." Religious celebrations turned into outbreaks of coarse lust, the cultic orgiastity turned into indecency. With that, the meaning of the world "orgy" changed "from its original meaning of secret worship to licentious revelry, the meaning it still has today." Orgiastic festivals revealed the basic religious idea. "What remained," according to Schubart, "is nothing more than the indulgence of lust. The *venus vulgivaga* resided in Caesar's Rome not as the goddess of life-giving motherhood, but as a demon of nerve-wracking lecherousness. Thus the East took revenge on Rome. Thus woman took revenge on man." The phallus cult became secularised and simultaneously weakened.

At this point let us risk a bit of psychoanalytic speculation by claiming that the shift from Greece to Rome was also a shift from the primacy of the phallus to genital primacy, with the dominance of the male organ, a shift that takes place ontogenetically in each individual development. In childhood development only one genital, the male, originally played a role. This is the difference to the final genital organisation of adults. "There exists not so much genital primacy but rather a primacy of the phallus," Freud notes in his text on "infantile genital organisation." Under the primacy of the phallus, the male and the female were still united, as expressed in the form of the male-female Dionysius. From this point of view, a disassociation of the two areas into two different gender identities must be seen as a negative development.

The lost religious dimension was finally replaced by spreading Christianity, which was also contemptuous of what remained: the sexual organs. But since the phallus is a "radical" in the human psyche, it remained present in hidden rites, festivals and ceremonies, despite all persecution. Thus the phallic symbol appears in witch cults in the form of the "horned." The maenads became witches, Priapus and Pan turned into shaggy, clubfooted versions of the devil and the fight against "heathens" turned sacred rites into sodomy and worship into whoring. "It is pretty much irrelevant whether the witches believed in a phallic god and worshipped him," Vanggaard writes, "or whether the Inquisition and the rest of the population invented him. At any rate, the people seriously believed in the 'horned one.' The fanaticism of the church confirmed the power of phallic symbols." On the other hand, the church's fight against this witch cult led to increased oppression of all openly phallic symbolism. This characterises our civilisation up to the present day.

To the extent that the phallus represents what is alive, Christianity is hostile to life. No one felt this "wrathful, vengeful resistance to life itself" as deeply as Nietzsche: "Christianity represented from the beginning, essentially and thoroughly, disgust and antipathy of life toward life, which it only disguised, only hid, only dressed up as belief in a 'different' or a 'better' life." "Christianity," writes Nietzsche in *Beyond Good and Evil*, "gave Eros poison to drink – he did not die of it, but was deformed, to vice." What was once worship mutated to excess, licentiousness and perversion.

143. Merenyi, 1925.

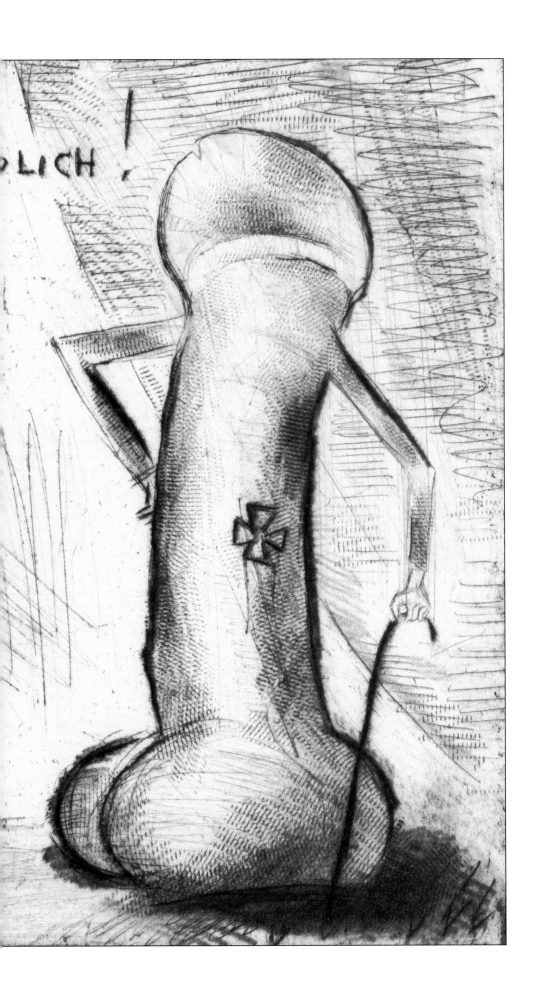

144. Michel Fingesten, 1917.

al palo di sacrifizio

This cultural discrimination is reflected as well in the psyche of individuals. In his essay *Eine Kindheitserinnerung des Leonardo da Vinci* ("A Childhood Memory of Leonardo da Vinci"), Sigmund Freud explains, "One will not be able to really develop a relationship to the activities of childhood sexuality ... as long as one does not relinquish the standpoint of our cultural derision of genitals and sexual functioning overall. To understand the sexual life of the child, one needs analogies to primeval times ... From the collections of cultural researchers gathered in arduous labor one may receive the impression that the genitals were originally the pride and hope of the living, enjoyed the adoration of the gods and that the sacred nature of their function was transferred to all the newly learned activities of humans. Countless god figures rose up from them through sublimation and at the time, since the link between official religion and sexual activity was already hidden from general consciousness, secret cults tried to kept it alive among their members. In the course of cultural development, eventually so much godliness and sacredness was extracted from sexual activity that the exhausted remainder became contemptible. But because of the indestructibility inherent in the nature of all spiritual changes, that one should not be surprised that even the most primitive forms of genital worship can be documented up until very recent times and that today's language use, customs and superstitions contain traces of all the phases of this development."

The holiness of the rites is no longer comprehensible to the western human of modern times. "Europe," Schubart writes, "went through a long period of erotic ostracism. The phallus was transformed into a disgusting symbol of depravity. In Dante's *Divine Comedy*, Lucifer's sexual organ represents Hell, the Satanic centre of the earth: a phallus service under a negative sign. The moral convictions that Christianity created have, according to Schubart, "affected or touched all of us in western countries, albeit if with varying intensity, including other kinds of believers, like Jews, or nonbelievers, like atheists. Who among them still has the pure, objective eye of the Dionysian?"

We banned devils and witches to a world separated from us and damned. What disturbed us was removed, but with it went the orgiastic and liberating element as well. This had a flattening effect on eroticism. For at the deepest level, according to Bataille, it is a tragic experience. "Today we prefer to ignore the fact that eroticism is a world of insanity and that its ethereal forms represent only a thin covering of an infernal abyss ... As long as we are not conscious of the bottomless nature of eroticism, we avoid the truth. Eroticism is in the first place the most exciting reality, but it is also, and no less so, the most disgraceful. Even according to psychoanalysis, eroticism remains a world full of contradictions: its depth is religious, it is terrible, it is tragic, it is still inadmissible. All the more so because it is sacred."

The infernal abysses open before Aschenbach in his heathen-Dionysian dream. The worship of the phallus, once born of a great religion, damned over the last two thousand years by Christianity, nonetheless remains firmly entrenched in the human soul.

Not until the rediscovery of antiquity in the Renaissance did the view of the erotic change. Leonardo da Vinci spoke at various times of the respect due the male sexual organ: "Human beings do it an injustice when they hesitate to show it and speak of it, when they always cover and hide it. On the contrary, it should be decorated and proudly displayed like an emissary," – an emissary from the realm of Dionysius. We do not find priapic images in erotic art again until the Rococo, with its

145. Anonymous, 1910.

greater enjoyment of the pleasures of life. The libertinism of French aristocracy let the old gods re-emerge; aristocratic liaisons, in reality often infused with calculation and intrigue, were mystified and celebrated as liaisons of the gods.

The "erotic universe" of Czaress Catherine the Great, whose taste for amorous adventures was well known, is legendary. She used the Gatschina summer residence for romantic assignations with Count Orlov. As photos and witness statements attest, she had entire rooms decorated with erotica (see the excellently researched television film by Peter Woditsch, *Das verlorene Geheimnis von Katharina der Großen* (*The Lost Secret of Catherine the Great*). One of the rooms was panelled in wood; ceiling-high phalli decorated the walls. Among the carved pieces of furniture, a table predominates whose top is supported by four enormous phalli. These monstrous organs draw their strength from femininity: they have breasts instead of testicles. These rare examples of erotic art are considered lost.

The first half of the nineteenth century was devilish and did not conform at all to the Biedermeier style. Poitevin's relaxed and lovable little devils are genealogically related to Pan and his satyrs. What had been repressed and damned returned in devilish form.

When, however, priapic motifs in erotic art accumulate at the turn of the twentieth century, this has less to do with heathen sensuality then with demonstration of male fears. The phallus as an expression of power, virility and strength is at an end and a new danger threatens to sap its last strength. The emancipation of women rocks the traditional male sense of self. "Free love" and overcoming the barrier of bourgeois moral precepts of marriage and love were at the top of the agenda of the early women's movement. Fear of "female domination" evoked fantasy images in which women appeared as seductive and threatening *femmes fatales*, as sphinxes and vampires. For many men, feminism was nothing less than the threat of castration. The figure of Lulu is the literary perfection of the now-powerless drives. She is, as her creator Wedekind says, "cold-blooded and completely free of inhibitions"; the woman who no longer concerns herself with any erotic conventions; the female who has turned from a passive love object to an insatiable demon and now demands the right to free choices in love she had always been denied.

A strongly erect ideal of masculinity is being created as a dam against femininity, which always also means the femininity hidden within every man. The chaos that seems to threaten the male world was once the domain of Dionysius. Now the danger comes from the pan-sexual woman, from whom the male world must be protected. The wish for limitlessness is projected onto the woman, whose image thus grows into an ideal both seductive and threatening. This ideal construction, Weininger recognises in *Geschlecht und Charakter* (*Sex and Character*), could "rob him of the power of reason." The fear of loss of control is transferred to the woman, who abandons herself to orgasm. Weininger fantasises a "whore" who "wants to ... disappear within coitus as reality, wants to be ground up, destroyed, eradicated, lose consciousness out of ecstasy ... she wants to dissolve in him." In these coitus fantasies, the female body becomes the territory of all-encompassing lust. The phallus has a hypnotic effect upon the woman and fascinates her. "It is her fate and there is no escaping it. The phallus is something that makes the woman absolutely and finally un-free." No longer is fascination with the phallus anchored in the unconscious: Its power is externalised, with the result that hate of the "woman" is actually an expression of self-hatred. Hatred of the Other and self-hatred, both are rooted in the general debasement of the sexual drive. This too is late revenge

146. Jules Derkovits, *Pandemonium II*, 1920.

of the rejected god Priapus. The Dionysian wish for the erasing of borders falls victim to a sharpened control by reason. There should be nothing animal left in man. But the condemned part of himself whose existence he cannot admit returns in even more threatening form.

In many works of current erotic art, the phallus seems like a megalith that forms a more defensive bulwark. Internally, the Vendome column of masculinity has long since been worn down by self-doubt. This phallus no longer stands in the centre of a "Dionysian culture," on the contrary, it has become fossilised as an unmoving symbol of its defence. It no longer represents masculinity, power, virility, but is more likely to indicate a "masculinity complex" that cannot be helped even with penis extensions. The return of the phallus in erotic art of this time is the portent of its downfall. It has lost the ability to give itself to desire. In this fossilised state, it has become the embodiment of hostility toward life, not of the bliss of creation. As a god, Priapus has disappeared from the surface of Western life. But he remains in the unconscious, where his influence is no less great. This has led to a deep emotional conflict for modern man. In his dreams, Aschenbach succumbs to Dionysian forces. "And his soul tasted the lewdness and frenzy of extinction."

The realm of art is the most likely place where the Dionysian is most likely to be allowed expression – as something disruptive and confusing. This, because the artist "has an inborn, irrepressible and natural hang toward the abyss," as Aschenbach recognises in his dream. Art must be mistrusted, for how could someone with an irrepressible and natural hang toward the abyss be a good teacher? Knowledge sympathises with the abyss; it is abyss. He speaks of a "second naturalness." "Form and naturalness," Aschenbach continues, "lead to ecstasy and to desire, lead the noble man perhaps to gruesome emotional wantonness that his own ability to judge rejects as contemptible, leads to the abyss, they, too, lead to the abyss. We poets, I say, lead them there, for we are not able to rise to higher realms, only to fall into dissipation." Thomas Mann is putting words into Aschenbach's mouth, words that express an anti-idealistic agenda.

A "second naturalness" – does that not recall Kleist's sentence from *Marionettentheater?* "Consequently, I said, a little distracted, should we not eat again from the tree of knowledge, in order to return to the state of innocence?"

This knowledge would be tragic. It would reveal the split that runs through human beings, created by the tension between the world of reason and the enticing magic of the ecstatic Dionysian world, in the centre of which stands Priapus – that damned god.

"Worship of Dionysius was essentially tragic," writes Bataille in *Die Tränen des Eros* (*The Tears of Eros*). "At the same time it was erotic, marked by extreme dissipation, and we know that it was just as erotic as it was tragic … The eroticism only brought to completion the atmosphere of tragic horror that was part of it." A romantic death wish also draws Aschenbach in dreams down to this boundlessly erotic world, a world in which the individual, with all of his limits and norms, is lost in Dionysian self-forgetfulness. Art, according to Nietzsche, can offer protection and a remedy that helps us to bear this tragic knowledge.

147. Erler, *The Holy Priapus IV*, 1927.

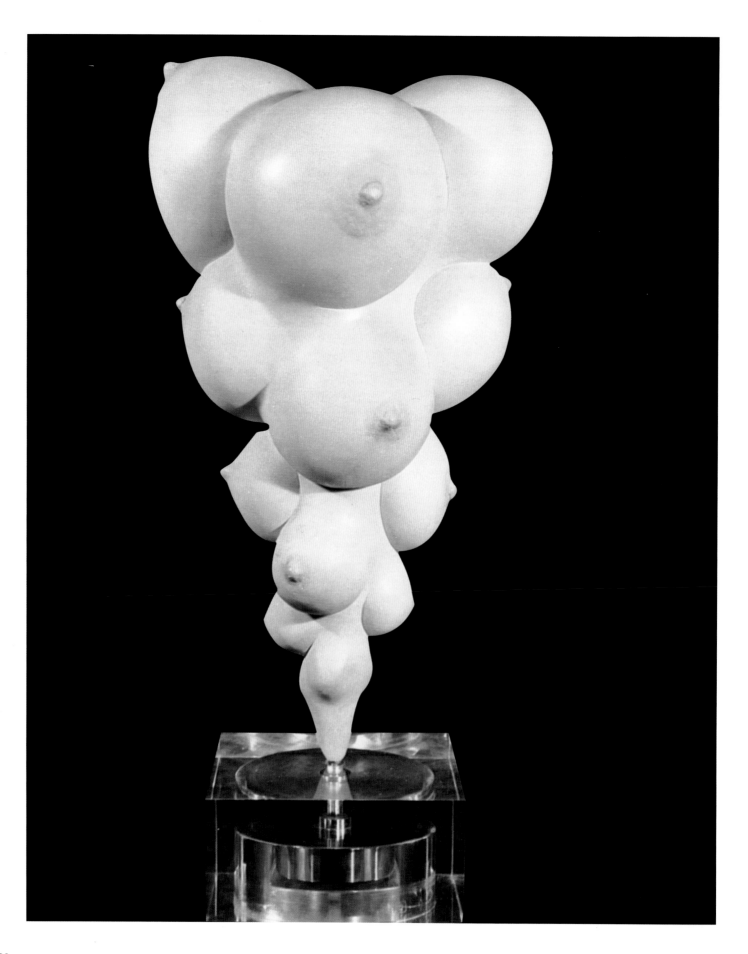

The Manipulated Breasts

"I felt as if I could kneel forever in front of her breasts and still not have seen enough of them. My intoxication was held in the sway of an ancient erotic magic" (from Jules Romains, *Der Gott des Fleisches* [*The God of Flesh*]).

What incredible fascination the female breast holds for us! And yet – what power it holds to disturb us and cause unease! Both men and women consider breasts as sexual jewellery, the crown jewels of femininity. This sexualised view of the female breast is by no means universal. In some African and South Pacific cultures, for example, where women's breasts have remained bare since primeval times, the breast does not have the primarily erotic significance that it has in the Western world. Non-western cultures, as Yalom indicates in her study, have their own erotic fetishes: tiny feet in China, the curve of the neck in Japan, a round posterior in Africa and the Caribbean. In every case, fascination with whatever part of the body laden with sexual significance is due to partial or complete covering of that part.

"We must return to the earliest times of human existence," says Moreck, "we must question ancient man, we must look for evidence in the oldest demonstrations of artistic expression about what was found most attractive about women, what was most enticing to male sexuality, which physical details of the female body awakened his longing and his imagination." The earliest depictions of human beings, from the Middle Palaeolithic and drawn in caves and on earth strata, are images of women that exist almost completely of breasts and posteriors.

Breasts and posteriors are seen both as the sensory totality of the female appearance and created symbolically as such. They form the targets of an original sexual urge and up to the present day have not lost their attraction for men. Paul Verlaine sang hymns to the beauty of the cheeks of the behind and to the breast, which he described as a heavenly pair of twins and a double altar of lust, and Michael Fingesten, in his drawing *Ecce Femina*, twists the female body so that breasts and posterior form a simultaneous frontal attraction.

Our love of breasts – and this "we" includes both men and women – goes back to our own early history, to childhood. For the infant, the world consisted of a soft round breast, a paradise from which milk and honey flowed. This "nourishing breast" promised safety, warmth and security. Hunger and love still come from the same source. It is the centre of the "feeling of oral lust." When we speak of the "aesthetic ideal of breasts," we are abstracting from these sensual origins.

The breast is a demonstrative organ of female maturity. No other part of the body demonstrates the interweaving of nature and culture more clearly: what has been seen as "beautiful" in the form and emphasis of the breast, up to and including its negation, follows historical and aesthetic developments, the course of which itself took on a breast-like form, if one may use the expression. Thus, the breast, as a "gift of nature," was always forced into the form of societal morality, with the consequence of a shape that was excessively pointed, even if perhaps covered fashionably. If the bourgeoisie of the

148. Hans Bellmer, 1968.
Bronze sculpture.

149. Louise Bourgeois, *Breast*, 1991.

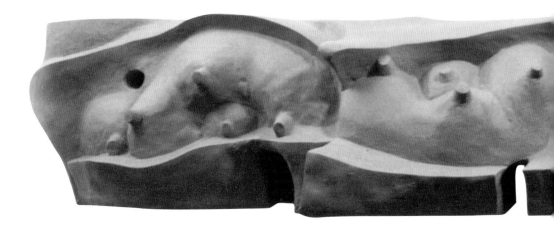

nineteenth century in its self-satisfaction and sense of well-being still appreciated the full bosom, the ideal of ampleness ended with the *fin-de-siècle.* The vision of voluptuousness was followed by a female ideal far removed from all that was maternal. Youthfulness dominated and shaped the male view of a woman whose characteristics were to be found in pre-puberty. Now the ideal was the boy-like, narrow-hipped child-woman with small tight breasts.

The emphasis and formation of this body part, whether in the history of fashion or in artistic depiction, show us the extent to which longing for mature femininity was welcomed or repulsed. It is obvious that these changes correspond to the various self-images of masculinity. Thus, there is no form of the female breast that has not appeared as perfect and beautiful, as the ideal, at one time or another, in one culture or another, to one individual or another.

The most astonishing examples of the adoration of the breast in antiquity are considered to be the famous many-breasted statues of Artemis of Ephesus. Among the ruins of ancient Ephesus, a lively Greek city on the coast of what is today Turkey, two life-sized cult statues of the goddess Artemis were found in the ruins of the council hall. These statues with their double rows of breasts have traditionally been interpreted as symbols of an excess of food and prosperity, which the goddess had the power to dispense. In other interpretations, the rounded forms on the upper body of the statues are rows of bull testicles. This interpretation is based on the archaic ritual practice of attaching the testicles of bulls that had been sacrificed to wooden cult statues. Still, the "many-breasted Artemis of Ephesus" became a metaphor for a wonderfully inexhaustible source of milk and nourishment and an answer to an ancient and timeless human fantasy.

The enormous significance of the breast in pre-Greek and early Greek cults was gradually superseded by the dominance of the phallus. The old goddesses faded away behind the Hellenic gods. Zeus usurped Olympus, the seat of the oldest Greek deity, Gaia Olympia "with many breasts," and this god established himself as the undisputed ruler of the Olympic Pantheon. In Greek society, which revered the phallus, the power of the female breast existed only in old legends which continued to ascribe supernatural powers to female breasts. Thus, the myth of the creation of the Milky Way was connected to the breasts of Hera. Mortals could become immortal, it was believed, if they drank at the breast of the great goddess.

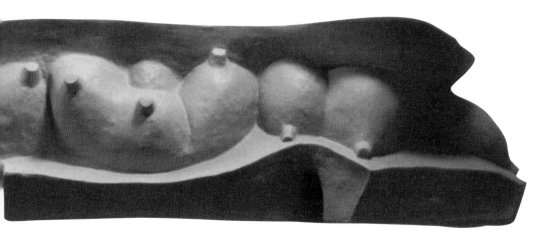

When Zeus wanted to give immortality to his son Heracles, whose mother was the mortal Alkmene, he laid the child secretly on Hera's breast while she slept. But Heracles sucked so fiercely that the goddess awakened and noticed the strange child. Outraged, she pulled her breast away with such force that milk spurted into the sky. Thus was the Milky Way created. Heracles, however, having already drunk Hera's milk, became an immortal hero and eventually took his place in the pantheon of gods.

The Greeks, who ascribed human characteristics to their gods, saw in Aphrodite the woman with "the breasts that arouse desire." From the fouth century onward, Aphrodite, the goddess of love, was always depicted naked or half-naked, with breasts clearly suggested or revealed. They followed the erotic ideal of the time: firm, slightly muscular, "apple-shaped," as classic texts describe them. This ideal was also associated with the beautiful Helena. "In the Hellenic period, Aphrodite became a figure similar to modern sex goddesses," Yalom writes, "the object of male desire and reverent admiration." Hellenic sensual desires were directed to the breasts as an attribute of female sexuality, while the actual sexual organs were considered aesthetically inferior. Hans Licht, an expert on Greek love life, points to the great significance of breasts: "Here literature and art in antiquity celebrated true orgies of beauty. The Greek enthusiasm for beauty for the female breast is illuminated nowhere better than by the history of Phryne and her defender Hypereides." Phryne has been charged with a serious crime. The tribunal is assembled, the scale has begun to tip, the beautiful sinner is about to be sentenced. But then Hypereides tears away her robes and reveals the radiant beauty of her breasts. The judges are so overcome with sacred awe before the goddess that they do not dare to execute the prophet and priestess of Aphrodite. "The judges' sense of beauty held them back from sentencing one who possessed such beauty. One can scarcely imagine a more ardent extolment of the breast." After the charges against Phryne were dropped, a decree was issued that prohibited defendants from revealing intimate body parts in court. The intention was to prevent someone else from making such an impression upon the court. Phryne was the most beautiful and famous but also the most dangerous of all the courtesans in Athens. Her immortality was due not only to her wonderful beauty but also to this scandalous story, which was the topic of the day in Athens.

The beauty of breasts also caused Menelaus to reconcile with Helen, although she had betrayed him with Paris. After conquering Troy, Menelaus wanted revenge for the violation of his honour and threatened Helen at sword point. She, however, revealed "the apples of her breasts" and so charmed Menelaus that he tossed the sword aside and took the beautiful Helen into his arms. According to the Greeks, Helen's breast was the model for the first wine goblet.

The Middle Ages in Europe were shaped by the Christian Church's negative view of physicality, which was transferred to a large extent to art. Depictions of the human body scarcely differentiated between male and female. With rare exceptions, the angels or human figures that decorated the portals of the cathedrals of the Middle Ages showed none of the curves or roundness we associate with the bodies of adults. Female breasts were often as flat as those of the men. When women were shown with naked breasts, it was in connection with negative symbolism. Naked women and men were shown being pushed into the mouth of Hell, while those who had been saved and were on their way to Paradise were clothed in tunics that covered their asexual body forms.

In the early fourteenth century, the painters of Tuscany began to depict the Virgin Mary offering her naked breast to Baby Jesus. This motif of Maria lactans became widespread in the Renaissance. All of these depictions, as Yalom notes, have certain characteristics in common: "The Virgin reveals one small breast, the other remaining covered under her robes. Baby Jesus drinks from the visible breast, which appears unrealistic, almost glued on, as if a halved fruit - lemon, apple or pomegranate - had accidentally fallen onto the canvas and stuck there."

The *blason* represents a pretty and light side of Renaissance eroticism. These poems celebrated every part of the female body. In his 1535/36 poem *Le Beau Tétin*, Clément Marot describes the perfect breast as a small ivory ball globe in whose middle sits a strawberry or cherry. He praised the object of his longing:

> ... Quant on te voit, il vient à maintz
> Une envie dedant les mains
> De te taster, de te tenir
> Mais il se faut bien contenir
> D`en approcher, bon gré ma vie.
>
> Car il viendrait une autre envie ...,
> A bon droit heureux on dira
> Celuy qui de laict t'emplira
> Faisant d'ung tetin de pucelle
> Tetin de femme entière et belle.

(When they see you, many / feel the desire in their hands / to touch you and hold you / but one must be satisfied with / being near you – or beware! / Else another longing will awaken (...) One must praise the good fortune / of he who fills you with milk / and transforms the breast of a virgin / into the breast of a perfect beautiful woman.)

Marot speaks only of the effects upon the male viewer at the sight of the female breast. The breast not only evokes his longing but is also the source of male pride, for it is the man's semen that will impregnate the woman and turn her into a creature with swelling, milk-producing breasts. Erotic *blasons* are in effect coats-of-arms of female body parts. Instead of the whole body, only fragments are celebrated, which amounts to a fetishist glorification of the body.

150. Artemis of Ephesos, 200 B.C.

151. *Birth of Aphrodite*, detail of the
"*Ludovisi Throne*", circa 470-460
B.C. Marble, h: 90 cm, I: 142 cm.
Museo Nazionale Romano, Rome.

Hartmut Böhme shows us that the *blasons* - and counter-*blasons* - form a tight network of rules, commands and prohibitions that dictate the female body more than they describe it. The woman herself does not exist as a person. "The women of the *blasons* are not only nameless, they do not exist at all. The *blasons anatomiques* have no women in them." Rather, they are an expression of male sexuality: "woman" is seen as a collection of body parts that arouse lust in men. This courtly, cultivated dissection of the woman serves male fantasy. Thus, the female body made anonymous becomes a plaything of desire. In the twentieth century, Hans Bellmer was to extend this logic to a lust based on dismemberment. The breast, emancipated from a religious context, now serves to arouse male fantasies. It does not yet belong to the woman.

The most famous French poet of the time, Pierre de Ronsard (1524 - 1585), was an unmistakable admirer of the bosom. In a cycle of love poems dedicated to Cassandra, he speaks repeatedly of her "beautiful breasts," "virginal buds," "milky meadows," "milk mounds," "ivory breasts," her "inviting bosom," "much too chaste bosom," "alabaster bosom," and so on. If he could only touch her breasts, he enthuses, even his dismal prospects would seem better than those of kings.

> I wish to God, I had never, so raging with desire,
> Touched my lover's bosom …
> Who would have thought that cruel fate
> Hides such a great fire
> Under such a beautiful bosom, in order to make me its prey?

In order to preserve the beauty of their breast, many women of the upper classes gave their infants to wet nurses. Breastfeeding was not considered attractive for women of rank. Elisabeth Badinter shows in her study *Mother Love* that disdain for nursing became a sign of social status: since aristocratic women had long set an example, not breastfeeding quickly became a sign of distinction for others. "Nursing one's child oneself was the same as admitting that one did not belong to better society."

The breast's erotic potential displaced its function as a provider of maternal nourishment. "In Renaissance society there were two kinds of bosoms," Yalom notes, "small firm 'upper class' breasts that were intended to entice men and full, large, milk-producing 'lower class' breasts of the women who nursed their own children and those of their rich employers."

The last of the royal mistresses, a woman whose beauty fit perfectly into the Renaissance gallery of "high culture pin-ups" (Yalom), was Gabrielle d'Estrées. She was famous for her beauty and for the influence that she exerted upon the king. Her gesture in the famous painting that shows her together with one of her sisters in the bathtub is considered to be a reference to her pregnancy. Gabrielle died in childbirth at the age of twenty-six.

"The female nude," according to Yalom, "was, during the Renaissance in France and Italy, the high-culture equivalent of today's foldout Playboy poster."

After the Italians and the French caught the fever, it soon spread to all of Europe. Even the German principalities were, in the words of Luther, "breeding grounds of forbidden lust." Women and children, he thundered, had begun to go about exposed in front and back and nobody was willing to order them to behave themselves or to punish them.

152. Pierre-Auguste Renoir,
Blonde Bather, 1903.
Oil on canvas, 92 x 73 cm.
Kunsthistorisches Museum,
Vienna.

It was different in England. In the Elizabethan period, sensual pleasures collided with religious convictions. "The British were never able to fully embrace the Mediterranean image of female nature as generous and friendly; the Nordic-Christian tradition of hostility toward the body and the rejection of sensual pleasure was too old and too deeply entrenched in their culture."

Yalom summarises: "Since the Late Middle Ages, worship of the erotic breast in western civilisation has remained nearly unchanged. All that changed were notions of the ideal size, form and function of the bosom. Painters and poets of the Middle Ages preferred small, high breasts above rounded bellies that suggested pregnancy. In France, the preference for small breasts together with slender, tall bodies remained until the late sixteenth century. The Italians of the High Renaissance liked a broader chest and somewhat fuller hips and thighs. Elizabethan men were obviously less interested in size than in oral gratification; breast metaphors were apples, cream, milk or luxuriant gardens. Since the Late Renaissance, the trend of male preferences was generally toward larger, fuller breasts. The small girlish mounds of the Late Middle Ages gave way five hundred years later to the voluptuous curves of Jane Russell in the 1950s, Carole Doda in the 1970s and Cindy Crawford in the 1990s. Women who wanted to attain this male ideal enlarged their breasts with padded brassieres and silicone implants; the latter often resulted in the loss of erotic sensation that had been the sexual value of the breast in the first place." It is clear that a trend is being described here that took root particularly in the United States.

The breasts were freed – for men, not for the women themselves. The image of the woman remained one defined, projected and established by men. A process that is as old as history itself. The female breast: an imaginary screen upon which men project their longings and fears.

The Covered Breast

Even if a sense of shame tried to deflect sexual longing for the breast by covering it and thus deflecting lecherous looks, this only intensified the erotic effect. Every effort at covering provoked the desire to lift the veil. This desire was increased by the cleverest tricks of veiling. We learn from Martial and Juvenal that at festive meals and orgies the clever presentation of the breast played a decisive role and that the strict prophets of the Old Testament complained about the silken robes that enticingly revealed the body and its fleshly glories. For Samuel, Jeremiah and Salomon, naked breasts were a sign of a harlot. Since then they have been seen as an advertisement for prostitution, for shamelessness was the privilege of prostitutes. Fashion repeatedly accentuated the presentation of the breasts, even if it claimed to veil them.

Ovid emphasised repeatedly how a beautiful female breast gives pleasure to the hand and the eye. In his *Art of Love*, he advises women to contribute to this pleasure: "... encircle a breast that is too full or of which there is too little, with a strap." This breast strap, the strophium, was an early form of the brassiere. Indian and Oriental dancers covered their breasts only to make their gradual unveiling all the more effective and overwhelming to the senses. With the advent of low-necked garments, the décolleté, baring the breast became a principle of clothing.

As early as the eleventh century, Saint Anselm railed against wearing a bodice to give the breasts an enticing form. With the baring of flesh came the wish for fullness. And soon the effect upon men began to spread. A minnesinger had to reprimand his comrades and make clear to them that it was not courtly and appropriate to reach into women's clothing and grab their breasts.

153. Bouliar Aspasia, 1794.

Numerous clothing regulations and contemporary reports document the opportunities women took to bare their breasts. "And in particular," says a Strasbourg decree of between 1370 and 1380, "it is of primary importance that the breasts should not be seen." Representatives of the Christian Church described the openings in women's bodices as "the gates of Hell." Jan Hus (1369 – 1450) also spoke out against this female fashion: "The women wear their clothing so widely cut out at the throat that anyone can see the radiant skin of nearly half of their bared breasts, in the temples of the Lord in front of the priests and spiritual leaders just as in the markets, but even more so at home and what is left of the breasts have been so artificially enlarged and protrudes to such an extent that they almost appear as two horns upon the chest." Who would not think of the horns of the devil? Bishop Jean Jouven des Ursins criticised the promiscuous lifestyle at the court of Charles VII. The declared target of his attacks were openings in women's bodices, "through which one sees the women's breasts, nipples and flesh," in his opinion, specific proof of a general atmosphere of "whoring and licentiousness and all the other sins." But despite churchly lectures on morality, the bosom continued to be shown, to the outrage of the critics and the pleasure of cosmopolites.

In the fourteenth century women wore low-cut garments, particularly in France, Germany and Lombardy that showed half of the bosom. "If you have a beautiful body, uncover your breasts," poet Pierre Michaud advised women at court in 1466. The waist moved higher and higher and pushed the breasts upward, thus emphasising them. Women were becoming increasingly free and independent in public life of the time and revealing their breasts demonstrated their power and superiority over men. The introduction of uncovered breast at court is ascribed to French queen Isabelle of Bavaria; chroniclers report about her court that "parties were given where the whole court, men and women, married and unmarried, did the most disgusting things with each other under the cover of masks and darkness."

In the seventeenth century, the Baroque poet Logau wrote:

> Womenfolk are open-hearted:
> the way that they clothe themselves
> sends a signal from the mountain
> that heats up the valleys.

The eighteenth century tightened clothing more and more. Part of the coquetry of the Rococo was that the breasts jumped out of the bodice at the slightest movement so that one could see the nipples.

The Revolution's trend toward freedom led to a loosening of clothing. The shirt, called "costume à la grecque" in democratic reminiscence, was cut out so far in front that in addition to the arms and neck, the breasts were often fully visible. The laced-up bodice (*Schnürbrust*) was rejected in favour of the brassiere of antiquity, which however, gave way again to the corset at the order of the *directoire*. Not until consolidating middle-class morals again held sway did breasts again become a domain in which bourgeois respectability could be demonstrated. Respectability expressed itself in modest covering. Still, there were enough opportunities to reveal physical temptations, in the main festive occasions. "The ballroom became a hotbed of exhibitionism, the realm of the décolleté, which was allowed in any form and in fact was required," Moreck writes. "The festive evenings at the court of the beautiful Empress Eugenie are a museum of naked shoulders and breasts, but the bourgeois balls of all nations are the same, and in the loges and rows of the great opera houses, fashion reveals the masses

154. F. Zettl, *The Spanish Singer*, 1889.

155. Anonymous, 1925.

156. Anonymous, 1925.

of flesh of the ladies, with the deepest of décolleté, between the white shirts of the gentlemen. The hot breath of the gallant cavalier caressing a breast is the most beautiful ovation for these women. They use Phryne's arguments of antiquity to win the power struggle of life, they triumphantly present what Zola once called the 'sensual trademarks' of the Second Empire."

The crinoline became the model for women and made the corset, with its deep décolleté, world famous as a delicious bag of breasts. Corsets became indispensable prerequisites for a lady's dress. "It was the hope of the flat-breasted and comfort to those who had too much flesh," in Moreck's judgment, "for it covered flaws, was a support for the elderly and expressed the longing of the plain. It was a hallmark in the service of vanity."

With the beginning of the twentieth century, the time of the corset, that instrument of torture that had restricted and deformed women's bodies for centuries, came to an end. Women's clothing was now inspired by sports clothing, which focused on freedom of limbs, and the strophium of the Hellenic world returned in the form of the brassiere. Not until the last decades of the twentieth century, however, were attempts made to "liberate the breast."

The Breast in Psychoanalysis

In his novel *The God of Flesh* (*Le Dieu des corps*), Jules Romains describes the overwhelming power of the physicality of the woman, particularly her breasts: "His lover, he admits, had made him an obsessed man. This had primarily to do with her beauty, which was completely fleshly, but less in the sense of animalistic fullness; it was such that one was intoxicated and could not resist becoming enslaved to it; that the entire universe dissolved into the mounds of two glorious breasts and the swelling of two thighs and that one became completely consumed in the service of this immeasurable treasure." The sight of breast, whose form the lover can only sense, evokes in him the most ardent declarations of passion:

"I knelt before her. She must have sensed that my eyes rested on her breasts admiringly and almost with desire, so glorious were they in their roundness and their movements. That was why she laid her right hand on the breast. The hand remained motionless, but the breast rose and fell with ever-greater urgency. And now I saw this hand, which in a mysterious way was similar to her face, press firmly and then slowly move somewhat higher, hesitate and then again come to a decision and then with quick decisiveness and with a skill that only musicians possess, open her dress at the top, push back the material and reveal her shoulder. Then she released the strap that held the shirt together, without stopping or allowing herself any hesitation. With a quick turn of her upper body, she let the shirt slide down her arms. Her breasts rose out of the shimmering material. But I had such fear of hurting her that I fought back the urge that propelled me to this glorious flesh... And while she bent down to me and touched my throat with her hands, the tips of these wonderful breasts moved toward my face. The blissful euphoria with which my face moved toward them was so free, so outside myself, so impersonal almost, that it became adoration... I admired her two breasts like a traveller who stands on a square in Venice and suddenly sees the cathedral dome. I was as astonished as a mathematician who suddenly finds an unexpected perfect drawing of a mathematical formula. As soon, however, as my euphoria threatened to become too conscious, the lightly crinkled and spiraling nipples, pink and brownish, the colour of a young flea, touched me, enticing me almost animalistically, reminding me of all the pleasures that move us most strongly, of the blindest destruction of flesh by flesh. I looked up into Lucienne's face..."

157. Anonymous, 1836.
Royal Museum, Naples.

Where does the powerful attraction come from that women's breasts have to men? They become an object of desire that activates both the desire to melt together and the fear of doing so. Only the quantum leap into the world of conscious rationality saves *homo faber* from sinking into intoxication.

Here too we must look back at early history, this time the ontogenetic:the first erotic object of every human is the maternal breast. It is known that the first five years have a determining influence on human life that cannot be reversed by later experiences. The strongest influence comes from those influences that a child receives before its psychological apparatus is fully able to absorb them. These impressions can scarcely be remembered; but they return in dreams, in the form of symbols. As psychoanalysis sees it, the female breast is the source of the oldest and deepest emotions of an individual.

Freud cites a dream that a then thirty-five year old man claims to have had at the age of four: the notary with whom his father's will was deposited – the father had died when the man was three – brought three large pears with him, one of which he was given to eat. The other one lay on the windowsill of the living room. He woke up with the conviction of the reality of what he had dreamed and demanded the second pear from his mother. His mother laughed. Freud interpreted the two pears as the breasts of the mother, replaced by symbols, that nourished him; the windowsill is the shelf of the bosom. "The dream can be translated as follows: mother, give (show) me the breast again that I used to drink from. The 'earlier' is represented by eating of one pear, the 'again' by the demand for the other."

Female breasts were represented in dream symbolism as apples, peaches, pears, and fruit in general. Thus Freud cites a section from Goethe's *Faust* (Walpurgisnacht, V,3772):

Faust, dancing with the young witch:
"Once I had a beautiful dream,
I saw an apple tree,
Two beautiful apples gleamed thereon,
They appealed to me, I climbed to them."

The boy:
"You desire the apples very much
and it was already thus in Paradise:
I am moved by joy,
That my garden also bears such fruit."

Freud comments: "There is no doubt about what is lying under the apple tree and what is meant by the apples." As we saw, apples were used as a metaphor for the breast already in antiquity.

The word "breast" refers to an anatomical organ. But as we saw in the historic overview, it is also a male fantasy. In the imagination of the conscious subject, it becomes the object of oral wishes, fantasies and also fears.

The female breast reactivates traces or memory of the maternal breast, it is the primal object of childish feelings of love. The experience of being nursed, according to Montague, is the basis of all human interaction and the communication the child receives through the warmth of the mother's skin is the first step toward integrating it into human society. The contact between the child's lips and the breast is the basis of the child's later sexual development.

158. Léon Bakst, *Erotic Scene*, 1920.

In his *Drei Abhandlungen* (*Three Treatises*), Freud writes: "The first and most essential activity of the child, nursing at the breast of the mother (or her surrogate) must already have made it familiar with this desire. We would say that the child's lips have acted like an erogenous zone and the stimulation through the warm milk was probably the source of the feeling of desire... Sexual activity is initially tied to a function that serves the preservation of life and only later becomes independent. Whoever has seen a satiated child sinking back from the breast and falling into sleep with reddened cheeks and a blissful smile will come to the conclusion that this image will remain decisive for the expression of sexual satisfaction in later life."

Psychoanalyst Sandor Rado noted that a satisfying feeling of satiation and a diffuse sense of comfort are an essential result of nursing. He used the term *Sättigungsorgasmus* (satiation orgasm).

In the final analysis, the moment of orgasm probably always brings together the internal image of the mother and that of the satiated child asleep at her breast. For Reimut Reiche, this image is more than an analogue: it is a background image that is later overlaid by other, differentiated images of man and woman. Sexuality begins at the maternal breast, for both sexes. It is known that mothers feel something similar to sexual arousal while nursing while the child experiences something that in a certain sense is much like later sexual satisfaction. Moreover, the primary experiences of the world, that is of the breast, seem to prefigure the child's entire later relationship to the world.

Erasmus Darwin, grandfather of Charles Darwin, wrote about the relationship and the development of human behavior in the book *Zoonomia or the Laws of Organic Life*, first published in 1794. Long before Freud, he wrote: "The most varied of pleasures are associated with the maternal breast, which the child embraces, against which it presses its lips, which it sees and whose form the child senses more clearly than the smell and feeling of warmth that his other senses convey. When in mature years we see something whose movement or line corresponds to the female breast, whether a gently rolling landscape, an antique vase or a work of the pen or the chisel, we feel a sense of inner joy. If the object is not too large, we are moved to embrace it and press our lips against it as we did with the maternal breast in early childhood."

Romains' lover thinks of the Venetian cathedral dome, of a mathematical formula, but in this situation there is no recollection of the female forms that are just at the tip of his nose. Here a process of objectification and distancing is taking place through associations that lead away from the breast. Behind this geometric and other abstraction one senses all too clearly the mechanism of rejection. Are architecture and mathematics not typical male domains? With their help it is possible to construct dams that prevent a flood of feelings. But where does this fear come from?

In the primary narcissistic phase, the child experiences itself as part of the mother, that is, the breast that gives milk is felt as part of one's self. In this undifferentiated period, the infant is unable to distinguish between itself and its surroundings, nor between psyche and body, nor between ego and id.

What Romains fantasises as "destruction" is based on these fantasies of melting together which would result in the dissolution of a male identity carefully constructed through the process of development and maturation. (Freud even compared the process of ego formation with draining the Zuider Zee). These breasts exert a regressive pull that undermines the Vendome columns of maleness. Architecture and mathematics offer an ego threatened by dissolution techniques of self-preservation. "I looked up into Lucienne's face." In that face he recognises the other as his opposite and thus regains his own borders. He has defended himself against the maternal breast with all its enticements. He is saved.

For women as well, breasts are associated with ambivalent fantasies. In her study *Die Sexuelle Brust* (*The Sexual Breast*), Friedl Früh examines the question of why the female breast, "one of women's most

159. Léon Bakst, *Erotic Scene*, 1920.

important erogenous zones," is not seen as a sexual organ, although arousal of the breast undoubtedly makes an essential contribution to the female orgasm. She suspects that the "trinity" of physical sources of lust for women – the vagina, the clitoris, the breast – are not allowed to be recognised because that would accord the breast, a place that serves the nourishment of babies, the significance of a sexual organ. The breast has a double meaning for both sexes: it represents the world of sexual desire and the world of maternal love. It is the place where sexual passion and childish or maternal devotion meet. Because the breast is the first place of exchange between the erogenous zones of mother and child, it is suited like no other place to be fixed as a sexual site. But recognition of the sexual implications of maternity could cause the idealisation of motherhood to come into question. Thus the two images lead to internal psychic conflicts and confusions: The sexually desirous character threatens to compromise "innocent mother love"; the sexual significance of the breast conflicts with its function as nourishment. Finally, the sexual image falls victim to denial or repression, with consequences for woman's struggle with her feelings.

A case cited by Marylin Yalom demonstrates the implications of a woman's admission that a baby sucking at her breast was a source of sexual feelings. The woman, from New York, was stripped of her parental rights to her two-year-old child after she admitted that she became sexually aroused while nursing. She was accused of having sexually abused her child. Although the court found that no abuse had taken place, the child was placed with its grandparents. The woman's relatives, social workers, the police and the judicial apparatus all judged her feelings to be "abnormal."

We find a parody of obsessive male desire for the breast in Philip Roth's novella *The Breast*, in which the protagonist is transformed overnight into an enormous breast. He comments on his unfortunate situation: "Why this primitive identification with the object of infantile adoration? What unfulfilled desires, which primal confusions, what fragments of my most distant past could have collided to bring about a delusion of such classic simplicity?"

In Roland Topor's *The Most Beautiful Bosom in the World*, a girl drapes her breasts onto a young man in an elevator. Janet is overjoyed: "How often she had wished that these bothersome sponge-like breasts, toward which men stretched out their feelers, would disappear! These tits that she had regarded as a malformation since youth. Oh! To get rid of the hated glands that dictated how she dressed, walked, acted, that had the gall to dictate her way of life! A wonder had taken place! ... She ripped off her brassiere and threw it, once and for all, into the garbage can." Simon, however, becomes a media star. Women fall all over him because he could offer something no one else could: breasts that no other man had and that woman had believed they could never possess within accepted sexual relationships. As a feminised man, he became the object of obsessive female desire for breasts. Two images that cannot be brought together: the real breast is viewed by its owners as constraint and restriction. As an imagined object of desire, as a fantasy, however, it is an organ that promises happiness to both sexes.

In psychoanalytic theory, the term "phallus" is not identical with "penis," which describes the anatomical reality of the organ. "Phallus" has symbolic meaning. For Lacan, it is the "significant of the wish." Analogously, there should be a term for the breast that differentiates between visible anatomical reality and symbolic meaning. All conflicts and confusions result from the lack of visibility of the symbolic. "Phallus" stands for power, but the larger power opposing the phallus is the breast. The phallus draws power especially from the fact that there is no special term for the breast. The female counterpart to the phallus

160. Achille Devéria, 1840.
Romantic lithograph.

is not the vagina, it is the breast. Fear of the vagina ("vagina dendata") is a later phase in sexual development that supersedes the original fear: fear of the regressive pull of the first object of desire. Only those who have the strength to admit that this fear resides in them can free themselves of it and enjoy the delights of the breasts.

The Liberated Breast

The image of the real breast was overlaid for centuries by the symbolic meaning of breasts. In that sense, it was consistent when the women's liberation movement in the USA initiated a symbolic action that became known by the slogan "bra-burning." In 1968, members of the Women's Liberation Party blocked the Miss America competition in Atlantic City with a demonstration and called on the women there to throw away their bras, girdles, hair curlers, false eyelashes and other objects that symbolised the "stupid little woman."(Yalom notes that the "bra-burning action" was a myth: the despised symbols of oppression were not burned but simply tossed into a trashcan. The reporters who coined this term doubtlessly wanted to create a link to other politically motivated burnings like those of flags or draft cards for the Vietnam War).

Two years after this event, the English author Germaine Greer wrote *The Female Eunuch*, a provocative depiction of the disempowerment of women by patriarchal society. Greer gives an extensive description of the exaggerated attention men pay to female breasts. Full breasts are "a millstone" around a woman's neck, she writes. Her breasts are admired only as long as they do not give any indication of their function. As soon as they darken, shrivel or become flabby, however, they are viewed only with disgust and revulsion. Breasts are not part of a person but only lures that a woman carries around her neck and that can be formed and shaped like wax. Like the American bra-burners, Greer also rejected breast fetishism and told women that they should not dress in such a way as to encourage male fantasies of the eternal full bosom. Many people critical of bra-burning saw it as an affront to the dictates of respectable society and male-influenced notions of physical beauty, which insisted on large, round, firm, clearly delineated breasts. The unconfined breasts of the late 1960s represented a kind of anarchy, a releasing of the breasts that allowed them to sway freely.

In the 1970s and 1980s, revealing one's breasts became a provocation. Bare-breasted demonstrators were able to insert a broad spectrum of women's issues into the public sphere. In 1984, for

161. Frazos, 1830. Lithograph.

example, a demonstration of sixty women (and men) paraded bare-chested through the streets of Santa Cruz, California. They protested against the degradation and abuse of female bodies in advertising and pornography. One of the feminists, who had worked as a model in New York, read a speech saying that "If women's breasts were not hidden out of shame or viewed as obscene or depraved, how could Madison Avenue, pornographers, film and television continue to profit from revealing them? ... We say 'No!' Our bodies are not the property of advertising agencies, organisers of beauty pageants, topless bars, peep shows and the like. We demand our birthright to our own bodies."

Posters bore statements like "The myth of a perfect body oppresses us all." But slogans like "Our breasts are for the newborn, not for men's porn" more clearly suggested female castration: would it not be most important to first discover desire for one's own body – something admittedly difficult in a Puritanical society. While in the USA such provocations grew into collective demonstrations, in Europe there were only single cases during the 1970s in which women revealed their breasts with the obvious goal of political provocation.

One is reminded of the breast demonstration against Theodor W. Adorno: It was on 22 April, 1969, not the first time that students had disrupted his lecture "Introduction into Dialectic Thought" with catcalls; nor was he the only professor whose courses were disrupted by small activist groups. Three long-haired, leather jacketed female students approached him, encircled him, tried to kiss him and tore open their jackets, under which their breasts could be seen. Adorno felt humiliated and left the lecture hall.

Another form of protest against the bosom fetish developed in fashion of the 1960s. The new fashions reduced the breasts, with their associations with motherhood, to a minimum and emphasised long youthful legs. The figure of Twiggy signalised sexual enticement that had to do neither with traditional femininity nor with maternity. This top London model, originally Leslie Hornby, was the absolute ruler of the runways of the fashion world for a time. With her small breasts and fragile build, Twiggy incorporated the youthfulness of pre-adolescence. In comparison with the feminist struggle to gain control of breasts, Twiggy represented something more like a strategy of avoidance.

The fight for a sense of self, independent of men, was also reflected in art.

Similar to the *blasons* of the Renaissance, French-American artist, Louise Bourgeois, (born 1911) often dismantles the human body into its parts, into pairs of eyes, hands, arms, feet and innumerable breasts, and reassembles them in new configurations. Breasts play a major role in her work. Her sculpture *She Fox* from the year 1985 is a depiction of the "Great Mother," with four powerful breasts that provide care and love. With *Mamelles* (1991), she criticised the attitudes of the Don Juan. This work consists of a frieze of pink rubber breasts that flow into one another. The breasts are presented as things that are thrown blindly into a gutter. Bourgeois explains that it is the depiction of a man who drew his life force from the women he seduced and who wandered from one to another. "He nourishes himself with them, but he gives nothing back and his way of life is consumerist and self-obsessed."

The work of Cindy Sherman, who became known for her shocking depictions of women, also reflects the objectification of the female body. Her photographic scenarios try to breakout of the usual ways of presenting women and femininity. Her series *Historic Portraits* (1988 – 1990) emphasises the traditional focus on the female breast with the uses of sculptured breasts. Never does she try to deceive us about the lack of authenticity of these props. According to Yalom, they destroy the illusion that the body has a natural history. "In Sherman's view, the history of the body is the history of its societal construction and manipulation."

162. *Triumph*, Lithograph, 1830.

Marilyn Monroe, for example, was an artificial product, built for men from head to toe. Even her name was strategy. Psychologists explained that American men were so fixated on breasts because they had been weaned too early. "MM, – the name was like a smacking sucking sound, breast fetishism translated into sound." The Fifties was the American decade. Hollywood was a temple and MM the altar figure. Marilyn even wanted to see her physical proportions memorialised on her gravestone: "Here lies Marilyn Monroe, 96-58-91 [centimetres]."

It is estimated that more than seventy percent of young women are dissatisfied with their bodies. Advertising and the mass media present them with an ideal that is unreachable for nearly all women. In light of the flood of such pictures, many women consider surgical alteration of their breasts. The business journal *brandeins* reported that in 1999, 167,318 American women had their breasts enlarged with silicone implants, 413 percent more than only seven years previously! In fewer than half of these cases, the operation was to reconstruct a breast lost to breast disease. "The remaining women hoped that larger breasts would bring them greater chances in life," according to the magazine. "Prominent women like Jane Fonda and Cher have made artificial femininity acceptable and they present it as a sign of their emancipation."

In Germany, on the other hand, many women seem to accept their breasts. Silicone, according to the magazine, is used here primarily as a substitute for amputated breasts. Breast enlargements make up only twenty percent of the operations. The fact that the queen of the German porno branch, Dolly Buster, with her immense body proportions (106-58-87 centimetres) was so successful has to do with archaic male fantasies.

Plastic surgeons worked with the female breast as early as the 1930s. They studied Greek statues and came to the conclusion that "the ideal breast lies vertically between the third and seventh rib and the nipples should lie parallel to the fourth rib, nine to nineteen centimetres from the midline and fourteen to sixteen centimetres below the collarbone." As a result, surgeons suddenly saw themselves as artists, who tried to replace the variety of real breasts – no body part exists in so many variations – with the "official breast."

The Hippocratic Oath prohibits doctors from causing their patients unnecessary pain. Therefore, the gap between ideal and reality had to be bridged as an illness. The result was the creation of mammahypoplasia or small-breastedness. According to medical textbooks and assessments, small breasts lead to minority complexes and reduce the quality of life. Doctors became psychologists who decided which woman was acceptable for silicone and which was not. "I want to get it done for myself" is the declaration of the suitable candidate. She does not realise that this "I" is societal manipulation.

Women around the world now submit to the western ideal of beauty. The Chinese used to value flat-breasted woman as moral and modest. Since the Second World War, larger breasts are modern in China as well. The demand for silicone is increasing. Plastic surgery has become the chief source of income for many surgeons in Japan, China and South Korea.

"Liberated breasts," however, are breasts that, according to Yalom, "belong to women who know what they like and who reject being manipulated." Women of the most disparate origins today consciously seek "emancipation of the breast" that does not follow the standardised ideals of beauty. It is to be hoped that men will also increasingly turn away from clichéd notions of female beauty and learn to accept the comprehensive significance of the breast. Only then can lust filled with shared feelings arise between the sexes.

163. Roberty, circa 1890. Watercolour.

Notes

1 Blasons auf den weiblichen Körper, hg.v. L.Klünner, Berlin 1964.

2 Hartmut Böhme, Erotische Anatomie, in: C. Benthieu/Ch.Wulf (Hg.), Körperteile. Eine kulturelle Anatomie. Reinbek 2001, p. 228.

3 ibid. p. 231.

4 ibid. p. 236.

5 ibid.

6 ibid. p. 237.

7 Norman O.Brown, Zukunft im Zeichen des Eros, Pfullingen 1962.

8 ibid. p. 49.

9 ibid. p. 47.

10 ibid. p. 251; sh. Auch S.Sontag, Norman Browns "Zukunft im Zeichen des Eros", in: Kunst und Antikunst, Reinbek 1968, p. 251-257.

11 D.Kamper / Ch.Wulf, Die Parabel der Wiederkehr, in: D.Kamper / Ch.Wulf, Die Wiederkehr des Körpers, Frankfurt 1982, p. 12.

12 Max Horkheimer / Th.W.Adorno, Dialektik der Aufklärung, Frankfurt 1969, p. 247.

13 sh. Jan van Ussel, Sexualunterdrückung. Geschichte der Sexualfeindschaft, Reinbek 1970, p. 39.

14 Rudolf zur Lippe, Am eigenen Leibe. Zur Ökonomie des Lebens. Frankfurt 1978, p. 143.

15 sh. dazu H.Schipperges, Am Leitfaden des Leibes. Zur Anthropologie und Therapeutik Friedrich Nietzsches, Stuttgart 1975.

16 Friedrich Nietzsche, Werke in drei Bänden, Hg. K.Schlechta, München 1968, Bd.II, p. 1181.

17 ibid., Bd.II, p. 301.

18 ibid., Bd.III, p. 476.

19 ibid., Bd.II, p. 300.

20 Horkheimer/Adorno, a.a.O., p. 249.

21 sh. dazu auch K.Theweleit, Männerphantasien, Frankfurt 1978, Bd. II, p. 185.

22 R. zur Lippe, Anthropologie für wen? In: D.Kamper / V.Rittner (Hg.), Zur Geschichte des Körpers, München 1976, p. 94.

23 E.Schorsch, Sexuelle Deviationen: Ideologie, Klinik, Kritik, in: E.Schorsch/G.Schmidt, Ergebnisse der Sexualforschung, Köln 1975, p. 88.

24 ibid., p. 88.

25 S.Freud, Drei Abhandlungen zur Sexualtheorie, 1905, GW V, p. 65.

26 V.Sigusch, Perversion als Positiv der Normalität, in: V.Sigusch, Neosexualitäten. Über den kulturellen Wandel von Liebe und Perversion. Frankfurt/New York 2005, p. 82.

27 ibid., p. 84.

28 ibid.

29 Blasons auf den weiblichen Körper, a.a.O.

30 This is a pun in German too. (Translator's note).

31 i.e. when it is very fat. (Translator's note).

32 12. Feb. 1862-5 Feb 1937; writer of theoretical papers on psychoanalysis.

33 Physicist, born 7. Oct. 1929; Alternative Nobel Prize Winner, 1987.

34 The rest of this quote is obscene/nonsense rhymes in German; untranslatable since they are words, or phonemes, which rhyme with DRECK. (Translator's note.).

35 Sic. Presumably this is meant to be a parody of the Biblical quote. (Translator's note).

36 English in original. (Translator's note).

37 Austrian behaviourist, whose research is primarily devoted to the possibilities of communication between human beings and animals.

38 Greek courtesan.

39 A town in south-eastern Sicily found by the Greeks.

40 30 June 1807-14 Sept 1887; writer and philosopher.

41 In English in original.

42 In English in original.

43 Our Mutual Friend, Chapter 4.

44 20 Apr. 1492-21 Oct. 1556; Italian poet.

45 This is a translation of a translation; that is, I have translated the German translation of the Italian original.

46 Nonce-word or neologism, obviously coined for this article. (Translator's note).

47 2 July 1740-2. Dec. 1814; French officer and writer.

48 14 Aug. 1840-22. Dec. 1902: researcher and psychiatrist.

49 In French in original. (Translator's note).

50 Poet, author of radio dramas, gained Büchner Prize in 1963 and the Heine Prize in 1998.

51 May mean "complexion" in this context. (Translator's note).

52 c. 450-404 B.C. pupil of Socrates, Athenian general and politician.

53 The word "tribade" as a synonym for "Lesbian" does exist, according to the O.E.D, but is rare. (Translator's note).

54 The word is "Pädiaktion", which appears to be a neologism coined by the author by analogy with "Pädophilie", etc. (Translator's note).

55 b. Perleburg, 21. March 1935; d. Hamburg, 8. March 1986.

56 Sic! veilchenfarbene Schöße is the term used - possibly, though, he does intend to convey the idea of "laps filled with violets". (Translator's note).

57 c. 160-220 C.E, Church Father.

58 Probably means "dressed in men's clothing". (Translator's note).

59 She was still executed, but was at least allowed a quick death. (Translator's note).

60 4. May 1904-6 Nov. 1997; Professor of Philosophy.

61 14. Aug. 1840-22. Dec 1902; psychiatrist and researcher into sexual pathology.

62 12 Feb. 1847-17. Sept 1921; Ambassador in Vienna, friend of Kaiser Wilhelm II.

63 The word used here is Gegengeschlechtlichkeit, which definitely means heterosexuality according to the DUDEN; but it does not seem to make sense in this context, since what he seems to be trying to say is that there are people who try to suppress their homosexual tendencies. (Translator's note).

64 14 May 1868-15 May 1935; neurologist and researcher into sexuality.

65 May mean "after the menopause?". (Translator's note).

66 American sexologist.

67 In English in original. (Translator's note).

68 Heinrich Heine, b. 13.12.1797, Büsseldorf, d. 17.2.1856, Paris; poet.

69 Wilhelm Bölsche, b. 2.1.1861, Cologne, d. 31.8.1939, Szklarska; writer.

70 Charles R. Darwin, b. 12.2.1809, near Shrewsbury (GB), d. 19.4.1882, in Dream House ; founder of the theory of evolution.

71 Irenäus Eibl-Eibesfeldt, b. 15.6.1928, Vienna; Austrian biologist and behavioural researcher, professor in Vienna.

72 Desmond J. Morris, b. 24.1.1928, Purton (GB); Bristish behavioural researcher.

73 Johann W. von Goethe, b. 28.8.1749, Frankfurt am Main, d. 22.3.1832, Weimar, German poet, scientist, graphic artist.

74 Georg Simmel, b. 1.3.1858, Berlin, d. 26.9.1918, Starsbourg; philosopher and sociologist.

75 Roland Barthes, b. 12.11.1915, Cherbourg, d. 26.3.1980, Paris; French critic of contemporary culture.

76 Marcus V. Martial, lived from c. 40-102 AD in Bilbilis (Spain) and for a while in Rome; poet.

77 Oscar F. O'Flahertie Wills Wilde, b. 16.10.1854, Dublin, d. 30.11.1900, Paris; Irish dramatist and narrative write.

78 Shere D. Hite, b. 1942, USA; sociologist who has made studies of human sexual behaviour.

79 Alfred C. Kinsey, b. 23.6.1894, Hoboken (USA), d. 25.8.1956, Bloomington ; zoologist and sexologist.

80 William H. Masters, b. 27.10.1915, Cleveland; American gynaecologist and co-founder of experimental sexology.

81 David H. Lawrence, b. 11.9.1885, Eastwood (GB), d. 2.3.1930, Vence (France); English writer.

82 Nancy Friday, American sexologist.

83 Octavio Paz, b. 31.3.1914, Mixcoac, d. 19.4.1998, Mexico City; Mexican diplomat, lyric poet, writer.

84 Alexandre Davy de la Pailleterie, b. 24.7.1802, Villers-Cotterets, d. 5.12.1870, Puys; writer.

85 Franz Grillparzer, b. 15.1.1791, Vienna; d. 21.1.1872, Vienna; Austrian poet, lawyer and philosopher.

Index